Peregrine Man

From the Desk of Ms. Margaret Gladstone, Innkeeper

Dear Mr. January,

I am writing to solicit your P.I. services in investigating some disturbing occurrences at my B and B, Peregrine Manor. I ~~can't afford to pay you cash~~ am offering in exchange a month at one of the most charming inns in the Northwest, with ~~overflowing toilets~~ distinctive rooms decorated Victorian style.

At the manor, you'll be able to relax ~~at least until the next arson attempt~~ and enjoy the ~~rain, rain and more rain~~ splendors of the Washington coast in ~~off-season~~ winter, a special time of the year here. Each morning, you'll have a hearty breakfast personally cooked by me ~~as the chef left~~ and in the afternoon you'll be served tea and freshly baked scones. ~~the freezer conked out but the oven still works…occasionally.~~

Enjoy cozy evenings by the parlor's fireplace ~~since the furnace is busted~~ in conversation with ~~elderly chaperons who'll watch you like a hawk~~ the permanent guests of the manor. My residents ~~have crackpot theories for you to investigate while they sneak into each other's bedrooms~~ are eager to assist in your investigations in any way.

Come join us at Peregrine Manor and indulge yourself in the tranquil environment of this lovely, unspoiled ~~innkeeper~~ setting.

Sincerely,

Maggie Gladstone

Jayne Ann Krentz is one of today's best-loved authors of women's fiction, with an astounding twelve million copies of her books in print. Her novels regularly appear on the *New York Times* and *USA TODAY* bestseller lists. First published in 1979, Jayne quickly established herself as a prolific and innovative writer, delving into psychic elements, intrigue, fantasy, historical and even futuristic romances. Jayne lives in Seattle with her husband, Frank, an engineer.

Dani Sinclair says she wrote her first romance novel because her sister asked her to. She was so pleased by the results, she wrote two more, and joined a writers' critique group. Three members of the group, including Dani, became published authors—and RITA® Award nominees! Dani says, "Thanks to the loving support of my very own hero and the two sons we raised, I've written over twenty books. I'm proud to call myself a writer. And hopefully I've given to others some of the pleasure I've derived from a lifetime of reading."

Julie Miller attributes her passion for writing romance to all those fairy tales she read growing up—and to shyness. Encouraged by her family to write down those feelings she couldn't express, she developed a love for the written word. This award-winning author and teacher gets continued support from her fellow Prairieland Romance Writers, and has published several paranormal romances as well as romantic suspense. She lives in Nebraska with her husband, son and smiling guard dog, Maxie. Write to Julie at P.O. Box 5162, Grand Island, NE 68802-5162 U.S.A.

JAYNE ANN KRENTZ

The Private Eye

Plus original stories by Dani Sinclair and Julie Miller

HARLEQUIN®

TORONTO • NEW YORK • LONDON
AMSTERDAM • PARIS • SYDNEY • HAMBURG
STOCKHOLM • ATHENS • TOKYO • MILAN • MADRID
PRAGUE • WARSAW • BUDAPEST • AUCKLAND

ISBN 0-373-83598-1

Copyright © 2003 by Harlequin Books S.A.

The publisher acknowledges the copyright holder
of the individual works as follows:

THE PRIVATE EYE
Copyright © 1992 by Jayne Ann Krentz

KEEGAN'S BLUFF
Copyright © 2001 by Dani Sinclair

COP NEXT DOOR
Copyright © 2002 by Julie Miller

Visit us at www.eHarlequin.com

Printed in U.S.A.

CONTENTS

THE PRIVATE EYE

Jayne Ann Krentz

PROLOGUE

IT NEVER PAYS TO PLAY HERO.

One of these days, he'd finally learn that lesson once and for all, Josh reflected. He sat on the edge of the emergency-room examination table and scowled at the closed door. He was not in a good mood. He didn't like hospitals and he didn't like realizing he'd been unlucky enough or stupid enough or slow enough to end up in one tonight.

Could have been worse, he reminded himself. If Eddy Hodder's knife had struck a few inches lower, he would have been spending the night in the morgue.

Josh took a cautious breath and winced. The doctor had just told him his ribs were bruised, not broken, but it was hard to tell the difference. The big question now was whether or not the ankle was fractured or just badly sprained. The X rays would be back any minute.

Everything else had been patched up fairly easily. The raw scrape on his shoulder had been bandaged quite neatly and the gash on his forehead where Hodder's knife had caught him had been closed with sutures. Unfortunately the local anesthetic was already wearing off. He deserved everything he got, Josh told himself grimly. He was in the wrong business. Or maybe he'd just been in it too damn long.

He was about to continue with the self-recriminations when the door of the emergency room swung open. A young man in a white coat sauntered in looking far more authoritative than any young man had a right to look. Josh wondered why doctors, cops and other such professionals were all starting to look so incredibly young to him. Maybe it was only private investigators like himself who aged rapidly.

"Good news, Mr. January. It's only a sprain. We'll tape it up for you and have you out of here in no time."

"Terrific." Josh eyed his swollen left ankle, feeling a sense of dark betrayal. *Stupid foot.* "How long?"

"How long for what?" The doctor opened a white drawer on the other side of the room.

"How long until I can walk on it?"

"Could be quite a while," the doctor said, sounding cheerful at the prospect. "You'll want to rest it for at least a week and it will probably bother you a bit from time to time, after that. We'll send you out of here on crutches."

"Crutches?" Josh swore with great depth of feeling.

The doctor turned around, holding an elastic bandage in his hand. His smile lit up the room. "Could have been worse. Heard you nearly got yourself killed when you went into that building after that Eddy Hodder character. The cops are in a room down the hall with him right now. If it's any consolation to you, Hodder's in worse shape than you are."

"Yeah, that really makes me feel a whole lot better," Josh growled.

"Thought it would. But you're going to be hurting for a while, yourself. No getting around it. I'll give you some pills for the pain when you leave. My advice is to take some time off from your job, Mr. January. You need a few weeks of R and R. That means rest and relaxation.''

"I know what it means." Josh set his teeth as the doctor went to work on his ankle. "Take it easy, damn it. That hurts!''

"Sorry. Every jarring movement is going to annoy you for a while," the doctor announced happily.

Josh glowered at him. "You enjoy your work?"

"Love it."

Josh winced again as the doctor tugged on the elastic bandage. "It shows."

MCCRAY WAS WAITING for him out in the hall. Short, balding and comfortably rounded at the waistline, McCray was the closest thing to a friend Josh had. He was also Josh's partner in Business Intelligence and Security, Inc., one of the biggest private security agencies in the Pacific Northwest.

McCray shook his head ruefully as Josh swung forward on the crutches. "Well, well, well. Aren't you a sight. How do you feel?''

"Like hell.''

"Yeah, that's kind of how you look, to tell you the truth. I've signed the paperwork for you and I've already talked to the cops. Gave them a full report. We're free to go.''

Josh shifted his shoulders, trying to get more comfortable on the crutches. All he succeeded in doing was sending shock waves through his bruised body. "The girl okay?''

"The girl's fine. Mad as hell at you for ruining her life, she says, but fine. Her boyfriend, Hodder, was on parole when he pulled this kidnapping stunt. He's headed straight back to prison and will probably stay there awhile. The young lady's father, our client, is everlastingly grateful, of course.''

''Send him his bill first thing in the morning. Might as well take advantage of the gratitude.''

''My, you are feeling nasty tonight, aren't you?''

McCray pushed open the glass doors of the emergency room and Josh hobbled out into the cold Seattle night. ''You know what, pal?''

''What?''

''You need some time off. Maybe a month or so.''

''Now listen, McCray—''

McCray held up his palm. ''I'm serious, January. You're burned-out, you're beat-up and you've got a real bad attitude. What you need is a month of easy living. You need someone to wait on you hand and foot. You need home-cooked meals, tea and scones in the afternoon, and a stress-free environment. In short, you need a complete change of scene.''

''You got any special place in mind?'' Josh asked, irritated.

''As a matter of fact, I do.'' McCray opened the passenger door of his faded blue Oldsmobile. ''Get in. I've got a letter I want you to read.''

''Who's it from? *Ouch!* Damn it to hell.''

''Here, let me have those crutches. I'll put them in the back seat. The letter's on the dash.''

Josh lowered himself gingerly onto the car seat, grimacing as he eased his left leg inside. He saw the envelope sitting directly in front of him on the dash. He picked it up and glanced at the letterhead. The bright lights outside the emergency room provided enough light to read the words ''Peregrine Manor.''

Josh opened the envelope. A colorful brochure depicting a fanciful Victorian mansion fell out, along with a neatly typed letter. A glance at the brochure showed that Peregrine Manor promised the ultimate in cozy luxury and gourmet dining on the spectacular Washington coast.

The letter promised a job.

"I think you should take the case," McCray told him as he got behind the wheel.

Josh scanned the contents of the letter. "This isn't a case. It's a joke. This Ms. Margaret Gladstone obviously has a vivid imagination."

"That's the whole point," McCray said patiently as he pulled out of the hospital parking lot. "A cushy setup. A piece of cake. A snap. You get all the perks of a fancy luxury inn for a month and in exchange all you have to do is a little sleuthing for the sweet little old lady who wrote that letter."

"Piece of cake, huh? What makes you think this Miss Gladstone is a sweet little old lady?"

"Who else would write a letter like that except some old-fashioned little spinster lady? What have you got to lose? You need to get away for a while, Josh. We both know it. You aren't going to be any good to us at BIS until you get out of this lousy mood you've been in for the past few months. Like I said, you're burned-out, pal. You've been in the business too long."

"You've been in it just as long," Josh muttered.

"Yeah, but it hasn't been nearly as hard on me. I don't get personally involved the way you do. I'm a deskman."

It never pays to play hero, Josh thought again. He glanced down at the letter lying on his knee. Something told him Miss Margaret Gladstone was not a little old lady, sweet or otherwise. And his hunches were almost always reliable.

Josh wondered why he was suddenly consumed with curiosity to know more about the woman who had written the crazy letter promising an even crazier job.

Maybe he did need to get away for a while.

CHAPTER ONE

A BLACK CAR TURNED into the driveway and drove straight up to the front door of Peregrine Manor. It was five o'clock and already dark. A driving November rain drummed against the windows of the parlor so that the people gathered there could not see who was driving the vehicle. But there was little doubt as to the identity of the new arrival.

"I reckon that'll be our man," the Colonel said with satisfaction. He pulled a gold pocket watch out of his well-worn dinner jacket and peered at it. His white mustache twitched. "Right on time. Good sign. I admire a man who knows the importance of being punctual."

"I do hope we've done the right thing," Odessa Hawkins murmured in a worried tone. She was seated next to the Colonel, a glass of sherry in her beringed hand. She, too, was dressed for dinner. Her faded blue gown was almost as old as the Colonel's jacket, but she wore it with the poise and elegance that had been bred into her over sixty-five years.

"We've been over this a hundred times, Odessa. It wasn't like we had a lotta choice, you know. Maggie's right. Sometimes you gotta get yourself a hired gun to handle this kinda thing." Shirley Smith took a swallow of her martini and shot Odessa an irritated glance through the lenses of her rhinestone-studded glasses.

Shirley was about the same age as the other woman but her background was considerably different. No one had taught Shirley Smith the social niceties at a tender age. To her, dressing for dinner meant slipping into a pair of stiletto heels and an extremely tight, strapless dress of shocking-pink satin that ended well above her bony knees. She was wearing her entire collection of rhinestones this evening. She even had a tiara perched on her heavily teased, brassy blond hair.

The Colonel nodded solemnly and patted Odessa's hand with deep affection. "Shirley's absolutely right, my dear. You mustn't fret. We had no choice in the matter. It was time to take decisive action."

Maggie Gladstone scanned the faces of the three permanent tenants of Peregrine Manor and mentally crossed her fingers. She sincerely hoped she had done the right thing. Hiring a private investigator was an entirely new experience for her. Nevertheless, she'd read enough mystery novels to be fairly certain what to expect from the man in the black car. Excitement bubbled up in her. She was about to meet a real live private eye!

"I'll go introduce myself and get him checked into his room. He's had a long drive from Seattle. I'm sure he'll want to change before dinner." Maggie put down her glass of sherry and leaped to her feet.

"Yes, of course," Odessa said regally. "Remind him that we dress for dinner here at Peregrine Manor." She pursed her lips. "I do hope he is a *proper* sort of detective. One of the old-school types that one always finds in those lovely British mysteries—not one of those brash young men who are always dashing about waving their guns on television.''

"Strikes me we might need a man who knows how to handle a pistol," the Colonel declared ominously.

"Dang right," Shirley agreed. "The last thing we need is some snobbish little wimp. This is a job for a guy with guts, as my Ricky always used to say."

Maggie paused in the doorway of the parlor. "He's from Business Intelligence and Security, Inc. It's one of the most exclusive security firms on the West Coast. We were very lucky to get him. I'm sure he's no wimp. Now, please hush, all of you. We don't want him to hear us discussing him."

"Run along and greet him, my dear," Odessa said.

"Yeah," added Shirley with a grin. "We'll behave."

Maggie hurried out into the hall and caught a glimpse of herself in the huge, gilded mirror that hung near the front desk. She had chosen to wear a black silk jumpsuit that she thought complemented her slender frame. Her mass of tawny brown curls had been swept up on top of her head, caught with a gold clip and allowed to cascade down her neck to her shoulders.

Maggie frowned critically at her own image and hoped she was projecting a savvy, with-it attitude. She wanted the fancy private investigator to consider her sophisticated and businesslike. High-powered city people sometimes thought they could bamboozle folks who lived in small towns such as Peregrine Point. She didn't want this expensive security expert to get the idea he could stay here at the manor for a month rent-free, write up a short report and then leave. Maggie wanted action.

Something thumped against the door. It didn't sound like a polite knock. Maggie grabbed the knob and yanked open the door.

She stared in amazement at the man who was standing on the front porch. Her heart sank in disappointment. He was clearly not the private investigator they'd all been anticipating, after all.

The poor man had obviously just been released from the nearest hospital emergency room. He was balanced on crutches and his left foot was heavily taped around the ankle. There was a large white bandage on his forehead. Both of his eyes were outlined with dark, purple bruises.

"Oh, dear," Maggie said. "I was expecting someone else."

The man scowled down at her. The glowering frown only served to make an already hard-looking face appear downright ferocious. The shadow of what looked like a day's growth of beard emphasized the effect. His black hair was wet from the rain, as was the denim of his work shirt and jeans. Could her first impression have been erroneous? He was certainly tall enough to suit her image of a professional man of action, and he was built along the lean, solid lines she had envisioned. Furthermore, there was something extremely dangerous about the expression in his cold, gray eyes.

But it was a safe bet that no real private investigator would show up for a case looking like the walking wounded.

"Do you mind if I come in?" the stranger growled in a low, raspy voice. He sounded as if he'd endured a number of hardships recently and was getting fed up with practicing the virtues of tolerance and patience. "It's damn wet out here."

"Yes, of course. Come on inside and dry off." Maggie stepped back quickly. "But I'm afraid you can't stay. We aren't taking visitors until after the first of the year. Maybe not until spring. We're, uh, refurbishing. You didn't have a reservation, by any chance, did you? I thought I notified all the confirmed reservations. Who are you?"

"January."

"Yes, that's what I said. We hope to be open again in January. It all depends, you see. Now, if you do have a reservation and you weren't notified that Peregrine Manor has had to close for a while, I'm very sorry. I can probably get you a room for the night at one of the other bed-and-breakfast places in town. No one is full at this time of year except on the weekends."

The man moved into the hall, managing the crutches skillfully but with obvious annoyance. "I said, I'm January. Joshua January." He quirked one black brow. "I believe you sent for me."

Maggie's mouth fell open in shock. "You're January? The private investigator from Business Intelligence and Security, Inc.?"

"Right." He transferred both crutches into his left hand and ran his right hand through his dark hair. Raindrops splattered the worn Oriental rug on the floor. "Now, if I could have some help with my luggage, I'd appreciate it. It's a little tough to manage suitcases when you're on these things." He indicated the crutches.

"But, Mr. January—"

"Call me Josh." He shot an impatient glance around the small lobby. "Where's your bellboy?"

"We don't have one anymore. Look, Mr. January, there must be some mistake."

"No mistake." Balancing precariously on the crutches, he fished a familiar-looking sheet of paper out of his front pocket. "This is Peregrine Manor, isn't it?"

"Well, yes, but—"

He opened the sheet of paper and started to read aloud in a grim monotone. "'In exchange for professional investigative services, I am prepared to offer a month's lodging at one of the most charming bed-and-breakfast inns in the Northwest. Peregrine Manor is a truly fine example of delightful Victorian architecture, offering unique and distinctive rooms furnished in period style.'"

"Yes, but—"

"'At the manor,'" Josh continued in a relentless tone, "'you'll be able to relax and enjoy the splendors of the Washington coast in winter, a very special time of year here. You'll awaken each morning to a hearty, home-cooked breakfast and in the afternoons you'll be served tea and scones.'"

"Please, Mr. January—"

"'In the evenings we encourage you to enjoy conversation and sherry with the other residents of the manor before proceeding on to dinner in our gourmet restaurant. After dinner you'll be treated to cozy evenings by the fireside. Come join us at Peregrine Manor and indulge yourself in the tranquil environment of this lovely, unspoiled—'"

"*All right,* Mr. January. That is quite enough, thank you. I recognize my own words."

He looked up and for the first time Maggie realized how cold his eyes really were. They were a chilling, icy shade of gray that reflected no warmth and even less patience. Joshua January had been well named.

"Good. So much for that." Josh refolded the letter and stuck it back into his front pocket. "You, I take it, are Ms. Margaret Gladstone?"

"Well, yes."

"Fine. I'm the licensed investigator you hired. I think that settles the matter. Right place, right people, so let's get on with it. I'd like the key to my room, if you don't mind."

Maggie stared at him. "But you...you're..." She waved a hand in a small, embarrassed gesture that indicated his crutches and bandages. "You're not quite what we had in mind, Mr. January. I'm very sorry about your obvious difficulties, and I mean no offense, but we feel we need a man of action—if you know what I mean. We have a problem here at Peregrine Manor and we need an investigator who is in good physical condition."

His mouth curved briefly in a humorless smile. "Good physical condition? On top of everything else? That's expecting rather a lot, considering what you're paying, isn't it?"

Maggie was incensed. "Now, see here, Mr. January, I am providing room and board at one of the choicest inns on the coast for an entire month. That is hardly a pittance."

"Do you have any idea what the usual hourly billing rate is for round-the-clock BIS services, Ms. Gladstone?" Josh asked very softly.

"Well, no." Of course, she hadn't bothered to inquire. Maggie had known full well she didn't have

the kind of cash it would take to pay for full-time
security service. She could barely pay the electricity
bill these days. "I didn't inquire as to your usual rates
because I assumed that what I was prepared to offer
in exchange for services rendered was adequate com-
pensation."

"Not even close, Ms. Gladstone."

"Then why did you accept the case?" she shot
back.

"Let's just say I happened to be feeling in a real
charitable mood when your letter arrived. You're my
good deed for the year, lady. Now, if you don't mind,
I'd like to get my room key. I would also like to have
my luggage brought upstairs as I am in no condition
to handle it myself. I am supposed to be waited on
hand and foot, according to my partner."

"Why do I have the distinct impression that you
are rarely given to acts of charity, Mr. January?"

He grinned without any warning and there was
something extremely predatory looking about his excellent teeth. "Perhaps because you are a very per-
ceptive female, Ms. Gladstone. Shall we get moving,
here? It has not been a good day. In fact, it hasn't
been a good week or even a good month. I am more
than ready to indulge myself in a little tranquillity."

Maggie considered throwing him out and decided
that was an impossible task, even if she could get the
Colonel to assist. Josh January might be hobbling
around on crutches and appear somewhat the worse
for wear, but he still looked awfully solid. "I suppose
that since you're here now, you may as well spend
the night."

"Ah, a touch of the gracious charm I was told to

expect." Josh inclined his head in a mocking bow. "Thank you, Ms. Gladstone."

"I'll get your key." She stalked past him and went behind the desk to take a key out of one of the little boxes on the wall. "Number 312."

"The third floor?" He gave her a disgusted look. "Forget it. I'm not climbing up and down two flights of stairs every time I leave the room. You said most of the guest rooms were empty. There must be something available on a lower floor."

He had a point, but Maggie was too annoyed by his tone of voice to admit it. She snatched another key out of a box. "Number 210 in the east turret." That was the room right next door to her own, she realized with a start. Not that it mattered, she decided. She automatically fell into the standard sales pitch. "Quite a nice room, if I do say so, myself. Excellent view of the sea. Canopied bed. Your own fireplace with wood supplied. Now, then, if you go on up, I'll see to your luggage."

Josh frowned and glanced through the open door to where the black car was parked in the rain. "Have you got someone around who can give you a hand?"

"Certainly," Maggie said, lying through her teeth. "Your luggage will be no problem. It will be brought up shortly."

"Suit yourself." He shrugged and then adjusted the crutches under his arms. "I smell something cooking. I'm starving. What's the deal on dinner around here?"

"We, uh, were expecting you to join us here at the inn," Maggie replied uneasily. "But perhaps you'd rather drive into town," she added a touch eagerly. "There are a couple of nice seafood places."

"Too much trouble. I'll eat here. I'm supposed to eat home-cooked meals. I'll be down as soon as I've showered and changed. Lord, I could use a drink. It's been a hell of a drive." The crutches thunked on the bottom step.

Maggie bit her lip, watching him progress heavily up the staircase. "I don't believe I mentioned it in my letter, but we—that is, the other residents of the manor—have established a little tradition of dressing for dinner. I go along with it." She eyed his jeans and work shirt. "I rather assumed you might do the same."

"Don't worry," Josh said from halfway up the stairs. "I'll dress. I rarely go out to dinner buck naked."

Maggie closed her eyes in momentary despair and then opened them again when she felt a cold blast of rain sweep into the hall through the open door. She grabbed an umbrella from the old-fashioned stand, gritted her teeth and went out into the downpour to fetch Joshua January's luggage.

She was beginning to wonder if she had made an enormous mistake in hiring a private investigator, sight unseen. Furthermore, she had a hunch it would be extraordinarily difficult to undo the error. Mr. January did not appear to be someone who would take kindly to being fired.

In fact, Maggie decided as she opened the rear door of the black car, Joshua January didn't look like the kind of man who did anything he didn't want to do. Rain thundered on the umbrella as she peered into the dark interior of the vehicle. She groaned aloud when she saw the luggage looming there. Apparently Mr. January didn't believe in traveling light.

She reached inside and lifted out one of the smaller cases. It was surprisingly heavy and was constructed of metal. She scurried back to the front door of the inn and set the case down in the hall. The Colonel appeared in the parlor doorway. His eyes brightened when he saw the metal suitcase.

"Oh-ho, a computer, I see." The Colonel nodded to himself, looking eminently pleased. "Our man is a high-tech sort of investigator. Excellent. Excellent."

Maggie glanced at the case and felt a wave of relief. The computer was a very positive sign, she told herself. Perhaps Joshua January *did* know what he was doing, after all. "I've heard that most modern investigations are done with computers."

"I'm sure the old methods are still employed," the Colonel said. "No substitute for fieldwork, I expect. But there's no doubt computers are the key to all the records that are maintained on people in this day and age. Yes, sir. Our man appears to know what he's doing."

Maggie wondered if the Colonel would still feel that way once he got a look at the crutches and bandages "our man" was currently sporting. She turned and dashed out into the rain for another suitcase.

Five minutes later she had two suitcases, a garment bag and the computer all safely in the hall. She eyed the stairs with a silent sigh.

"Need a hand with those, my dear?" the Colonel inquired gallantly.

"No, thanks. They're light as a feather." Maggie managed a bright, reassuring little smile. The Colonel, being the gentleman he was, was more or less obliged to make the offer, but they both knew his doctor had sternly forbidden him to put his bad back at risk. "I'll whisk them upstairs and be back down in a few minutes. Mr. January said he would be delighted to join us for dinner.''

"Excellent." The Colonel turned and sauntered back into the parlor.

Maggie waited until he was out of sight and then she bent down to hoist the two suitcases. She staggered toward the stairs, wondering if the weight of one of the bags was caused by a very large gun of some sort.

At the second-floor landing she paused to catch her breath and then took a fresh grip on the suitcases before plodding down the hall to 210. January had been right, she reflected. The third floor would have been a bit much.

A moment later she set the suitcases down a second time and rapped sharply on the turret-room door.

"Hang on. I'll be there in a minute," January growled back.

Maggie used the short wait to catch her breath. By the time the door was open a crack, she was no longer panting. But the sight of Joshua January wearing only a towel around his lean waist and the remains of some shaving cream on his face was enough to take her breath away all over again.

"Oh, it's you." Josh glanced at his luggage, reached down and hauled first one and then the other suitcase into the room.

"I could have done that." Maggie's mouth was suddenly dry and her pulse seemed to be pounding as hard as it had when she'd climbed the stairs with the suitcases. Then she noticed the huge dark, blotchy bruises on his ribs and shoulder. "Good heavens! It must have been a really miserable drive for you."

He followed her gaze, glancing down at his chest. "Bruises always look the worst a couple of days after the accident."

"Can I get you something?"

"A shot of whiskey and a decent meal when I get downstairs will take care of everything. Where's my computer?"

"In the hall. I'll bring it and the garment bag right up." Maggie whirled and fled back down the corridor. The sight of January's broad, muscled shoulders gleaming in the soft light of his room was having an odd effect on her nerves.

Perhaps it had been the glimpse of the canopied four-poster bed behind him that had created the disturbing sensation. The whole scene had been far too *intimate*.

When she got the computer upstairs she knocked quickly. "I'll leave it outside the door, Mr. January," she shouted through the wood. "See you downstairs."

BACK IN THE BATHROOM, Josh scraped the rest of the shaving cream off his jaw and listened to the sound of Maggie Gladstone's footsteps scurrying down the hall. *Nice going, January. Apply the chill factor, why don't you, and send the only interesting female you've encountered in God knows how long running in the opposite direction.*

His hunch had been correct. Maggie Gladstone might be a spinster, but she sure as hell wasn't elderly. In fact, she was extremely attractive in a rather unusual way. There was a sweet, wide-eyed innocence about her, even though she had to be close to thirty. He was willing to bet she'd been a small-town girl all her life. Maybe a schoolteacher or a librarian. She probably read a lot of mystery novels and thought private eyes were the last of the paladin kings—lone crusaders who fought for truth and justice on the side of the little guy.

Definitely not his type.

Nevertheless, Josh could not deny he had felt an almost-irresistible urge to thread his fingers through the mass of tawny curls that had cascaded down Maggie's neck. She had looked sleek and lithe, yet rounded in all the right places in that black jumpsuit she'd been wearing.

He was thinking about sex. He must be feeling better.

He gazed broodingly at his dark, forbidding reflection in the mirror and wondered what the hell he had gotten himself into by accepting this bizarre job in Peregrine Point.

He'd been crazy to let McCray talk him into it. Half out of his mind from the painkillers they had given him at the hospital. That was the only explanation.

He surveyed his bruised and battered body. None of the damage was permanent. *This time.* But there was no getting around the fact that a man who was about to turn the big four-oh didn't bounce back the way he would have five, ten or fifteen years ago.

He was definitely getting too old to be dashing into dark buildings after people who had no strong inhibitions about smashing other people with tire irons, knives and assorted other implements of destruction. *Too old to play hero.* When in hell was he going to learn? Josh wondered grimly.

He stifled a groan as he leaned over the sink to rinse the shaving cream from his face. Maybe this time he *would* need a month to recuperate, just as McCray and the doctor had suggested.

And there was always the book, Josh reminded himself. He needed to bite the bullet and take a crack at writing that mystery novel he'd been contemplating for the past couple of years. Peregrine Manor was just the kind of place where a man could settle in and find out whether he was meant to be a writer.

Josh bit back a savage oath as he limped heavily out of the tiny bathroom. The ankle was only sprained, not broken, but when he accidentally jarred it, the damn thing seemed to ache a lot more than a fracture would have. At least the bruises would fade in a few more days.

He gave the frivolous room a single, disparaging glance and shook his head. The place looked like something out of a fairy tale with its rounded tower walls, heavy velvet drapes and the gingerbread trim on the furniture. The bed itself was an ornate monstrosity. Josh knew he was going to feel like an idiot when he levered himself up into the thing via the little wooden steps on the side. He wondered if the management would supply an old-fashioned bed warmer at night.

For some reason that thought brought Maggie Gladstone to mind again.

Josh jerked a suitcase up onto the silly-looking bed and opened it. Inside he found a clean white shirt and a silk tie. There was a fairly decent Italian jacket and a pair of slacks in the garment bag. It was beyond him why anyone would bother to dress for dinner in a place like this, but he was willing to go along with the program. Up to a point.

He grinned fleetingly at the thought of what Maggie Gladstone's expression would be when she saw him wearing a pair of unlaced running shoes with his Italian jacket and silk tie. There was no way he was going to get a pair of dress shoes onto his still-swollen left foot.

Twenty minutes later, Josh made his way slowly and carefully down the carpeted stairs. There was a tantalizing aroma in the hall that indicated dinner was a real possibility. Things were looking up. He almost regretted the way he'd snapped and growled at poor little Ms. Maggie Gladstone.

Then he reached the inn's front parlor, saw the rest of his clients waiting for him and changed his mind again.

Maggie turned toward him at the sound of the crutches on the hardwood floor. She gave him a polite but extremely wary smile. "Oh, there you are, Mr. January. Allow me to introduce you. Mrs. Odessa Hawkins and Miss Shirley Smith."

"Ladies." Josh inclined his head as he lowered himself cautiously into a chair. "Call me Josh." The two bright-eyed women on the sofa twinkled at him.

"We are ever so grateful you were able to accept our offer, Josh," Odessa said with a gracious smile.

"You can say that again," Shirley declared. The rhinestones in her glasses flashed in the light as she examined the crutches and bandages. "What the heck happened to you, anyway? Have a shoot-out with some bad guys?"

"I had an accident," Josh answered smoothly.

"Oh. Sorry about that." Shirley looked disappointed. "Thought maybe it was bad guys."

Maggie took charge again, nodding at a patrician-looking gentleman with a magnificent white mustache and ramrod posture. "And this is Colonel Amos Boone."

"Retired," murmured the old soldier as he strode forward to shake Josh's hand. "U.S. Army. Everyone calls me the Colonel."

"I see."

"What sort of hand weapon do you favor, sir?" the Colonel asked with professional interest. "Automatic pistol or revolver? Always carried a Colt single action, myself. Back when I was on active duty, that is."

"I'm not particularly interested in guns," Josh replied.

Maggie frowned. "You mean you don't carry one?"

"Not if I can avoid it. Which is most of the time, believe me."

The Colonel nodded wisely. "Martial-arts man, eh? Not surprised. You've got the look. Always could tell those martial-arts types."

Maggie's attractive mouth tightened as she gave the crutches a pointed glance. She smiled a little too sweetly. "Let's hope that's not his forte, Colonel. If it is, we're in trouble, aren't we? A martial-arts expert on crutches does not inspire confidence."

"Don't worry, Maggie," Josh said very gently. "My crutches have been licensed as lethal weapons."

The Colonel cleared his throat and hastened to interrupt before Maggie could respond to the goad. "I say, sir, what can I get you to drink?"

"Whiskey, if you've got it." Josh glanced doubtfully at the liquor cabinet.

"Certainly, we've got it." The Colonel opened one of the doors on the cabinet and removed a bottle.

"Good Tennessee sippin' whiskey. Just the thing on a night like this." He splashed a modest amount into a glass and handed it to Josh with a flourish.

"Thanks." Josh took a swallow and enjoyed the heat all the way down. He caught Maggie studying him covertly. It was easy to read her thoughts. He smiled blandly at her. "The answer is no."

She blinked and Josh took some small satisfaction from the flash of surprise in her eyes.

"I beg your pardon?" Maggie said.

"I said the answer is no, I am not a lush. Hard-drinking private eyes exist only in novels. Heavy drinking isn't conducive to clever sleuthing, and we real-life types have a living to make. I hope you're not too disappointed?"

"Relieved is the word," she answered dryly. "Discovering you had a drinking problem in addition to being accident-prone would have been somewhat discouraging under the circumstances."

"Yeah. I can see that." Josh leaned his head back against the cushion and deliberately narrowed his eyes with lazy menace as he watched her. He realized he was beginning to enjoy himself. He swirled the whiskey in his glass and said absolutely nothing until Maggie began to fidget uneasily. It didn't take long. The lady was out of her league when it came to wars of nerve. "Now, then, suppose you all tell me just what it is you want done in exchange for a month's free room and board?"

Maggie straightened her shoulders and fixed him with a determined glare. "Now, see here, Mr. January. I have contracted for first-class professional investigative services. We expect an investigator who is fully capable of taking on the responsibilities of

this job. Do you really believe you can handle this
assignment in your present condition?''

Josh smiled slowly. ''You get what you pay for,
lady. And believe me, for what you're paying, I'm
the best that's available.''

CHAPTER TWO

MAGGIE DID NOT LIKE Josh's smile. It made her more uneasy than ever. It also made her angry. It occurred to her that her emotions had been all over the place in the short time January had been at Peregrine Manor. In the past forty minutes she had experienced everything from hopeful expectation to extreme irritation. Somewhere in the middle, she was forced to admit, there had also been a powerful element of pure, physical attraction.

Physical attraction was all it could be, she assured herself firmly. The man was certainly not going out of his way to endear himself to her. In fact, it would take very little at this point to make her dislike him intensely.

It was time to take charge of the situation. She had set this whole thing up so she would have to see it through. Maggie returned Josh's taunting smile with a stiff, mockingly polite one of her own.

"Mr. January—"

"I thought I told everyone to call me Josh."

It wasn't worth an argument, Maggie reflected. "Very well, Josh. I'll be blunt and tell you straight out that you are not what I expected when I set out to hire a private investigator."

"I rarely am. What people expect, that is. For some reason I always seem to come as a surprise."

"I can understand that," Maggie said. "Now, then. As we appear to be stuck with you—"

"Really, Maggie," Odessa interjected reproachfully. "There's no need to be rude to Josh."

"Yeah, he ain't really done nothin' yet," Shirley added. "Give the guy a chance."

The Colonel cocked a disapproving brow at Maggie. "Quite right, my dear. We must give our man an opportunity to do his job. Personalities should not enter into the equation."

Maggie flushed under the gentle rebukes. She could see the laughter in Josh's eyes. "I fully intend to give our—I mean—Josh a chance. As he himself has just told us, we appear to be getting what we paid for."

Josh held up a hand. "I have an idea. Why doesn't one of you tell me why you all think you need a private investigator? I believe Maggie's letter said something about 'disturbing occurrences' here at Peregrine Manor. What disturbing occurrences?"

Predictably, everyone started to talk at once.

"The most unsettling incidents..." Odessa began in a worried tone.

"Felt we should get a professional to look into them," the Colonel confided. "A lot at stake, you know. Potentially millions."

"Warnings," Shirley said eagerly. "That's what they are. Warnings. And I don't mind tellin' you I'm scared."

Josh held up his hand again. "I said one of you should give me the details. Not all of you at once." He looked straight at Maggie. "You wrote the letter and you're apparently paying my fee, such as it is. Tell me what, exactly, is going on around here."

The Colonel cleared his throat in an attention-getting manner. "He's quite right, Maggie. If we all talk at once we'll only cloud the issue. Lay out the facts for our man."

"All right." Maggie crossed her legs and absently started to swing her foot as she gathered her thoughts. Josh January was the kind of man who dealt in hard facts. He wouldn't be interested in hunches and intuition. "A series of incidents have occurred here at the manor which have alarmed all of us to some degree. In fact, the real reason we're closed for the offseason this year is because of those incidents."

"Give me some specifics," Josh urged, his gaze on her swinging foot.

"First, there are all the mechanical and structural problems that we've been experiencing." Maggie realized he was watching her foot, which was half out of her patent-leather pump. She carefully uncrossed her legs and slid her stocking-clad foot back into the shoe. "At the height of the season the large freezer and the refrigerator we use in the kitchen went on the fritz. We lost several hundred dollars' worth of food. But worse than that, we had to close the dining room on the biggest weekend of the year. A lot of people with reservations for dinner were very upset. The inn was full and everyone was irritated at the inconvenience."

"Go on," Josh prompted.

He seemed to have lost interest in her foot since she'd put it back inside her shoe. Now, Maggie realized, for some reason he was watching her hands.

"We've had continual problems with the furnace, although it was installed less than two years ago." Maggie finally realized that her fingers were fluttering as she talked. She folded her hands in her lap. "Then

one day I happened to do a routine test on the smoke
detector in the basement and discovered that the batteries had been disconnected. That really worried me.
The Colonel keeps all his equipment and files in the
basement, you see. A fire that started down there
would be disastrous.''

"Equipment and files?''

The Colonel shrugged modestly. "I do a bit of ex-
perimenting. We'll get into that later, if you like.''

"I see.'' Josh switched his gaze back to Maggie.
"Anything else strange going on?''

She bit her lip. She was afraid Josh wasn't very
impressed so far. "As I said, there have been a variety
of little, annoying breakdowns. The new hot-water
tank went out. The guests were very irate over that,
I can tell you.''

"Some of them shouted at Maggie in the rudest
possible terms. Very upsetting,'' Odessa confided.
"The Colonel was forced to speak to one man who
was exceptionally ill-mannered.''

"'Conduct unbecoming,' as we used to say in the
military.'' The Colonel shook his head with a frown.
"I sent the fellow packing, of course.''

Maggie smiled wryly. "Unfortunately you sent him
packing before he had paid for his room.''

"Maintaining standards is considerably more important than money,'' Odessa declared.

"Right,'' Shirley agreed. "Gotta have standards.''

"Very true,'' the Colonel murmured. "Can't tolerate just any sort of behavior, you know.''

Maggie stifled a small sigh. It was much easier to
take the high road on that subject when one wasn't
trying to keep the books balanced. She realized Josh
was watching her intently again. She hurried on with

the rest of the tale. "In addition to the trouble with the hot-water tank, we had trouble with the toilets. Then the rooms with fireplaces, such as yours, all developed problems in the chimneys. The rooms filled up with smoke whenever the guests lit their fires. The fire trucks were here every night for a week before we had to make a rule that no one could use the fireplaces."

Shirley shook her head grimly. "We finally got 'em cleaned out and working, but it was one thing after another and first thing you know, word started getting around."

Josh glanced at her. "What word?"

"You know. Like the manor was not a nice place to stay anymore. Too many problems. Old-fashioned wiring. Inconvenient. In need of repairs. Folks said the new management was letting the place go down the tubes. Maggie started losing bookings."

Josh gave Maggie a thoughtful look. "Is that right?"

She nodded unhappily. "After the trouble with the fireplaces, I decided it would be better to say we were closing for the off-season this year. I told everyone repairs were going to be made over the winter and that things would be back in tip-top shape by spring. But the truth is, the place is already in good shape. Great-Aunt Agatha saw to that."

"Who's Agatha? Besides being your great-aunt, that is," Josh inquired.

The Colonel answered that one. "Agatha Gladstone was one of the finest ladies you'd ever want to know. She owned this place for forty years. Died last year and left the manor to Maggie, here."

Josh absorbed that. Maggie could see questions in

his eyes but he didn't ask them. Instead, he focused on his original line of inquiry. "Okay, let me get this straight. There have been a series of small but annoying mechanical and electrical problems here at the manor. The inn started getting a bad reputation and you decided to close the place down except for your three regular guests, here."

Maggie blinked at him in surprise. "Odessa, Shirley and the Colonel are not guests. They are permanent residents. The manor is their home, too. Aunt Agatha made that very clear."

The Colonel nodded. "Had an understanding, don't you see? We're a family. Agatha's gone, rest her soul, but now we've got Maggie."

Josh eyed Maggie. "Uh-huh. Just one big happy family."

Maggie frowned. "The point is, we don't believe all the incidents over the past few months have been due to sheer bad luck. We want you to find out who or what is behind them, and what his motive is. Before you begin, you should know that we all have different theories you really ought to check out."

Josh sipped his whiskey. "Would anyone mind if we ate dinner before we explored these theories? I'm hungry. I was promised home-cooked meals, if you'll recall."

Maggie stood abruptly and managed a tight smile. "Not at all. If you'll excuse me for a minute, I'll go check on the casserole."

"I'll come with you," Odessa said.

The Colonel rose gallantly as the two women headed for the door. "Maggie and Odessa do the cooking around here these days," he explained to Josh. "Had to let the chef and kitchen help go when we closed down for the winter. Shirley and I clean up."

"Just one big happy family," Josh murmured again.

"Don't knock it," Shirley remarked. "It works."

Maggie glanced back over her shoulder as a thought occurred to her. She paused in the doorway, wondering how a man could simply take off for an entire month. "Do you have a family, Josh?"

"No," said Josh. "The only one I have to worry about is myself. I like it that way."

Maggie shivered under the wintry chill of his words and hurried down the hall after Odessa.

"What do you think of him?" Maggie hissed under her breath when she caught up with the older woman.

"Seems quite a capable young man," Odessa answered cheerfully as they entered the kitchen. "I feel we're in good hands, dear."

"Capable? The man's on crutches, for heaven's sake. And he doesn't seem all that professional to me. His attitude seems wrong. And he doesn't even carry a gun. I thought all private eyes carried guns."

"Perhaps that's only true in those novels you're always reading, dear. Have you ever actually met any private investigators?" Odessa opened the refrigerator door and removed the tossed green salad she had prepared earlier.

"Well, no. But I've read enough mysteries to have a good idea of what to expect in an investigator." Maggie grabbed a set of hot pads and opened the oven door. Fragrant steam wafted upward. "It occurs to me that maybe Josh January accepted this job because he thought the manor might be a nice place to recuperate from his accident. He probably thinks our problems will make for a real cushy assignment.''

''I wonder what happened to him?'' Odessa tossed the salad greens with the dressing that had been made from her own secret recipe. ''Do you suppose it was an automobile accident?''

''More likely someone got really annoyed with him and pushed him down a flight of stairs,'' Maggie muttered darkly as she hoisted the casserole out of the oven.

''You're not far off,'' Josh said from the doorway. He leaned with one shoulder propped against the wall, both crutches in one hand. Somehow he managed to look casually arrogant and mildly predatory, even though he was precariously balanced. ''Someone did get really annoyed with me.''

Maggie set the casserole down very quickly. It was the heat of the oven that was causing a flush to rise up her neck, she assured herself. She glanced pointedly at his crutches. ''I didn't hear you coming down the hall.''

Josh grinned evilly. ''I know. Moving stealthily is child's play for us professional private eyes. We take special courses in it.'' He tapped the crutches soundlessly on the Oriental rug in the hall. ''The carpeting makes it easy, you see. Even with crutches. You might want to remember that.''

''I will,'' Maggie snapped.

''Pay no attention to Maggie,'' Odessa said lightly. ''She was just being clever. Maggie has quite a sense of humor.'' She smiled serenely as she carried the salad past him out of the kitchen. ''Do have a seat at the big round table in the dining room, Josh. We'll have dinner ready in a moment.''

"Thanks." Josh waited until Odessa had disappeared into the dining room before turning back to Maggie. "Anything I can do to help?" he asked blandly.

"I doubt it," Maggie replied. "Not in your present condition." She swept grandly past him, casserole in hand.

"Remind me not to be standing at the top of any staircases when you're around," Josh murmured to her back.

MAGGIE HAD BEEN DEAD-ON, Josh reflected midway through dinner. He had taken on this ludicrous excuse for a case primarily because it had seemed like a cushy job and because he needed some time to recover from his "accident." Very clever lady, that Maggie Gladstone. He would have to keep an eye on her. It would be one of the perks of the job.

The case itself was going to be a cinch, of course—just as McCray had predicted. The situation here at Peregrine Manor was a clear-cut case of some unfortunate luck coupled with some vivid imaginations. Things were constantly going wrong in big old houses. His client had obviously panicked over a few minor incidents that were actually nothing more than perfectly normal problems.

The trick would be to stretch out this so-called case for an entire month. If he did stay the four weeks, as planned, he could get some good solid writing done on the book. He would do it, he decided promptly. When he was feeling fit again and had decided whether or not he was cut out to be a mystery writer, he would prepare an imposing report to present to his client. She and her "family" would be suitably impressed and probably relieved to be told no one was behind the incidents. *Piece of cake.* In the meantime, he could sit back and get himself waited on, hand and foot. Maggie's cooking was excellent, if this first meal was any indication.

Josh polished off his second helping of the very tasty vegetable-and-cheese casserole. He was considering a third serving when Odessa, with the unfailing graciousness of the born hostess, offered it to him.

"Do have another helping, Josh. A gentleman recovering from a serious accident needs to build up his strength." Odessa smiled warmly.

"You talked me into it." Josh scooped out some more of the casserole. "I'm ready to listen to your theories now. Why don't you start, Odessa?"

"Certainly." Odessa put down her fork and pursed her lips in a disapproving fashion. "I am convinced that one of my nephews is behind the effort to close down Peregrine Manor. I have three, you know. Nephews, that is."

"Why would any of your nephews want to close down the manor?"

"Retaliation for my having recently written all three of them out of my will, of course," Odessa stated. "A nasty, ungrateful, selfish lot, those nephews. I have finally decided not to leave any of them a single share of my gold-mining stock. I hold a considerable interest in a company called Lucky, Inc. I fear my nephews have learned about my intentions to disown them. They think they can terrorize me into changing my mind."

Josh managed not to smile at that. It was highly unlikely that any lady who held a "considerable amount" of valuable stock would be wearing a gown as faded and worn as the one Odessa Hawkins had on tonight. Odessa may have been wealthy at one time, but the air of faded elegance about her now was unmistakable. He was certain someone had hocked the diamonds in her massive dinner ring years ago. That was glass glittering on her finger. He would bet on it.

"I, however, have a different theory," the Colonel intoned portentously from the head of the table. "I believe I mentioned earlier that I am conducting some experiments down in the basement. I don't mention the fact to just anyone, but the truth is, I am something of an inventor. I have been making tremendous progress on a potentially valuable alternative fuel that would make oil-based fuels obsolete. I venture to say it will revolutionize the automobile industry, as well as the manufacturing sector of our economy."

"Interesting." Josh abruptly swallowed an oversize bite of casserole and remembered the disconnected smoke-detector batteries down in the basement. *Just what I need,* he thought ruefully. *A month spent in a mansion with a crazy inventor who likes to play with flammable substances.*

"Naturally, I've suspended all experimentation until you get this matter sorted out for us," the Colonel went on. "Can't risk the results of my experiments falling into the hands of the wrong parties."

"No," Josh agreed quickly. "Can't take the risk. Suspending your experiments for the time being is very wise." *Wait until I'm out of town before you go back to playing inventor.*

"Well, I don't happen to think these incidents have anything to do with Odessa's terrible nephews or the Colonel's experiments," Shirley announced. She peered shrewdly at Josh through her rhinestone-studded glasses. "It's *him*. He's sending me a warning."

Out of the corner of his eye Josh saw Maggie nibble anxiously on her lower lip. A sure sign that she was uneasy. Josh wondered what it would be like to nibble on Maggie's lip, himself. The idea was very appealing. He forced his attention back to Shirley. "Who's sending you a warning, Shirley?" he asked patiently.

"Ricky." Shirley's eyes suddenly filled with tears. "Excuse me. Didn't mean to make a scene." She yanked off her glasses and dabbed at her eyes with her napkin. "It's just that every time I think about him, I get scared."

Josh sighed and turned to Maggie. "Do you know who this Ricky is?"

"He's a gangster," Maggie muttered, looking embarrassed. "Shirley says she used to be his, uh, girlfriend."

"That's right," Shirley sniffed. "Ricky 'The Wrecker' Ring. Twenty years ago they didn't call him 'The Wrecker' for nothin', you know. But he was a gentleman, through and through. Always treated me like I was a queen. Until the day they hauled him off to prison, that is. I know he probably thinks I betrayed him, and now he's going to get revenge."

Maggie coughed discreetly. "Shirley says she changed her last name fifteen years ago when she moved out here to the coast. She's been worried ever since that Ricky would find her when he got out of prison."

Josh lifted his brows. "When was he due for release?"

"He was supposed to get out a few years ago," Shirley replied, wiping her eyes again. "I expect it's taken him this long to find me. But now he has and he's lettin' me know he's going to get even for what he thinks I did. I'd run if I could, but I can't afford to go anywhere. Peregrine Manor is my home."

Josh wondered whether he should mention to this little group that if a powerful mob figure wanted to kill someone like Shirley Smith, the job would probably have been done by now. Then he reminded himself that he had a whole month ahead of him here at the manor. He didn't want to start punching holes in his clients' theories too quickly. They might fire him if they thought they didn't need him. He had a hunch it wouldn't take much to convince Maggie she could dispense with his services.

"All right," Josh declared in an authoritative tone that clients generally responded to quite readily. "That takes care of three of your theories." Privately he had begun to reflect on the possibility of dessert, but forced his attention back to the matter at hand. "What's your explanation for the incidents, Maggie?"

"Perhaps I should go over it with you later, Josh," she said hastily. "You've been given enough to analyze for the moment. Dessert, anyone?" She jumped to her feet and began clearing the table with quick, anxious movements.

Josh watched her with amusement. Her gaze slid away from his as she loudly stacked dishes. It was clear she realized that the pet theories of her fellow residents at Peregrine Manor were ridiculous. She wasn't anxious to give him another explanation to mock.

"Dessert sounds great." Josh was surprised to discover he actually felt quite content sitting in Peregrine Manor's dining room surrounded by the engaging bunch of eccentric lunatics.

Things were looking up. Either that or he was losing it fast.

"Always did like a man with a healthy appetite," Shirley remarked as she got to her feet. "Now, never mind those dishes, Maggie. You know the Colonel and me are the ones who do the clearing up around here. You know, my Ricky would eat like a horse. 'Course, he needed a lot of energy in his line of work. Expect you do too, eh, Josh?"

"Yes, ma'am," Josh agreed. "I lost my appetite for a while after my accident, but I seem to be getting it back." He deliberately caught Maggie's eye. "For a lot of things."

"I'll get the apple pie," Maggie said. She vanished into the kitchen as if pursued by small demons.

Odessa smiled knowingly at Josh. "You're having quite an effect on our Maggie."

The Colonel gave Josh a man-to-man look. "You go easy with her, sir. Don't tease her unless you're serious. Our Maggie is a small-town girl. She isn't used to dealing with men of your stamp."

"Men of my stamp?" Josh arched an eyebrow.

"Now, you know what I mean," the Colonel continued calmly. "You've got the look of a man who's accustomed to going after what he wants. All I'm saying is, don't go after our Maggie unless you're real sure you want her. We're right fond of our Maggie. Wouldn't want to see her get hurt, if you take my meaning."

"I take your meaning." Josh leaned back in his

chair and eased his injured foot carefully out in front of himself under the table. He tried to recall the last time he had been warned off a woman but could not. "You all know Maggie well?" he asked casually.

"Oh, my, yes," Odessa offered. "We all saw a lot of her when she was growing up. Her parents lived in Washington. Maggie spent most of her summer vacations here at Peregrine Manor. Haven't seen as much of her in recent years, of course. Not until Aggie died and left her the manor. But we've all kept in touch. Her folks have retired to Arizona but they get up here at least once every summer."

Josh fiddled idly with his coffee cup as he delicately probed for information. The technique was second nature to him after all these years in the business. "What's she been doing with herself in the past few years?"

"After she got out of high school she went off to college and became a librarian," Odessa explained. "She's been working at it ever since in a couple of different towns around the state. She gave up her last position when she inherited this place. Her folks were against the notion, but Maggie insisted."

"Her boyfriend must have had a few thoughts about Maggie changing careers and moving here to Peregrine Point," Josh observed. He realized he was suddenly tense, waiting for the response that would tell him if Maggie was involved with someone.

"Boyfriend? Maggie doesn't have any boyfriends." Shirley gave a snort. "Not unless you count that Clay O'Connor fella."

"O'Connor?" Josh repeated gently.

"New in town as of last year," the Colonel said, looking concerned. "Opened up a real-estate office.

Seems to be doing fairly well. He and Maggie have started going out to dinner together lately. Took in a movie last week.''

Josh listened to the nuances in the Colonel's tone. ''You don't approve of O'Connor?''

The Colonel shrugged. ''Nothing wrong with the boy, I guess. Polite. Successful. Just seems a bit soft around the edges, if you know what I mean. The kind who should have done a stint in the military to toughen him up.''

'''Soft around the edges' is right. Not the kind of man my Ricky would have wanted behind him in a fight,'' Shirley declared forcefully. ''Maggie can do a lot better than Clay.''

''I'm not so sure about that,'' Odessa countered with a small sigh. ''Clay is really a very nice man, as Maggie says. No different than most men these days and better than a lot of them. At least he's got a steady job and he knows his manners, which is more than I can say about some.''

''That don't say much for men in general these days,'' Shirley muttered. ''A good job and slick manners don't necessarily make for a good man. Like I said, Maggie can do better.''

''Maybe you're all a bit overprotective of Maggie,'' Josh suggested thoughtfully.

The Colonel smiled with just enough steel to remind Josh that the man had once trained other men for war. ''Maybe we are. Like I said, we're a family.''

CHAPTER THREE

SEVERAL HOURS LATER Josh lay propped against the overstuffed bed pillows and stared sleeplessly up at the chintz canopy overhead. It cut off his view of the high ceiling, but he probably could not have seen much there, anyway. He had opened the heavy velvet drapes earlier but a dense cloud-cover was obscuring the moon tonight. There was almost no light coming in through the window.

His thoughts shifted restlessly back and forth between three subjects: Maggie in the room next door, the book, and the idiotic case he had accepted here at Peregrine Manor. Of the three, it was his awareness that Maggie was sleeping in the room next door that was having the strongest effect on him. Inwardly, he sighed. He was too old to be reacting to a woman with this kind of sudden, intensely erotic need.

But the truth was, Josh admitted, he had been strangely fascinated by her from the moment he had opened her crazy letter. Perhaps it had been the incredible audacity of her appeal for help in exchange for a month's free rent that had intrigued him. And most people would never have approached a major security firm for this ridiculous little situation here at Peregrine Point.

No doubt about it, it had taken nerve to write that letter. Josh admired nerve.

He turned on his side, wincing as his bruised ribs protested. He listened for sounds from the room next door. All was silent. Earlier he had heard the water running in the tiny bathroom and his imagination had fed him tantalizing images of Maggie getting ready for bed.

He tried to decide what it was about her that appealed to him. She wasn't stunningly beautiful. She had a surprisingly sharp tongue for a sweet little small-town girl. And Josh just knew that she was going to be one of those demanding clients who wanted a lot more than they were willing to pay for in the way of service.

But something in her had struck a responding chord within him and the more he thought about it, the more he was afraid he knew just what that chord was.

He recognized in Maggie the same naive, misplaced desire to ride to the rescue of the weak and innocent that had once driven him into his present line of work. That explained what she was doing here trying to keep this white elephant of an inn going, of course. She was going to do her best to protect the home of those three aging eccentrics down the hall.

Maggie Gladstone clearly hadn't yet learned that playing knight in shining armor was a thankless task and generally a waste of time.

The clock on the bedside table ticked softly, recording the passage of what was apparently going to be an endless night.

The hell with it, Josh decided. If he wasn't going to get to sleep, he might as well get some work done. He would get started on the book tonight. Sooner or later he was going to have to find out whether he could pull off the task of getting the characters in his head down on paper. *Make that computer disk,* he told himself as he pushed aside the heavy quilt.

Josh levered himself to an upright position and rolled off the edge of the high bed with a sudden surge of enthusiasm. It was not until he was halfway off that he belatedly remembered the small set of steps on the side. By then, of course, his right foot had missed them entirely and he was off balance.

He grabbed for the ornately carved bedpost. The damn thing was apparently broken. It turned beneath his hand, providing no support at all. His fingers slipped off it. In a reflexive movement that he regretted an instant later, Josh put his injured left foot down to catch his full weight. His heel hit the floor and waves of pain shot through him.

"Damn it to hell." Josh gritted his teeth against the agony in his leg and grabbed desperately again for support. His fist closed around a handful of the chintz bed hangings.

Unfortunately the bed hangings had not been designed to bear weight. They tore free of the canopy frame. There was no time to clutch at anything more substantial. Josh toppled awkwardly back onto the edge of the bed, promptly slid off it, and landed heavily on the floor. His bruised shoulder and ribs, which had been healing rather nicely up to that point, took the brunt of the fall.

Josh closed his eyes, clenched his teeth and waited for the agony to recede. While he waited, the torn bed hangings drifted lightly down to settle on top of him.

Josh remained on the floor, tangled up in chintz, and gathered his strength to fight off the pain. He was amusing himself by running through a list of four-letter words that seemed suitable to describe quaint, charming Victorian inns furnished with period pieces when he heard anxious pounding on the door. He knew at once who it was.

"Josh? Josh, are you okay?" Maggie's voice was filled with concern.

Hell. Just what he needed, he thought, disgusted. It wasn't enough that he already felt like a damn fool. No, now he had to face the ignominy of having his client race to the rescue. Somehow his restful, relaxing month on the coast was not getting off to a good start.

"I'm fine, Maggie," he managed. "Go back to bed."

"You don't sound fine. You'd better open the door. I thought I heard something heavy fall in there."

"A little accident," Josh gasped, spitting out a mouthful of chintz drapery.

"Another accident?" she asked in obvious dismay.

"Don't worry about it," he got out through teeth that were still set against the roaring protest of his battered body. The woman was clearly forming the opinion that he was a clumsy idiot. He could hardly blame her.

"Josh, you sound terrible. I'm coming in."

"No." That threat galvanized him into immediate action. Josh lurched to a sitting position beneath the shroud of bed hangings and had to suck in his breath as a new wave of pain surged from his ankle and bruised ribs. "Damn."

The door opened on the far side of the bed. A narrow shaft of light cut a swath across the floor as Maggie stuck her head inside the room. "Josh? Where are you?"

He realized she couldn't see him because he was

lying on the other side of the huge bed. "Over here. Look, Maggie, there's no need to get excited, okay? I'm all right."

"What on earth happened?" She flipped the light switch beside the door. "Good grief, what have you done to the bed?"

"It's more a question of what your bed has done to me. Did you know one of the posts is loose?" Josh inhaled deeply as he tried to free himself of the enveloping fabric. He promptly sneezed. "And when was the last time you washed these things? They're full of dust."

"Oh, dear. I'm sorry about that. It's been a while. This was my aunt's room. I didn't see any reason to keep up the regular housekeeping in the unused rooms. Here, let me help you."

He heard her bare feet padding across the carpet and resigned himself to the inevitable humiliation of being found on the floor. "As long as you're here, you might as well give me a hand. Just get this stupid drapery off me."

"Of course. Josh, I really am sorry about this. Did you miss the step when you tried to get out of bed? Sometimes people get disoriented and forget how high these old beds are. You're not going to sue or anything, are you?"

"That's a thought," he muttered darkly.

"It wouldn't do you any good, you know. The only major asset I've got is this inn and you probably wouldn't want it." She started to lift the chintz fabric away from him and then paused abruptly just as she got it free of his face and shoulders. "Good grief."

"Now what?" He looked up and saw that she was

staring straight down at him. She was blushing furiously.

He also saw that her hair was down, forming a delightfully sleep-tousled cloud around her face. She had put on a quilted robe but hadn't taken the time to tie the sash. Tiny flowers and bits of lace trim adorning an old-fashioned, high-necked flannel nightgown peeped out through the opening of the robe.

Maggie looked warm and cozy and ready for bed. In spite of the pain, Josh felt his body responding in an unmistakable fashion. He wondered idly why nature had made it possible for the male of the species to feel desire and pain simultaneously.

"I'll get you a robe," Maggie said in a small voice and promptly started to drop the draperies back down on top of him.

"*Wait*. Damn it, don't bury me under that stuff again." Realizing belatedly what the problem was, Josh managed a rueful smile. "Guess I should have warned you I sleep in my shorts, huh? Look, if this is too much for your maidenly modesty, just get out of here. I can take care of myself."

"Don't be ridiculous. I'll help you back into bed." She swept the remainder of the fabric away from him and turned quickly to deposit it on the nearest chair. A small cloud of dust wafted upward. "I suppose I really should get these washed as long as they're down."

"Good idea." Josh grabbed on to the edge of the bed and started to hoist himself up off the floor. The movement brought more protest from his ankle and ribs. He bit back another groan.

Maggie whirled around at his small sound of stifled pain. The embarrassment in her gaze was immediately replaced by concern. She reached out to grasp his arm. "Here, lean on me. When we get you back on the bed, I'll run downstairs and get you some ice for that ankle. Would you like some for the shoulder, too?"

Anger at the embarrassing situation in which he found himself swept through Josh, mitigating some small portion of the pain. "I don't need any ice and I don't need a nurse. Just leave me alone, okay? I'm not dying. Not even close." It was only his masculine pride that was on the critical list, he decided.

"No, but you are obviously hurting." She released his arm as he heaved himself into a sitting position on the bed. "Just stay there. I'll be right back with the ice. Is there a robe in your closet?"

"No. Don't own one."

"Oh. Well, I'll be right back."

Before he could stop her, Maggie was out the door. Josh swore under his breath and sat very still, waiting for her to return. As long as she was going for ice, he would be a fool not to use it. Hell of a way to impress a client, he reflected. *Hell of a way to impress a woman.*

By the time he heard Maggie's returning footsteps on the stairs a few minutes later, the pain had receded to a dull throb in both ankle and ribs. He was going to live, after all, Josh told himself grimly as the door to his room opened. Furthermore, he had his raging hormones back under control.

"Luckily we keep some ice bags around for emergencies," Maggie said cheerfully as she came back into the room. "Just lie down and I'll put one on your ankle. I brought one for your shoulder, as well."

There was no point protesting. Josh propped himself in a sitting position against the pillows and winced as Maggie carefully positioned the ice bags. "Thanks." He knew he didn't sound particularly gracious.

Maggie straightened and regarded him with a worried expression. "Do you have any pain pills?"

"Yeah, but I don't need any. I'll be all right in a few minutes. The ice will do the trick." He slanted her a hooded look. "I'm really doing my best to shatter your romantic notions about dashing private investigators, aren't I?"

She smiled at that. "Well, yes, as a matter of fact. You certainly aren't anything like the ones in the novels I've read. I've never heard of one falling out of bed, for instance. But I guess I can cope with reality. Do you still think you can handle this case?"

"With one hand tied behind my back."

She swept an assessing gaze down his bruised and battered frame. "How about with one hand and one foot tied behind your back?"

"I'll manage."

"How?" She gave him a frankly inquiring look.

"What do you mean, how? The usual way."

"I'm serious." She sat down in the chair near the bed and carefully folded her robe around her knees. "How do you intend to approach this case?"

Josh shrugged and tried to compose his words so that he sounded halfway professional. "Well, I think in this particular case, my initial approach will be to eliminate everyone's pet theories. I don't think any of your permanent residents is going to be satisfied with the results unless I've definitely proven them wrong first."

"Hmm." Maggie was quiet for a moment. "You

could be right. I take it you don't believe that any of
the theories you heard explains what's been going on
around here?''

Josh cautioned himself not to say too much too
soon. He didn't want to talk himself out of the job.
''I didn't say that. I said I think they should each be
checked out thoroughly. You know the old saying,
'When you have eliminated the impossible, whatever
remains, however improbable, must be the truth.'''

Maggie's expression brightened. ''Sherlock
Holmes. *The Sign of the Four,* I think. I'm so glad
you've studied the classic detectives.''

''Uh, yeah. The classics.'' Josh decided not to tell
her that it had been nearly thirty years since he had
read Sir Arthur Conan Doyle, and that he had long
since forgotten the origin of the quote. The only reason he had remembered it at all was because it so
frequently fit his cases.

''I suppose you'll be using your computer to eliminate the impossibles in this case?''

''Huh? Oh, yeah. The computer.'' Josh mentally
crossed his fingers. He hadn't planned on using his
computer for anything except working on the book.
''We do a lot of investigative work on computers
these days.''

''Yes, I know.''

There was nothing like having a mystery enthusiast
for a client. He was going to have to watch his step.
Josh sought for a way to change the subject. ''You
never told me *your* pet theory, Maggie. You implied
you had one.''

She gave him an uncertain glance. ''Well, yes, I
do. But you'll probably think it's pure fantasy.''

''Try me.''

"Well…" She hesitated. "To be perfectly frank, I've begun to wonder if someone is after Aunt Agatha's emerald brooch. I haven't been able to find it since she died, you see."

Lord, Josh thought in amusement. *Now we've got emeralds involved in this thing.* "Why would anyone go to the trouble of creating a lot of trouble here at Peregrine Manor because of a brooch?"

Maggie leaned forward intently. "It's my theory that whoever is causing the trouble is actually trying to force the manor to close down entirely so that he or she can search the premises for the brooch."

Josh tried to look suitably impressed. "You think it's hidden somewhere here in the house?"

"It's possible. You see, my aunt died very suddenly from a heart attack. She had no time to give last-minute instructions. She had been in excellent health and had no reason to worry about her future. She always loved that brooch and she kept it in her jewelry box rather than in a safety deposit box. But when I went through her things after the funeral, the brooch was missing."

"Who was supposed to get the brooch after her death? Was it mentioned in her will?"

"Yes. It was to come to me, along with the manor. She left very specific instructions that it was to be treated as a sort of long-term investment."

"An investment?" Josh frowned.

"Yes. For the manor. Aunt Agatha told me privately that I was to sell the brooch if it ever became necessary in order to keep Peregrine Manor running."

"But why? What's so important about keeping the manor open?"

Maggie gave him a startled glance. "It's their home."

"Whose home? You mean Shirley's, Odessa's, and the Colonel's?"

"Right. If the day ever came when the inn could no longer pay its own way as a hotel, Aunt Agatha wanted to be sure it could still shelter her friends."

Josh whistled softly. "Are you telling me your aunt left that kind of responsibility on your shoulders?"

Maggie frowned. "She didn't exactly force it on me. She talked it over with me many times before we made the decision. I didn't mind, really. You see, I've always thought running Peregrine Manor would be fun. And it is. To me, it's the ideal job. I learned a lot about innkeeping while working here during the summers. And I must say, the manor was doing very well before the trouble started a few months ago."

"But now you're not doing so well," Josh suggested. "And the brooch is gone. Probably stolen long ago by some thief who posed as a guest in order to get access to it."

"I don't think so," Maggie said slowly.

"Did your aunt wear the brooch in public?"

"Certainly. Once in a while."

Josh nodded grimly. "Then a lot of people knew she owned it and that she didn't keep it in a safe-deposit box. Believe me, Maggie, it's probably long gone."

"Even if you're right, that doesn't mean my theory about the reason behind the trouble around here is wrong," she pointed out, looking stubborn all of a sudden. "Someone might have decided the brooch is lost somewhere in this house, which is very likely, and has decided to look for it. In order to do that, he has to get the rest of us out. At least for a while.''

Josh drummed his fingers on the bed, trying to be patient. ''Tell me something, Maggie. What are you going to do if you can't save the manor for your aunt's friends?''

She sighed unhappily. ''I don't really know. None of them have much in the way of financial resources. I know Odessa talks about her stock holdings, but Aunt Agatha once told me Odessa had purchased that mining stock years ago and never seemed to get any dividends.''

Josh smiled briefly. ''Which pretty much eliminates one theory, doesn't it?''

Maggie returned his smile with a wry one of her own. ''You mean the one about the three nephews who are furious about being left out of the will? Yes, I'm afraid so. But I haven't had the courage to tell Odessa that. She's so proud. Being a possessor of stock is very important to her.''

''Well, I'll check it out—just to be thorough. If I discover that the stock really is worthless, maybe I can find a tactful way of telling Odessa her nephews aren't trying to terrorize her without having to inform her that the stock is no good,'' Josh suggested.

''That would be very nice of you.''

''So, what will you do if you can't find a way to keep the manor open for those three, Maggie?'' he asked again.

''I don't know,'' she admitted. ''All I can do is try.''

He had been right, Josh thought. A naive little lady Don Quixote, tilting at windmills on behalf of the weak and the innocent. "It's a waste of time, you know."

"What is?"

"Playing hero. Never pays."

She gave him a searching look. "How would you know?"

"Experience," he said, and was amazed at the sudden harshness in his own voice. "How the hell do you think I got started in this business in the first place?"

"Because you wanted to rescue people?"

His jaw tightened. "When I first started, the last thing I planned to do was create a corporation like Business Intelligence and Security. I was just a one-man operation in the beginning. I had some damn fool idea that I could help balance the scales of justice for those who couldn't do it on their own. Like I said, I wanted to play Sir Galahad. I wanted to charge off to protect those who couldn't protect themselves."

"What happened?" she asked gently.

Josh wished he had never started this conversation. But for some reason he couldn't seem to stop it now. "What happened was that I eventually learned that it's damn tough to play hero because it's often impossible to tell the bad guys from the good guys. That's what happened."

"I don't understand."

"Hell, Maggie, during my first five years as an investigator I took on every sob-story case that walked through my front door. And none of them were what they seemed."

"Tell me," she whispered, her eyes wide and searching.

"You want to know what being a private eye is

really like?'' he asked roughly. ''I'll tell you what it's like. Parents came in with tears streaming down their faces and asked me to find their little lost girl. I'd track down the kid and discover that she had run away from home because she was more afraid of being abused by her father than she was of life on the streets.''

''Oh, Josh.''

''I'd find missing wives for distraught husbands, and the wives would tell me they had gone into hiding because their husbands routinely beat them and threatened to kill them. They'd beg me not to tell my clients where they were.''

''How awful…''

''And then there were the child-custody cases,'' he continued, feeling savage. ''Parents wage war with each other and the poor kids get caught in the firing line. The children serve as the battle prizes. Spoils of war. A way for the parents to hurt each other. I was supposed to take the side of whichever parent had legal custody. No one gave a damn about the kids themselves.''

Maggie was silent. ''I think I see what you mean. It's not quite like it is in mystery novels, is it?''

''It damn sure isn't. At least, not most of the time. I finally got smart and decided that since I wasn't going to be able to save the weak and the innocent from the bad guys and since I seemed to have a talent for the business, I might as well get into the end of it that paid well. A friend of mine and I created Business Intelligence and Security, Inc. We got some plush offices in downtown Seattle, hired a staff and went after corporate business. The nice thing about white-collar crime is that there isn't so much emotion involved. And hardly anyone gets killed.''

"I suppose there is a big demand for corporate security consultants these days," Maggie ventured.

"Yeah, and although I never thought I'd say it in the old days, it's cleaner work than the kind of thing I used to do. Give me a nice computer-fraud situation or a loading-dock security problem anytime." Josh stopped abruptly, shocked at how much he had told her.

He knew what had gotten him started. It was seeing in her some of the same useless, naive nobility that he himself had once had. It had goaded him into trying to tear the rose-colored glasses from her eyes.

"You know," Maggie said quietly, "I didn't want to say anything, but I have been wondering exactly why you took this case. Frankly, I was surprised when your office called and said you were on your way."

Josh eased his shoulder into a more comfortable position and studied his throbbing ankle. "You weren't the only one."

"BIS was the last company I expected to get a response from. But I had tried every small agency in the Seattle phone book. No one was willing to come out here to Peregrine Manor in exchange for a month's free room and board. I was getting desperate, and I figured I had nothing to lose by approaching some of the big firms."

"I'll bet most of them laughed in your face," Josh responded glumly.

"Not exactly. But all I got from the rest of them were form letters telling me they didn't handle my sort of case."

"Your situation here is a little unusual," Josh allowed.

Maggie nibbled on her lower lip. "So why *did* you take this case, Josh?"

"Felt like a change of pace," he said simply, shifting again on the pillows. "Like I said. The case is unusual."

Maggie studied him for a moment longer and then got to her feet. "I think there was more to it than that." She smiled tremulously as she came over to the bed. "You know what I think?"

He slanted her a speculative glance, wondering if she had figured out that he was using Peregrine Manor as a place to convalesce. "Why do you think I took this case?"

"I think that, in spite of what you say, you're still playing hero." Her eyes were soft as she bent over the bed to adjust the ice pack on his ankle. "I think something in my letter appealed to your old desire to rush to the defense of the weak and the innocent. You don't want to admit it because you're much too macho. You're too used to hiding your real motives behind the facade of the tough, cynical private eye who's seen it all."

Josh shot out a hand and caught her wrist. Maggie made a small, startled sound. Her gaze flew to his and he took some satisfaction in seeing the dawning awareness in her bright sea-green eyes. "If you really believe that, lady, you're setting yourself up for a major fall. Take some advice. Don't waste your time attributing any fancy do-gooder motives to me. I'm a businessman. Period. You'll get what you paid for."

"You've already told me I'm not paying the going rate. So what, exactly, will I get?" Maggie made no attempt to withdraw her hand from his but Josh could feel the tension radiating through her.

"I'm not sure yet." His voice slipped into a husky growl as he realized just how soft her skin was. The scent of her filled his head. A new surge of arousal shot through him. Without even thinking about it, he used his grip on her wrist to tug her closer.

Alarm and sensual awareness flared simultaneously in her eyes. "Josh? Josh, stop it. For heaven's sake, I don't even know you."

He smiled slightly. "But I know you."

"No, that's not true." But she still made no effort to pull free. Instead, she was watching him with a fascinated look. "You don't know anything about me."

"I know you're small-town born and raised. You were a librarian until recently. I know you spent your summer vacations here at Peregrine Manor when you were growing up. I know your parents live in Arizona. I know you've been dating a real-estate broker named O'Connor." Josh smiled dangerously. "Want me to continue?"

Her lips parted in astonishment. "How did you…? Wait a minute. You grilled the Colonel and the others, didn't you?"

"I'm a private eye, remember? Digging up information is my business."

"You mean prying into other people's lives is your business."

He shrugged. "Same thing. You get used to it after a while. There is no such thing as real privacy in the modern world. In any case, I figured I was entitled to do a little digging where you're concerned. Your friends were warning me off, you see. It annoyed me.''

She frowned in confusion. ''Warning you off what? *Me?*'' She was clearly shocked.

''Right. The Colonel as good as told me not to try to seduce you unless my intentions were honorable.''

''How embarrassing.'' For the first time she started to struggle. Her hand twisted in his grasp. ''You can bet I'll have something to say to all three of them. They mean well, but I don't appreciate people interfering in my private life.''

Josh tightened his grip on her wrist for an instant, not wanting to let her go. But when she struggled again, he released her. ''Does that mean you're interested in being seduced, regardless of whether or not my intentions are honorable?''

''Don't be ridiculous.'' She stepped back quickly from the bed. ''I don't know the first thing about you. Why on earth would I want anything more than a business relationship with you?''

''Who knows? Maybe because I understand you better than you know. I told you, I used to have a few things in common with you.''

''Well, it certainly doesn't sound like we have anything in common now,'' she snapped.

''You never know. We might be kindred souls in search of each other.''

''That's crazy.''

''Life is crazy. Who would have guessed a week ago that I'd be lying in this bed having a midnight conversation with a prim little ex-librarian who reads too many mysteries?'' Josh leaned over and opened the drawer in the bedside table. He pulled out the notepad and pen he had stuck inside earlier in the event that he awoke with a brilliant idea for the book.

Maggie watched him with deep suspicion. "What are you doing?"

"Evening the score. Only fair that we go into this on an equal basis." Josh scrawled McCray's private phone number at the offices of Business Intelligence and Security—the one that bypassed the secretary. When he was finished, he tore off the page and handed it to Maggie. It was amazing how many people automatically took anything that was handed to them, even if they didn't want it. "Here."

"What's this?" Maggie reluctantly took the page and glanced at the phone number.

"You said you didn't know anything about me. Okay, I can fix that. The man who answers that number is named McCray. He's my partner. When you call him, tell him I said he was to tell you anything you want to know about me. He can provide proof of the excellent status of my health—sprained ankle and assorted bruises, aside. He can also give you my credit rating and verify that I have no criminal record or children. He'll even tell you my shoe size and the color of my favorite tie, if you want to know."

"But I don't have any questions about you." Maggie angrily crumpled the paper in her hand. "At least not any *personal* questions."

"You never know." Josh folded his arms behind his head and watched the bright flags of indignation flying in her cheeks. "If you decide you're interested in something more than a business relationship with me, you might suddenly have a lot of questions. Very sensible, these days. A woman can't be too careful, can she?"

"Apparently not. Look what I got when I tried to do something simple like hire a private investigator. Of all the nerve."

"I said the same thing when I read your letter offering me a month's free room and board here at Peregrine Manor. Nerve is something else we have in common, too, although I suspect I've got more of it than you do. Nature of the business I'm in, you know."

"I don't doubt that you are an extremely nervy individual, Mr. January." Maggie turned and stalked toward the door.

"Maggie?"

"Yes?" She paused, her hand on the knob.

"I'll be waiting for you to make that call. I want you to know exactly what you're getting into."

"Don't hold your breath."

Josh smiled. "But I will be holding my breath, Maggie. Because if you do make that call, I'll know you're personally taking down the Keep Off signs the Colonel posted around you."

She stared at him. "You're not really interested in me. Not as a person. You're feeling challenged. That's what it is. Your masculine ego is just acting up because my friends warned you to stay away from me."

"They warned me to stay away unless my intentions were honorable," he corrected softly.

She sniffed in disdain. "They could hardly be *honorable*."

"You won't know that or anything else about me for certain unless you make the call to McCray. This is the modern age, Maggie. A smart woman checks a man out before she gets involved with him."

"I do not intend to get *involved* with you. Good night, Mr. January. You are, if you don't mind my saying so, very well named. I have never met anyone quite so cold-blooded."

"Then you have lived a very sheltered life, Maggie Gladstone."

Josh watched with satisfaction as she started to slam the door on her way out of the room. At the last minute she apparently changed her mind, no doubt afraid the noise would be heard down the hall. She closed it very softly with a self-control that spoke volumes.

She was at least fully aware of him now, Josh decided. As aware of him as he was of her. The month at Peregrine Manor was going to prove interesting.

After a few minutes he removed the ice from his leg and levered himself carefully up and off the bed. This time he found the steps. Balancing on his good leg, he studied the ornately carved bedpost that had turned so easily beneath his wildly clutching fingers.

He recalled what Maggie had said about this room having once belonged to her Aunt Agatha.

Josh took a good grip on the post and slowly turned it counterclockwise. The post squeaked softly in protest and then the entire upper portion came loose.

Josh lifted that section of post off the joining portion and realized he was looking into a small, hidden "safe." There was a little jewelry box resting inside the hollowed-out bedpost. He plucked it out and opened it.

An old-fashioned emerald brooch winked in the light of the bedside lamp.

Was he a hotshot private eye or what? Just give him a clue and he was a regular Sherlock Holmes.

Grinning to himself, Josh replaced the lid and dropped the box back into the hidden chamber. Then he carefully repositioned the upper section of the bedpost and screwed it back into place.

There was no point in solving the mysteries of Peregrine Manor too soon, he reminded himself as he got back into bed. He had a month to kill here. A month in which to delve deeply into the mysteries of one Maggie Gladstone, spinster, amateur sleuth and reader of detective novels. He realized he was looking forward to the next four weeks with more enthusiasm than he'd felt about anything in a long, long while.

Josh went to sleep feeling as if some great weight had begun to be lifted from his shoulders.

CHAPTER FOUR

MAGGIE AWOKE the next morning feeling surprisingly rested and refreshed. She realized that she hadn't been sleeping very well lately. The nightly stress of listening for strange noises, the concern about whether she had double-checked every lock on every window, the growing worry about the future of Peregrine Manor— all had taken their toll on her during the past few weeks.

Apparently there was much to be said for having a man like Josh January in the house. In spite of the crutches and bruises, there was something oddly reassuring about his presence. It was unfortunate he had made that pass last night. Now she was going to have to make a point of keeping him in his place. *No more going to his rescue in the middle of the night,* she told herself.

Maggie showered and quickly selected a pair of jeans and an orange sweatshirt from her closet. When she had put them on, she went to stand in front of the dressing table and picked up a brush.

She had just finished tying her thick hair back into a ponytail when her eyes fell on the crumpled sheet of yellow paper lying on the table. Maggie went very still as vivid details of the night before returned to her.

There had been a disconcerting and thoroughly

devastating masculine arrogance about the way Josh
had sprawled on the big bed in the turret room. His
dark hair had been disturbingly tousled. The crisp,
curling thicket on his broad chest had fascinated her.
It had been all she could do to keep from staring. She
had wanted to run her fingers through that black mat
in the worst way. And she had ached with a desire to
soothe the massive bruise on his rib cage.

The brooding speculation in his eyes had ruffled
her senses as nothing else had ever done. When he
had talked of his bitter disillusionment with his chosen work, she had sensed the fundamental integrity of
the man. Only a man who had a strong sense of integrity would have become disillusioned. Obviously,
Josh hadn't gotten into the business for the money.

Maggie acknowledged with an uneasy little shock
that she would never forget that scene in the room
next door. It would haunt her for the rest of her life.

And even though she knew there must be no rep-
etitions, a part of her would always wonder what it
would have been like to go to bed with Josh January.
She had never in her life experienced such a powerful,
deeply feminine curiosity, and she felt ill-equipped to
deal with it. Her quiet, uneventful past had not prepared her for even a casual approach from a man like
Joshua January.

And casual was all it had been. Maggie's mouth
tightened as she finished surveying herself in the
dressing-table mirror. She would have been shaken to
the core to discover that Josh was even mildly interested in her, but it was a certainty that he hadn't been
half as affected by her presence as she had been by
his. She'd been well aware of his half-aroused body,
of course, but that meant very little. Men were very

physical creatures, very easily aroused. She was old enough to know that. Josh must consider her an amusing challenge—no doubt because he had been warned off her by the Colonel. But that was all there was to it.

She certainly was not going to call the number on that sheet of yellow paper, Maggie told herself firmly. She wondered if he started all his relationships with a mutual background check. Very likely. The man clearly had no romance in his soul. Maybe his profession had destroyed his sense of passion and discovery even as it had destroyed his faith in human nature.

Nevertheless, Maggie couldn't bring herself to throw away the piece of paper. She picked it up and scanned the boldly scrawled figures. There was a lot of male bravado in those numbers. Josh must have been sure she would make the call.

Disgusted, she opened a drawer in the dresser and shoved the crumpled sheet inside. She slammed the drawer shut and left the room.

Halfway down the stairs the aroma of freshly brewed coffee floated up to greet her. Odessa had apparently risen early. Maggie inhaled deeply and smiled with pleasure. The smile was still on her face when she swung the kitchen door open.

"Good morning, Odessa," Maggie said before she realized who was inside. "That coffee smells wonderful."

"Thanks," Josh drawled from the far side of the large room. "I make good coffee, even if I do say so, myself. Here, have a cup."

Maggie stopped short at the sight of him. He was leaning against the tiled counter, sipping coffee from

a mug. His crutches were propped beside him. He
looked very sexy in a denim shirt that was open at
the throat. And there was no getting around the fact
that the man looked good in a pair of jeans. His dark
hair gleamed in the wintry sunlight that streamed in
through the window.

Maggie forced herself to take a deep, steadying
breath as she stepped forward. She was going to be
dealing with Josh for the rest of the month, so she
had to get used to seeing him in the mornings.

The thing to do this morning, she decided, was to
establish the ground rules. It was clear that Rule
Number One was to act as if nothing at all had happened last night. After all, she thought with an odd
sense of regret, nothing *had* happened. He hadn't
even attempted to kiss her. He'd just invited her to
do a background check on him.

"Thank you." Maggie took the cup he held out.
"I take it you're an early riser?"

"Looks like you are, too." Josh grinned fleetingly,
his gaze holding hers over the rim of his cup. "One
more thing we have in common, I guess, huh?"

She shrugged, choosing to ignore the taunting
gleam in his eyes. "I'm one of the cooks around here,
if you'll recall. I have to get up early, whether I like
it or not."

"Ah, yes. I'm looking forward to the home-cooked
breakfast that was promised in your letter. And the
tea and scones mentioned in the brochure, too.
Haven't had a scone in years. Do you put raisins in
yours?"

Maggie nearly choked on her coffee. "The tea and
scones are only served when the manor is open for
guests. I would have thought that was obvious."

"Nope. Tea and scones are part of the deal."
Josh's expression was unreadable. "As far as I'm
concerned, I signed on for this job based on what was
promised in that letter and the brochure that accompanied it. It's a binding contract."

"Oh, for heaven's sake, Josh. I was merely listing
the amenities of the manor. Surely you understood
that. I didn't mean to imply that you were going to
be served as if you were a paying guest."

"That's exactly what was implied. And I'm holding you to what was promised." He ticked the items
off on his fingers. "A home-cooked breakfast, tea and
scones in the afternoons, and a gourmet dinner."

"Is that so? Well, when do I start getting some
investigation services in return?"

"Relax. I've been on the job since the minute I
walked through your front door. You're in good
hands, lady."

"Wonderful. So reassuring to know the future of
the manor is in the hands of an investigator who has
problems just getting out of bed," Maggie grumbled.
She caught her breath as she realized she had just
broken her own rule about not mentioning the pre-
vious night. Her gaze flew to Josh's and she knew it
was too much to hope that he would ignore the comment.

"I may have a little trouble getting out of bed,
Maggie, but I can guarantee you I know how to get
into one."

Maggie lifted her chin proudly. "I think I should
tell you I do not appreciate that kind of humor. Furthermore, as I am your employer, it is within my
rights to set the standards of behavior I shall expect
from you in the future. I wish to make it very clear

that I expect that behavior to be entirely businesslike and professional in nature. Do you understand?''

"Got it." He took a swallow of coffee and smiled again. "Going to make that phone call to McCray today?"

"No, I am not. I have no reason to make it."

"I'll give you a reason," Josh said softly.

Before Maggie realized his intentions, he set down his coffee mug on the counter and reached for her.

"Josh." Maggie looked up at him as tension suddenly rippled through her. She felt herself being tugged gently, inevitably, forward, and for the life of her she couldn't summon up the will to resist. Curiosity was swamping her good sense.

"I wanted to do this last night," Josh muttered.

He bent his head and his mouth brushed lightly across hers. The kiss was full of masculine invitation and tantalizing promise. Maggie tasted coffee and an intimate warmth that made her shiver.

Josh lifted his head almost at once, breaking the contact before she even had time to decide how to react. He watched her with lazy, glittering eyes as she instinctively touched her lips with wondering fingertips.

The brief embrace had been a hint of possibilities, not a full-blown kiss, she reflected. Still, she had felt it to the soles of her feet. Just as she had known she would. Just as *he* must have known she would.

"I didn't do it last night because I figured it would be a little too much for you. And a little too soon." Josh slid his hands slowly up her arms to her shoulders and then wrapped them gently around the nape of her neck. "You're not accustomed to making quick decisions about people the way I am. You don't know how to look into a person's eyes and see if you're being lied to. But me, I'm an old hand at it. I've been sorting out the lies from the truth for so long that it's second nature.''

"You're right," Maggie replied breathlessly. "I don't have that skill. So, how will I know if you're telling me the truth about yourself?''

"For starters, you can make the call to McCray,'' he said gently.

That brought Maggie down to reality with a thud. She stepped back quickly and Josh let her go. "No, thanks. Then I'd have the added problem of not knowing if I could trust McCray, wouldn't I?''

"Like I said, he can supply proof to back up anything he tells you.''

Maggie smiled nervously. "Excuse me, I'd better get started on your home-cooked breakfast. Wouldn't want you to say I'd stiffed you out of your fee.''

He chuckled. "Right. Word of mouth travels in my business, same as it does in yours. You might have trouble hiring another investigator in the future if you don't pay me.''

Odessa appeared in the doorway. "Squabbling again, are we, children? My, my. Never saw two people strike sparks off each other the way you two do.''

"She started it,'' Josh said cheerfully.

Maggie groaned. "And here I was just beginning to think you were man enough to take responsibility for your own actions.''

Josh sipped his coffee. "Depends on the actions.''

"Now, now, my dears, that's enough of that sort of thing.'' Odessa bustled about the kitchen, selecting grapefruits from the tray on the counter and a knife from a drawer. "Stop teasing her, Josh.''

"Yeah, Josh." Maggie arched her brows. "Stop teasing me. Your threat is meaningless, anyway. You know darn well I'm hardly likely to ever need a private investigator again in my entire life. What do I care if I get blacklisted by your union for nonpayment of your fee?"

"You never know," Josh murmured. "A lot of women are using investigators these days."

Odessa gave him a surprised glance. "Why on earth would young women be going to private investigators?"

"To have background checks run on the men they're dating," Josh explained. "BIS gets requests all the time, but since we focus on corporate security, we generally refer the potential clients to smaller agencies."

Maggie was startled. "You're serious, aren't you?"

"I'm always serious when it comes to business," he assured her.

Odessa looked thoughtful. "What kind of women go to investigators to have their boyfriends checked out?"

"Smart women." Josh shrugged. "One major group of female clients are women who have established careers and are financially independent. They're at risk of being married for their money, same as men are. They want to make certain they're not marrying con artists who will clean out their bank accounts and then split. Another growing group of clients are women who want to be sure they're not dating men who are secretly bisexual or using drugs."

"Makes sense to me," the Colonel remarked from the doorway. "In the old days a young woman's parents and neighbors knew a lot about the man she wanted to marry. They did the background checks, you might say. But these days there's no one to protect the ladies.''

"Or they won't listen if you do try to protect them.'' Josh slid Maggie a meaningful glance. "Give a lady a little friendly advice these days and she takes the bit in her teeth and runs in the opposite direction.''

"Speaking of running.'' Maggie set her cup down on the counter with a loud thud. "We'd better get breakfast on the table, hadn't we, Odessa? I'm sure Josh is eager to get started on his inquiries. Colonel, would you like to show him around Peregrine Manor this morning? You could point out all the places where we've had problems. He might be able to find a clue or something.''

"Certainly,'' the Colonel agreed. "Be delighted.''

"A clue.'' Josh looked politely enthusiastic. "What a good idea. Clues are very helpful in my line of work.''

"We'll just have to hope you can recognize one when you see it, won't we?'' Maggie murmured as she pulled a frying pan out of the cupboard.

"Not to worry,'' Josh retorted. "I brought along my handy-dandy official private investigators' manual. I believe there's an entire chapter devoted to finding and recognizing clues.''

"A manual, you say? How reassuring.'' Maggie measured flour for pancakes. "Did you see it advertised on the back of a cereal box and send away for it with a coupon?''

"Probably,'' Josh said. "I eat a lot of cereal. I almost never get real home-cooked breakfasts, you see.''

"Well, well, well. Fireworks already." The Colonel winked at Odessa. "Sounds like things are going to be lively around here for the next month."

Shirley walked into the kitchen, yawning. "You know what my Ricky always used to say about two people who went at it right off the bat like Josh and Maggie here?"

"No. What did Ricky 'The Wrecker' used to say?" Josh asked.

"He'd say they were either meant for each other or else they would wind up throttling each other. One of the two."

"An interesting choice," Josh observed blandly.

MAGGIE WAS RATHER surprised to discover that during the next few days Josh fitted himself very comfortably into the routine at Peregrine Manor. As his injured ribs and ankle improved, he even turned out to be surprisingly useful around the place. He was always up first and had the coffee going by the time Maggie came downstairs. Furthermore, he seemed to be quite handy in the home-repair department. He gave her a hand painting three of the guest bathrooms, fixed a broken toilet seat and rehung the canopy over his bed.

And he did not make any more passes.

"I still don't know if you're much of an investigator, but you're certainly saving me a bundle of money that I would normally have spent on Dwight," Maggie told him at one point.

"Who's Dwight?"

"Dwight Wilcox is a handyman in town. He usually takes care of the minor repairs around here for me," she explained.

By the end of the week Maggie realized she had already grown accustomed to Josh's presence. The intimacy of sharing the kitchen with him in the early-morning hours had become something she unconsciously looked forward to each day.

As far as she could tell, he was dutifully making inquiries into the incidents at Peregrine Manor. Josh spent a lot of time with the Colonel examining the basement where many of the problems had occurred, and he talked to Odessa and Shirley at length. He asked questions about the nephews and about Ricky "The Wrecker" Ring. Furthermore, he disappeared into his room for hours on end to work on his computer. It all seemed very professional to Maggie.

The only really annoying aspect of the situation was that she was getting very tired of making tea and scones at three in the afternoon.

"I wonder what he does on that thing?" Shirley asked on Friday. She was sitting at the kitchen table along with the others. They were all watching Maggie mix up the scone dough.

Josh had been up in his room for the past three hours and Maggie knew he would be down any minute demanding his afternoon rations.

"Checking out the information he's collecting." The Colonel looked knowledgeable. "Our man is a modern sort of investigator, just as I've suspected. Does most of his research on a computer, he told me. Quite bright, too. Shows a good grasp of technical matters, in general. Understood most of the details I gave him about my experiments, for example."

Odessa nodded, not looking up from her knitting. "Very easy to talk to, I'll say that much for him. I told him all about my three atrocious nephews. He certainly seemed to understood how nasty family can get. Said a lot of his early work in the investigation business involved unfortunate family situations.''

Josh appeared in the doorway, minus his crutches. "Those scones ready yet?"

Maggie glanced at him as she bent over to shove the pan of scones into the oven. "No. Not for another fifteen minutes. Where are the crutches?"

"I don't need them anymore. See?" Josh walked carefully into the room. He still limped but it was obvious he was again mobile. "I'll be all right as long as I don't try to run up and down the stairs. Boy, am I hungry."

"Yes, it has been a whole three hours since lunch, hasn't it?" Maggie muttered.

Josh glanced at his wristwatch and frowned. "More than three hours. What's happening around here? Says in the brochure that teatime is at three o'clock every afternoon. It's now 3:05."

Maggie shot him a narrow-eyed look. "Speaking of stairs, what would happen if you took an unfortunate tumble down a flight?"

"I'd sue," Josh assured her. "Tea ready?"

The wall phone rang before Maggie could tell him to fix it himself if he was in that big a hurry. She picked up the receiver.

"Peregrine Manor," she snapped.

"Maggie?" The familiar male voice on the other end of the line held a faint, inquiring note.

Maggie relaxed and leaned back against the wall. "Hello, Clay. Sorry, I was busy. How are you?"

"Just fine," Clay O'Connor said in his easy, pleasant tones. "Thought I'd check and make sure we're still on for this evening."

"Of course. Six o'clock, right?" Automatically Maggie glanced at the calendar beside the phone and saw where she had written "Clay - dinner - six" on that day's date.

"Right." There was a slight pause. "Listen, I hear you've got a guest staying at the manor. Thought you'd decided to close for the winter. Change your mind?"

Maggie realized with a start that she hadn't invented a solid cover story to explain Josh's presence to outsiders. Her gaze swung toward Josh who was watching her intently from where he was sitting at the table.

"It was kind of unexpected, Clay." She sought frantically for an explanation. Clay O'Connor was a very nice man, but she didn't want anyone outside the small household at the manor to know that she had hired an investigator. "I'll tell you all about it this evening. See you at six."

"Maggie—"

"Got to run, Clay. I've got scones in the oven. Bye." Maggie hurriedly hung up the phone and scowled at Josh.

"Problems?" Josh inquired softly.

"We've got to think up a good reason for your being here at the manor, Josh. I don't want the people in Peregrine Point to know I've hired a private investigator. It might get back to whoever is causing the trouble around here."

"That's right," the Colonel chimed in. "When we made the decision to hire you, we agreed to keep your real purpose here a secret."

Josh eyed Maggie. He looked very thoughtful.

"You don't think your friend O'Connor could keep his mouth shut?"

Maggie winced. "I'm not worried about him keeping quiet. I'm afraid he'll laugh at me. He thinks I'm getting paranoid about the incidents."

"Got it." Josh nodded. "Don't worry, I'll come up with a good cover story by the time he arrives to pick you up this evening. Six o'clock, wasn't it?"

"Yes." Maggie removed the kettle from the stove and poured boiling water into a teapot. For some reason she felt vaguely uneasy. She realized she didn't know how to read the expression in Josh's eyes.

Josh flashed a wicked grin. "Leave everything to me. I keep telling you you're in good hands, Maggie."

Maggie shot him a suspicious glance. She didn't like the sound of that. "Perhaps we'd better work on the cover story together, Josh."

"Forget it. This is my area of expertise."

"But, Josh—"

The Colonel interrupted. "Now, Maggie, he's right. Leave all that sort of thing to our man, here. He's a professional."

"I think the scones are done," Josh said helpfully. "By the way, we're almost out of jam. You'd better put it on your shopping list, Maggie."

"Thank you for reminding me," Maggie answered through set teeth.

"That's what I'm here for, ma'am. To check out the details."

Odessa smiled happily. "Such a relief to know you're on the job, Josh."

"Sure is," Shirley agreed. "Like my Ricky always

used to say, when you want something done right, hire a professional.''

Josh smiled. ''I'm sure Ricky knew all about hiring professionals, Shirley.''

MAGGIE DRESSED FOR DINNER with some trepidation that evening. She had been worrying all afternoon about the ''cover story'' Josh was supposedly inventing. The closer six o'clock got, the more she fretted about it.

She slipped into a long-sleeved black dinner dress that hugged her small waist and flared out around her calves in a rich swirl of fabric. She brushed her hair out so that it hung freely around her shoulders, and was pondering the question of earrings when a knock sounded on the door.

''Clay's here,'' Shirley called. ''Let's see how you look, honey.''

Maggie opened her bedroom door. ''Tell him I'll be right down, will you?''

''Sure. Hey, you know what? I've got a necklace that would be perfect with that dress. Hang on, I'll get it.''

''That's all right, Shirley, really....'' Maggie's voice trailed off as Shirley disappeared down the hall.

The older woman reappeared a few minutes later with a long rhinestone-studded necklace of ancient vintage. ''Here you go, honey. This'll be perfect.''

Maggie smiled weakly, unwilling to hurt Shirley's feelings by refusing the gaudy necklace. ''Thanks, Shirley.'' She put the long string of rhinestones over her head. It hung to her waist. The rhinestones twinkled cheerfully as they fell across her breasts. Maggie glanced in the mirror and smiled. The tacky, glitzy look was rather appealing in its own way.

"Have a good time, honey." Shirley waved from the top of the stairs. "Seeing you off like this always makes me think of the days when Ricky took me to all the best places."

"Thanks for the loan of the necklace, Shirley."

Maggie heard voices in the parlor as she went down the stairs. When she caught Josh's soft, deep tones, she hurried quickly down the last few steps. She had wanted to be present to monitor things when he gave his cover story. She was learning that, left unsupervised, Josh was somewhat unpredictable. She moved into the parlor just as Josh and Clay were shaking hands.

"Pleased to meet you, January," Clay said. "I heard Maggie had someone staying here. Thought she'd closed the place for the winter season."

"A mutual friend prevailed on her to make an exception for me," Josh explained easily. "I'm writing a book and I needed a quiet place to work. The friend suggested Peregrine Manor and talked Maggie into letting me come here for a month." He turned his head as Maggie walked through the door. "Isn't that right, Maggie?"

A writer. Of course. It was perfect. Why hadn't she thought of that? Maggie wondered. She smiled in relief and immediately felt more cheerful. Josh might be a pain in a certain part of the anatomy from time to time, but he really could be clever on occasion. Posing as a writer seeking solitude and inspiration was a wonderful explanation for his presence at the manor.

"Yes, that's right," Maggie added brightly. "A

mutual friend of ours talked me into it. And since Josh doesn't care that we're doing some refurbishing around the manor, I decided to make the exception. Ready to go, Clay?''

"You bet. You look lovely tonight, Maggie.'' Clay smiled warmly at her and the smile was reflected in his pale blue eyes. He was an attractive man with an engaging, friendly air that stood him well in the real-estate business.

Tonight Clay was dressed for dinner in an expensive wool jacket and slacks. There was a chunky gold ring set with a diamond on his hand and a thin gold watch on his wrist. His sandy brown hair had been moussed and blown-dry into a smooth style that made him look very sophisticated and urbane next to Josh.

Somehow the contrast between the two men had the effect of making Josh look decidedly tough and dangerous. That was primarily because Josh hadn't yet changed for dinner, Maggie decided, feeling charitable.

He was still wearing jeans, running shoes and a work shirt. His dark hair had probably never known the touch of mousse. Maggie wondered if he had deliberately come downstairs in his jeans and work shirt in order to make his cover story more realistic. He actually *looked* like a writer, she thought. Not that she had ever actually met one in person.

"We really should be on our way.'' Maggie smiled at Clay.

"Don't worry, honey,'' Clay said with a charming laugh. "This is Peregrine Point, not Seattle. We don't have to worry about losing our table at the Surf and Sand Restaurant.''

"Yes, I know, but I'm really very hungry.'' Maggie took his arm and urged him toward the door. She didn't want him hanging around asking questions. Josh's cover story might not hold up if Clay got inquisitive.

"Have a good time," Josh murmured from the doorway. The words were polite, but Maggie thought there was something strange about his tone—something she couldn't put her finger on.

"Thanks." Maggie glanced back over her shoulder and was jolted by the laconic gleam in Josh's eyes. She frowned.

"What time should we expect you home?" Josh asked. He propped one shoulder against the door frame and folded his arms.

"Don't worry about it," Maggie retorted with a cool smile. "I've got my own key. I own the place, remember?"

"Oh, yeah. That's right."

Maggie was relieved when the door closed firmly behind her and Clay.

"How long has he been here?" Clay asked as he helped her into the front seat of his silver Mercedes.

"Not long. A week."

"Seems to have made himself right at home." Clay closed the car door and went around to the driver's side. "Who's your mutual friend? The one who suggested he stay here?"

Maggie experienced a moment of panic. It was a perfectly natural question under the circumstances and she ought to have been prepared for it. Darn it, she *would* have been prepared if Josh had taken the trouble to tell her his cover story before Clay's arrival. But, no, he had to try to impress her with his cleverness. She would speak to him about that later, Maggie decided.

"Oh, just someone we both know in Seattle," she said airily. "To tell you the truth, as long as Josh doesn't mind staying at the manor while we're refurbishing, I don't mind having him there. Things are going to be a little lean this winter without any paying guests. Usually our weekends are booked solid, even in November and December."

Clay nodded with obvious concern. "I know. It's going to be rough for the next few months, honey. Sure it's worth it?"

Maggie sighed. "I have to try to save the place, Clay. I've told you that."

"Honey, I admire your kind heart, but take it from an expert—that old mansion is a white elephant. You'll wind up pouring all your income back into it and in the end, you'll probably have to sell, anyway. You'd be better off dumping the place now and clearing some profit."

Maggie's mouth tightened. This was not the first time Clay had suggested she sell the manor. She had to admit that from his point of view, it made perfect sense. Clay was in the real-estate business, after all. He knew about this kind of thing. "I know you're probably right, Clay. But the thing is, I've made a commitment to the Colonel, Odessa and Shirley. I have to try."

Clay took one hand off the wheel to reach over and pat her hand. "I understand. Just remember that if you change your mind, I'll be glad to help you find a buyer. And I won't even charge you my usual commission. How's that for a deal you can't refuse?"

Maggie smiled ruefully. "Thanks. I'll keep it in mind."

AT ELEVEN O'CLOCK that evening, Maggie was back on her doorstep, saying good-night to Clay. Unfortunately, it was getting harder and harder to find polite ways of getting rid of him.

Maggie knew in her heart that all she had ever wanted with Clay was a casual friendship, and she was starting to feel a little guilty about that. Clay was beginning to push for a much more intimate relationship. She wondered how much longer she should go on accepting his invitations when she knew she was never going to fall in love with him. Perhaps it was time to gently end it.

"Clay," she began as she fished her key out of her purse. "I've been thinking."

His mouth curved in amusement as he hovered close. "So have I. I see the lights are off in the parlor, which means the Colonel and the others have gone to bed. Why don't you invite me in for a nightcap and we'll do our thinking together?"

Maggie bit her lip. "The thing is—"

Before Maggie could get her key into the lock, the door opened. Josh loomed in the shadows.

"Thought I heard someone out here," he said as he reached out to flip on the hall light. "I was watching television in the study. Come on in. We can all have coffee or something. You play cards, O'Connor?"

Clay's eyes narrowed with obvious annoyance. "Sorry, I don't care for cards. Maggie says she has to get to bed early. I'd better be on my way." He nodded stiffly to Maggie. "Good night, honey."

Maggie smiled anxiously, aware that Clay was upset by finding Josh at the door. "It was a lovely evening, Clay."

"I'll call you." Clay stalked back down the steps and out to where his Mercedes was parked.

Josh shook his head sadly. "They all say that."

Maggie glowered at him as she stepped into the hall. "In Clay's case, it happens to be true. He *will* call me."

"Yeah, he probably will." Josh helped her out of her coat. "Come on into the parlor. I've fixed you a nice cup of hot chocolate."

"*Chocolate.* Josh, were you by any chance waiting up for me? The answer had better be no. Because if I thought for one moment that you deliberately staged that little scene at the door in order to make Clay go home early, I'd be furious."

He gave her an injured look as he limped into the parlor and turned on one of the lamps. "I thought you might want to discuss the progress I've made so far on your case."

Maggie stared at his broad-shouldered back. "You've actually made some progress?"

"You don't have to sound so surprised. It is my job, you know. How many times do I have to remind you that I am a trained investigator?"

"I don't know why that fact keeps slipping my mind," Maggie responded grimly.

CHAPTER FIVE

JOSH POURED the hot chocolate he had carefully prepared earlier. As he did so, he felt the tension that had been eating at him all evening dissolve at last. It made him realize that he had been waiting for Maggie to return from the moment she had walked out the door on another man's arm five hours earlier. It was only sheer willpower that had kept him from actually pacing the floor for the past hour.

The Colonel, Odessa and Shirley had assured him that Maggie never stayed out late with Clay O'Connor, but that hadn't relieved Josh's mind. He knew in his gut that it was just a matter of time before O'Connor tried to talk Maggie into staying out very late. Maybe even all night. Josh had seen the determination in O'Connor's eyes when Maggie had swept into the parlor to greet him at six. O'Connor was on the make. There was no doubt about it.

During the evening Josh had come to the decision that Maggie Gladstone was not going to fall into Clay O'Connor's bed while he, Josh, was anywhere in the vicinity. If she was going to fall into any man's bed, it was going to be his own, Josh told himself.

He'd known he was attracted to her from the instant he had seen her. He'd known he wanted her that first night when she had hovered over his bed, adjusting ice packs. But he'd learned just how severely he was hooked during the past few hours as he had tortured himself with thoughts of another man touching her.

The interminable wait for Maggie to come home tonight had taught Josh that in some subtle way during the past few days, he had come to think of Maggie as *his*. The surge of possessiveness he experienced at that thought made his hand tremble slightly. The pot he was holding rattled against the rim of Maggie's cup.

Maggie frowned in horror. "Don't drop that, whatever you do. Aunt Agatha once told me that pot has been in the family for generations."

"In spite of your obvious opinion to the contrary, I am not a complete klutz." Josh set the pot firmly on the end table. He wondered dourly what McCray and the rest of the staff at BIS would say if they knew his new client thought him clumsy and accident-prone. Hell of an image he had going for himself here, Josh reflected.

Maggie smiled with a hint of relieved apology when she saw that the pot was safe. "It's just that that particular pot is rather valuable. If I ever do have to sell this place, I'll be counting on making enough profit from the furnishings to provide the Colonel and the others with some financial security."

Josh lowered himself cautiously onto the sofa beside Maggie. "What brought that up?"

"What?"

"Selling the manor. Every time I've talked to you, you've always made it clear you're not even considering that alternative."

Maggie sighed and leaned back against the sofa cushion. She toyed absently with the long rhinestone necklace she was wearing. The stones sparkled like diamonds in the soft light.

"Clay and I were discussing it earlier in the evening," Maggie explained. "I told you he's a real-estate agent. A very good one, apparently."

"I know. I saw the Mercedes and the gold ring on his pinkie." Josh had also pumped the Colonel, Odessa and Shirley for every scrap of information they had on Clay O'Connor. He hadn't learned much more than he had already guessed.

"He really thinks I should dump the manor," Maggie continued. "Says I'm pouring money down a hole trying to keep it open. He's been after me to cut my losses for several weeks now."

"When did you start dating him?"

"Two months ago." Maggie fiddled with her teacup. "He's really very nice, you know."

"No. How would I know?"

"Well, he is," she muttered. Then she gave him a reproachful glance. "That reminds me. I had to fast-talk my way around the subject of our 'mutual friend' when Clay asked me about her. Or him. You really should have briefed me on your cover story, Josh."

"What did you tell him?" Josh asked, unconcerned.

"Not much. Just that the friend lived in Seattle. Then I changed the subject."

"Sounds like you handled it well."

"Nevertheless, I expect to be kept better informed in the future. And speaking of being informed, let's have your report."

Josh shrugged. "I think we can safely discard Shirley's theory of who's behind the trouble here at the manor. I made some inquiries about Ricky 'The Wrecker' Ring and the answer came back today.''

"Oh, yes. Your computer inquiries." Maggie smiled eagerly. "What did you learn?"

Josh decided there was no point in telling her he'd learned everything through a simple phone call to the home office where one of his staff had run a quick check. "Ricky Ring got out of prison five years ago. From all accounts he was a model prisoner—spent most of his time inside teaching other inmates how to read. Since getting out, he's routinely devoted twenty hours a week to a local literacy project. He's living a quiet life down in Portland and shows absolutely no signs of going back to his erring ways. His present income appears to be derived entirely from T-bills and government securities that he bought years ago before he went to jail. In short, Ricky is a reformed man."

"No indication that he's out for vengeance?"

"None."

Maggie gazed thoughtfully into her chocolate. "Well, I never did think Shirley's explanation was sound. What about Odessa's nephews?"

"I did some checking on them, too. All three nephews live on the East Coast. Not one of them has ever made a trip to Washington, and apparently not one of them has any intention of doing so. Furthermore, they are all doing quite well financially. Two of them are lawyers and one of them is in banking. I'm still checking on the mining stock Odessa owns."

"That leaves the Colonel and his fuel experiments, doesn't it?"

Josh was about to tell her that from what he'd seen of the Colonel's work, they could safely discard that theory, too. There was no way anyone was going to turn water into a combustible substance. At least, not going at it the way the Colonel was. But Josh thought he would save that revelation for later. He had to make his work last for the next three weeks.

"I'm still working on the Colonel's theory and your idea that someone is after your aunt's emerald brooch," Josh said smoothly.

"I suppose you think my theory is as nutty as all the others that are floating around here."

"What makes you say that?" He slanted her a surprised, assessing glance. Her tone of voice alarmed him. This was not the upbeat, gung-ho Maggie he had come to know during the past week. "You're kind of down tonight, aren't you?"

"A little," she admitted. She set her hot chocolate on the table, leaned her head back and gazed forlornly out the window into the darkness. "Clay talked all evening about how smart it would be to sell the manor. He meant well, I know. But still, it was depressing hearing him lay out all the practical reasons why I should get rid of the place. He says I'm not doing the Colonel, Odessa and Shirley any favors trying to save it."

"Yeah?"

Maggie nodded wearily. "He says they'd all be better off financially if I sold the manor and gave them a share of the profits. I don't know, Josh. Maybe I am being foolish, trying to save it. What if there really isn't something mysterious going on around here for you to find? What if it's just a big old house slowly fading away?"

"Hey, let's not jump to the worst possible conclusions so soon." Josh realized with a start that he didn't want Maggie to have to face reality quite so quickly.

To his chagrin, he was suddenly stricken with a wild, impulsive desire to help her salvage her dream. *Bad move,* he reminded himself. *It never pays to play hero.*

But it was too late. Josh knew he was already looking for ways to ride to the rescue.

"Maybe Clay's right, Josh. Maybe it would be doing Odessa and Shirley and the Colonel a favor if I sold the place now. I know they love it and think of it as their home, but—"

"Give me the rest of the month," Josh said quickly. "Just give me the amount of time you contracted for in the beginning. That's all I ask. Okay?"

She turned her head on the cushion and looked up at him with damp eyes. "But what can you do besides prove our theories wrong? What if there isn't anything odd happening?"

He framed her face gently with one hand and leaned close. "Maggie, you hired me to fix things. Let me do my job for the rest of the month and we'll see what happens." He grinned briefly and brushed his mouth lightly against hers. "What have you got to lose? I work cheap, remember?"

"Oh, Josh, I just don't know. I was so sure in the beginning, but Clay says—"

"Forget O'Connor, okay?" Josh stroked his thumb along her lower lip. "You haven't made that call to McCray, have you?"

"Well, no." She went very still as she looked up at him. Her mouth trembled slightly. "I really don't see why I should."

"Maggie, sweetheart, you are very kind, but a little

naive.'' He brought his mouth down on hers and this time he didn't pull away.

Maggie held herself tensely as he slowly deepened the kiss. And then, to his incredible delight, she began to respond. Josh felt his whole body react instantaneously to the promise of her stirring softness. His blood sang with the thrill of a desire that went all the way to his core.

When she moved again it was to put her arms tentatively around his waist. She was careful of his ribs. Josh probed gently and her mouth opened for him.

With a rush of passion he could barely restrain, he realized that he was already fighting for his self-control. The effect Maggie had on him was electrifying. He was suddenly insatiably hungry for her. But it was too soon to take her to bed. If he tried, he would no doubt scare her off entirely. He had to go slowly, he told himself. But he was no longer sure he could wait. It had never been like this. At least not for more years than he could recall.

''Josh?''

''Maggie, sweetheart. Just let me touch you. Please, love.'' He eased her down carefully onto the cushions of the old Victorian sofa and sprawled heavily on top of her. She was soft and sleek beneath him, the gentle contours of her body accepting all the hard, rough-edged places of his. He was overwhelmingly conscious of wanting to be careful with her, of wanting to let her respond to him in her own time.

Josh groaned; the husky sound of need chained by willpower emanated from somewhere deep inside him. He kissed the curve of Maggie's cheek and then her throat. When he raised his head to look down at her he saw the wonder and uncertainty in her beautiful eyes. And then he saw the sweet passion that was flickering to life within her.

Josh reached out to switch off the lamp and the shadows enveloped them.

"Josh. *Josh.*"

His name on Maggie's lips was a breathless whisper in the darkness. It sent a shudder of desire flaring through him.

"I'm right here, sweetheart." He stroked a finger inside the V-neck of her dress, tracing its outline down to the lowest point just above her breasts. Then he slowly drew his finger back up to her throat where her pulse beat warmly in the soft hollow.

"You are a very strange man," Maggie said seriously.

That made him hesitate. "Why do you say that?"

"I don't know. There's just something different about you."

"Different from what?" he demanded.

"Different from any other man I've ever met."

Josh relaxed slightly. He smiled in the shadows. "Okay, I can live with that, I guess. It's not the most inspiring compliment you could give a man under these conditions, but I suppose I can put my own interpretation on it."

She touched the side of his face with gentle, questing fingertips. Her shadowed eyes were still very serious. "What would be a more inspirational remark?"

He slowly started to undo the large black buttons that closed the front of the dress. "You could tell me I'm incredibly sexy."

"You are," she said with a simple, touching honesty. "But I figured you already knew that."

The words struck him like lightning. His hand

stilled on a button as he paused to gaze down at her. *"Maggie."*

"Hmm?" She was fingering the buttons on his shirt.

"Maggie, sweetheart, do you mean that? You really think I'm sexy?"

"Yes. The sexiest man I've ever met."

"Oh, Maggie." He choked back an exultant laugh and hugged her fiercely. "I forgive you for all the nasty cracks you've made about me during the past few days. I'll even forget you called me accident-prone."

She relaxed in his arms and giggled softly against his chest. "You like hearing you're sexy?"

"I like hearing it from you. I like it very, very much." Josh went back to work on the buttons of her dress. "Mostly because *I* think *you* are incredibly, astoundingly, amazingly sexy."

The laughter went out of her again. She clung to him with sudden urgency. "Josh, there has to be more."

Josh sucked in his breath as his ribs protested her abruptly fierce hug. "There *is* more, sweetheart." He took a cautious breath as she released him. "A lot more. Give me a chance to show you."

He had the front of the dress open now. Rhinestones spilled across the upper curves of her breasts. He eased his hand inside and found the softness of a warm globe cupped in lace. When he brushed his thumb over its sweetly shaped curve he felt the velvety nipple stir and begin to harden. He realized she was holding her breath.

"Relax, Maggie. Trust me tonight."

"I do trust you. It's crazy. But I do." She put her

arms around his neck and kissed the taut line of his jaw. Her leg shifted alongside his on the cushions.

Josh could feel the promise of surrender in her and he was awed. The soft, giving warmth of her made him powerfully aware of his own maleness. He sensed that he was being given a rare and wonderful gift and that he dared not ruin the experience by demanding more than Maggie was prepared to give at this point.

Josh reached down and found the hem of her dress. He eased it upward to her thighs and sighed when he felt the warmth between her legs. He lowered his mouth to one breast, dampening the nipple beneath the lace with his tongue. When she moaned softly, he began to explore her more thoroughly.

Slowly he eased the silky panty hose down her legs to her ankles. Then he peeled them off her delicately arched feet. He slid his hands back up her legs and gently pushed her thighs more widely apart. She resisted slightly and then surrendered to his gentle, insistent pressure.

His fingers brushed against the soft nest that sheltered her secrets.

"Josh."

There was a throaty passion in her voice. And uncertainty, as well. Josh couldn't tell if he had gone too far or if she wanted him to go further. He brushed his fingers against her again and felt the wet heat. He kissed her deeply. "Do you like that, Maggie?"

"Yes. Oh, *yes.* Please, Josh." She was starting to clutch at him, moving her head restlessly.

Josh took a deep breath to control his own skyrocketing need. He cupped her intimately with the palm of his hand. "You're burning up, sweetheart, aren't you? You're on fire for me."

Her answer was to arch herself against his hand.
Josh stroked one finger slowly inside her and felt her
shiver in response. "You're so tight," he said in wonder. "Tight and hot and wet. All passion and fire."
He stroked again—a little harder—and she gasped.

"I don't...I can't... Josh, I feel so strange. What
are you doing to me?"

He heard the confusion and excitement in her voice
and realized with amazement that Maggie didn't recognize her own impending climax. It dawned on him
that Maggie was going to learn the passionate power
of her own body at his hands—and a glorious exul-
tation roared through him. He felt simultaneously
humble and magnificently proud. He could give her
something almost as wonderful as what she was giving him; something no other man had ever given her.

"Don't fight it, sweetheart. It's going to be so
good. You're going to go up in flames. Tighten yourself, Maggie. Yes, that's it, harder, harder. Yes." He
stroked her gently, finding the small, engorged nub of
feminine sensation with his thumb.

He knew it was happening even before she did. It
was unmistakable. Her whole body suddenly clenched
and tiny, shivering ripples quivered around his invad-
ing finger. Josh almost lost his own self-control at that
moment.

"Josh."

She was going to cry out. Josh sensed it and as
much as he yearned to hear the sweet sound of her
release, he knew he had to protect her privacy. The
parlor was directly under the Colonel's bedroom.

Josh captured Maggie's mouth with his own, swal-
lowing the soft, joyous sounds. He held her while she
convulsed beneath him and took as much pleasure in

the release as Maggie herself did. It was an odd sensation to be so enthralled by a woman's passion that he could forgo his own without resentment. All Josh wanted in that moment was for Maggie to be happy and to know that he was the one who had made her so.

Maggie eventually collapsed into a soft, warm heap beneath Josh and for a long time he was content to just lie there on top of her, savoring the scent and feel of her. The minutes slipped past.

Maggie shifted slightly at last. "Josh?" she whispered.

"Mmm?"

"Josh, that was…quite wonderful."

He grinned to himself in the darkness. "Yeah, it was. Never seen anything like it."

She laughed softly. "You're teasing me."

"No, I'm deadly serious. It was wonderful." He finally raised his head and kissed the tip of her nose.

"Oh, dear. I didn't realize. I wasn't thinking. I mean, you didn't—" She broke off as he silenced her by kissing her mouth.

"No, I didn't. But that's okay, too," he assured her. "When it happens for me, I want to be deep inside you, Maggie. And it's a little too soon for that. You need time to get to know me better. I want you to be sure of me, sweetheart."

She shook her head in wonder. "You're playing the noble hero again, aren't you?"

He frowned. "I've told you, I gave that role up a long time ago."

"I don't believe you." She traced the line of his nose with a soft fingertip.

Josh opened his mouth to tell her not to get the

wrong idea about him, but something stopped him. A tiny sound from somewhere in the house. A sound that was not quite normal.

"Josh? What is it?" Maggie looked up at him. "Is something wrong?"

"Hush." He touched her mouth with his fingers, silently warning her. When he knew she had gotten the message, he sat up slowly on the sofa.

The sound came softly down the front hall—a small, muted click that could have been metal on metal. Maggie sat up beside Josh, fumbling with the buttons of her dress. He could feel her watching him and knew she wanted to ask questions. But she obviously knew when to follow instructions. She kept silent.

Josh touched her shoulder and put his mouth to her ear. "Stay here. Don't move."

She nodded and then put her lips next to his ear. "Call police?"

"No. Not yet. But be ready." He stood and moved to the door of the parlor. He listened intently, straining to hear the soft clinking sound before he stepped out into the hall. He caught it echoing faintly and knew for certain, now, that it was coming from the basement.

Josh limped forward and silently cursed the weakness of his still-healing left foot. He went quietly down the darkened hall, his bare feet making no sound on the carpet. When he reached the door that opened on the basement stairs he hesitated once more.

Silence.

Josh unlocked the door and opened it. The hinges made only the faintest whisper of sound. The stairs to the basement descended into an inky darkness. If there was anyone down there, Josh thought, he had the eyes of a cat.

But his instincts told him the basement was empty. Josh waited another moment and then decided to chance the light. He flattened himself against the wall and crouched low. There was no need to make a target out of himself, just in case someone was hiding among the wine bins and filing cabinets. He reached up over his head to flip the light switch.

The lights came on and Josh swept the large room below in a single glance. The basement was empty. He straightened slowly. "Maggie?" he called softly over his shoulder.

"Right here." She hurried barefoot down the hall. "Is everything all right?"

"Yeah, I think so. I was sure I heard something, though. I'm going to go on down and take a closer look." He started down the stairs, using the handrail to take the weight off his bad foot. Maggie floated along behind him like a nervous little ghost.

The cold draft that swept the room caught Josh's attention first. He glanced toward the two narrow, ground-level windows near the basement ceiling. One of them was open.

"Hell." He reached the bottom step and crossed the concrete floor. He sensed Maggie following him with her gaze.

"Josh, that window should be locked. We always keep it locked."

"It was locked," Josh told her quietly. "I checked it earlier, myself. But the latch is not much more than a toy. Easy to pry open from the outside. Hell, maybe it fell open on its own. It's old."

He contemplated the window for a moment longer

and then studied the arrangement of filing cabinets and boxes stacked beneath it. An ancient blanket had been placed on top of the metal cabinets. There were some bits of dirt scattered on it. Josh touched them with his fingers.

"What have you found?" Maggie came close. "Dirt?"

Josh nodded slowly. "If there was someone in here, he came and went through that window. Could have used these boxes and cabinets to climb down and back up again."

Maggie considered that. "It's a very narrow window, Josh."

"It's big enough for a slender man to crawl through."

"Or a woman." Maggie looked around the cold basement. She crossed her arms and hugged herself. A shadow flitted across her face, giving her a vulnerable look. "Josh, do you think someone was actually in here?"

"I think it's a real strong possibility," he said quietly.

"But what would he want? There's nothing of any great value here, except for the manor's wine supply. But it's safely locked up in that wire cage over there." Maggie nodded toward the wine-storage area on the other side of the room.

"The wine might be enough of a temptation to draw a prowler," Josh remarked thoughtfully. "Teenagers, maybe."

But Maggie's eyes were narrowing as a more sinister thought apparently struck her. "You know what I think?"

"Uh, no, Maggie. What do you think?"

"I think someone climbed in here to search for Aunt Agatha's emerald brooch."

Josh let that pass. The last thing he wanted to do tonight was shoot holes in Maggie's theory. He'd already shot holes in everyone else's. "What do you say we take a look around and see if any of the cabinets look like they've been jimmied open."

"Right." Maggie started determinedly toward the bank of file cabinets the Colonel used to house his research data and the reports on his experiments.

She stopped short with a soft shriek. "Oh, my God, Josh! Look! There's water pouring out of that pipe. If it gets into the cabinets it will ruin the Colonel's papers."

Josh looked up from a stack of boxes he was studying and frowned. Sure enough, a steady stream of water was leaking from a joint in the pipes that ran overhead. The volume of water increased even as he watched.

"Hand me that wrench hanging on the wall," he ordered as he lunged across the room, cursing his awkward, broken stride. "Damn it, not that one, the other one. The big one. Yeah, that's it."

Josh reached the file cabinets, planted his hands on top of two of them and hoisted himself up until he was standing amid the clutter on the metal surface. His shoulder twinged painfully but he ignored it.

Water was starting to pool and flow over the side of the filing cabinets. The cabinets, which were already groaning under the weight of the Colonel's accumulation of paperwork, trembled at this additional punishment. Josh could only pray they wouldn't collapse beneath him.

"Here, Josh." Maggie thrust the wrench up at him.

"Hurry. The Colonel will be brokenhearted if all of his papers are destroyed."

"You think I don't know that?" Josh fitted the wrench to the pipe joint and applied steady pressure. The flow of water diminished quickly. Josh gave the joint a few more turns, tightening it securely until the leak stopped.

When he had finished, he handed the wrench back to Maggie and slowly eased himself down to the floor. Maggie picked up some old cloths and began mopping up the water on top of the cabinets.

For a moment neither of them spoke. Hands on his hips, Josh stared up at the pipe and thought about the faint sound of metal on metal that had brought him down here.

"Someone was definitely in here, Josh." Maggie tossed the wet rags onto the floor. "Someone climbed into this basement and deliberately loosened the pipe joint."

"Looks like it," Josh agreed, still contemplating the pipe.

"If we hadn't discovered the water coming out of that pipe tonight, the entire basement would have been flooded by morning. It would have been a disaster."

"Yeah. It would have been a mess, all right." Tonight's incident put a whole new perspective on this cushy, piece-of-cake case. It was now clear to Josh that the things that had been happening at Peregrine Manor could no longer be written off as due to overactive imaginations.

"What are you thinking?" Maggie asked uneasily.

"That the problems you've had might be the work of a vandal. Maybe some local sicko who gets his kicks causing this kind of trouble. Or a kid who's bent on doing mischief just for the hell of it.''

Maggie chewed on her lower lip. ''The sheriff did suggest that possibility when I called him after the first couple of incidents,'' she admitted. ''He said to be sure I locked everything up securely at night. I haven't bothered calling him again. But, Josh, it's not just wanton vandalism. I know it isn't.''

Josh glanced at her and saw the anxiety in her eyes. He sighed. ''You still think this has something to do with your Aunt Agatha's emerald brooch? Maggie, I don't want to quash your theory, but it doesn't make sense that a prowler would try to flood the basement while he searched for a valuable piece of jewelry.''

Maggie frowned. ''It does look like he was trying to destroy the Colonel's papers, doesn't it? Do you suppose there might be something to his theory, after all?''

''No,'' Josh said flatly. ''I don't.''

Maggie drummed her fingers on a file cabinet. ''It's possible someone *thinks* he can create it and is after the formula.''

''Damn it, Maggie…''

''Okay, okay. It's highly unlikely.''

''Highly unlikely.''

''But not impossible,'' she said coaxingly.

He gave her a wry glance and realized for the first time that in her haste to rebutton her dress, she had put the top button through the wrong hole. The dress was skewed across her breasts. The edge of her lacy bra peeped out at him. He found the sight incredibly endearing.

''All right,'' Josh replied gently. ''I'll concede it is not completely beyond the realm of possibility that some other screwy inventor thinks the Colonel is on to something and wants to see how the experiments are progressing or wants to destroy them. But, to be brutally frank, I'm still ranking that theory very low on my list.''

She nodded. "Fair enough. In exchange, I'll agree to consider your vandalism theory.''

"It's a deal," he murmured. There was a short, suddenly charged silence as the conversation on possibilities and theories came to an end. The expression in Maggie's eyes started to change.

Josh recognized the exact instant when it occurred to her that they were still alone together and the night wasn't over. Uneasiness and a deep, feminine shyness shimmered in her sea-green eyes.

The moment was lost and Josh knew it. He reminded himself that he had never intended to take things any further tonight, anyway, no matter how tempted. He smiled with what he hoped was reassurance. "Why don't you go on upstairs to bed, Maggie? I'll relock the window. Tomorrow I'll rig up something to keep it from being opened from the outside. We can talk about this in the morning."

Maggie hesitated and then nodded quickly. "Good night, Josh."

"Good night, Maggie."

He watched her dash back up the stairs and felt as though she were taking a part of him with her. It was all he could do not to call her back.

But Josh knew he had to let her go tonight. She needed time. Besides, he told himself, the memory of Maggie shivering in his arms as she found her first real, exquisite release would be more than enough to warm his bed and his dreams tonight.

CHAPTER SIX

THE BEACH WAS shrouded in fog. On the horizon, the gray sea met the gray sky in such a seamless fashion that it was impossible to tell where one began and the other ended. Bundled up in a hooded down jacket, Maggie stood at the water's edge and tried to come to terms with the unsettling emotions that were churning inside her.

There was no getting around it. She was falling fast and hard for Joshua January. The realization simultaneously thrilled and terrified her. He was so different from every other man she had ever known. A part of her recognized something deep within him that mirrored a fundamental part of herself. She knew in her heart that Josh January was one of the good guys in a rough world.

And yet, for all her instinctive certainty about him, Maggie was forced to admit that there was a great deal she didn't know about Josh. She had always assumed the man she would someday love would be safe and comfortable. Josh was neither.

She should never have allowed him to kiss her and touch her the way she had last night. She was his employer, for heaven's sake. He was working for her. Where was her common sense? She ought to be keeping a strict, arm's-length distance between them. Things were complicated enough around Peregrine

Manor. She didn't need to add a potentially explosive affair with Josh to the brew.

But last night had been extraordinarily special, Maggie thought with a rush of joy. She had felt incredibly beautiful and passionate and free in Josh's arms. The exhilaration of the experience still hadn't faded entirely. If she closed her eyes, she could relive the glorious moment. Her body even began to respond to the memory.

"Hello, Maggie." Josh's deep, dark voice broke into the delicious spell that bound her. "I had a hunch I'd find you down here this morning."

She turned, with a tremulous smile on her lips, and watched as he emerged from the fog. He was wearing a shearling jacket over a pair of jeans. He had his hands buried in the warm pockets of the jacket and the fleece collar was turned up to protect his neck. He looked potently, vitally *male*. In some strange fashion his recent injuries only seemed to underscore the sensual danger the man projected.

"Hello, Josh." Maggie tried for the light, sparring tone that had characterized so much of their conversation till now. "I suppose you tracked me down to see about your home-cooked breakfast?"

He smiled. "Breakfast can wait. I wanted to talk to you, but you didn't come downstairs to the kitchen the way you usually do."

"I felt like a walk on the beach this morning."

Josh nodded. "Yeah. Me, too." He took his right hand out of the pocket of his jacket and held it out for her.

Maggie hesitated and then slipped her hand into his. His fingers curled warmly around her own. She couldn't think of anything to say as they started along the beach. It was one of the few times in her life that she had actually felt tongue-tied.

"It's okay, you know," Josh said after a bit.

She looked up quickly. "What is?"

"You don't have to be nervous, Maggie. I'm not going to pounce on you."

"I didn't think you were," she retorted.

"Yes, you did. But I told you last night I'll give you time, and I meant it."

She drew a deep breath. "I think it's only fair to tell you that I don't really want a brief affair with you or anyone else, Josh. I've never gone in for that sort of thing. I don't intend to start now. Not even with you."

"I know." He squeezed her hand gently. "I'm not into brief affairs or one-night stands, either. Messy and unsatisfying."

"So, what does that leave?" she asked carefully.

His mouth curved almost whimsically. "It leaves you and me and something else."

"Josh," she began in a little rush before she lost her nerve, "this probably isn't a good idea. You and me, that is. I mean, I am a client and you do work for me and I live out here on the coast and you live in Seattle and we're really very different people when you think about it—"

"Are we?"

"Well, yes," she said helplessly.

"I don't think so. I think we've got a lot in common. I knew it that first night. You just need time to realize it."

"Josh, please—"

"Have dinner with me tonight, Maggie."

"What?"

"Have dinner with me. In town. A real date."

"Oh."

He grinned fleetingly. "Is that an answer?"

"No."

"Is *that* an answer? Come on, Maggie. Take a chance."

She scowled. "All right, Josh. I'll have dinner with you. But you probably shouldn't read too much into it."

"You can't hold it against me if I look for a few clues. It's instinctive, you know? I'm a trained investigator."

She smiled unwillingly. "You're impossible, that's what you are."

"I'll be on my best behavior. After all, I am fully aware of the fact that I can be replaced at any moment by Clay O'Connor."

Maggie started to laugh. She couldn't help it.

"What's so damn funny?" Josh demanded.

"The thought of you selling real estate. It boggles the mind."

AT MIDMORNING A KNOCK on the kitchen door caused Maggie to put down the vegetables she had been peeling for soup. She peeked through the curtains and saw a familiar beat-up old pickup parked in the driveway behind the manor. She smiled as she opened the door for Dwight Wilcox, her faithful handyman.

"Hi, Dwight. How are you this morning?" Maggie wiped her hands on her apron.

Dwight ducked his head by way of greeting and gave her his customary morose expression. Maggie had never seen Dwight display any other emotion.

Today he appeared completely oblivious to the cold, driving rain that was pounding down around him.

He wasn't very old—perhaps twenty-five or twenty-six—but it was clear that Dwight had already found the world sadly wanting. Maggie sometimes wondered if he had ever, in his entire life, been happy.

Dwight was garbed in his handyman's uniform, which consisted of a peaked cap over his unkempt brown hair, a pair of twill pants and a shirt in a dull shade of green. He also had on his thick-soled boots and, as usual, he was chewing gum.

"Mornin'." Dwight was a no-nonsense speaker. Every word was clipped short and there were no extras. "On my way into town. Figured I'd see if you wanted that furnace checked. You said something about it the other day. I brung my tools." He hoisted the toolbox he was holding in his right hand.

"Great." Maggie stepped back to let him enter the kitchen. "I'm glad to see you. I don't want to take any chances on the heating system going down again. Not at this time of year."

Dwight nodded and tromped across the kitchen toward the door in the hall that opened to the basement steps. Maggie followed. She was unlocking the door when Josh appeared on the second-floor landing. He braced himself by putting both hands on the railing and looked over.

"What's going on down there?" he called easily.

Maggie looked up. "This is Dwight Wilcox, Josh. I told you about him. He takes care of things around here for us. He's going to service the furnace just to make certain it's running smoothly. Dwight, this is Josh January. He's staying here at the manor for a few weeks."

Dwight squinted up at Josh from beneath the peak of his cap. "'Lo."

Josh nodded and started down the steps, limping only slightly. "I'll come down there with you, Wilcox. I know a thing or two about electric furnaces."

"That right?" Dwight looked skeptical.

"Enough to figure out where to put the lubrication oil in," Josh assured him blandly. "Besides, I need the break. I've been writing all morning."

"Josh is a writer," Maggie said quickly, just in case Dwight had not gotten the point. Dwight was very helpful when it came to mechanical matters, but it was difficult to tell how much he was taking in when one spoke to him. His eyes always reflected a sort of wary bafflement, as if everything going on around him was almost too complicated to comprehend. The only things Dwight Wilcox seemed to feel really comfortable with were his tools.

"Suit yourself." Dwight went down the steps to the basement.

Josh followed. "How's lunch coming?" he inquired as he went past Maggie.

"Don't worry about it. You aren't in any danger of immediate starvation."

"Just making sure I get everything that's coming to me."

"You were only promised breakfast, tea and dinner," she reminded him.

"Yeah, but I figure the little extra work I'm doing on the side around here should be properly rewarded."

"What extra work?" Then a suspicion took hold. "Josh January," Maggie hissed, "if you're implying

I should reimburse you for your talents as a...a..."
Words failed her.

"Lover?" he supplied helpfully.

"I can think of more descriptive words."

"Such as?"

"Go on down those stairs before I decide to assist you," Maggie growled.

"Sure thing. By the way, I made reservations for us this evening at a place the Colonel recommended." Josh grinned and went on down the steps. He held on to the handrail, taking the weight off his left foot as much as possible.

Maggie stood in the doorway and watched both men for a while. Then she went back into the kitchen to finish the soup. She wondered why Josh had accompanied Dwight into the basement.

AT SEVEN O'CLOCK that evening Josh and Maggie were shown to their seats in a cozy little restaurant perched on the cliffs above the sea. Maggie glanced around expectantly. It was Saturday night and the place was crowded. The pleasant hum of dinner conversation mingled with the clink of dishes and glassware. The delightful smell of freshly broiled salmon drifted over from a nearby table.

As soon as their orders had been given to the waitress Josh leaned back with a satisfied look in his eyes. "It's a relief to get you out of that house, sweetheart. I hadn't realized until now what a dampening effect the Colonel and the others were having on our relationship. I have the feeling that if one of them catches me stepping over the line with you, I'm going to find myself facing a shotgun and a preacher."

Maggie knew she was blushing, but she tried to

keep her tone light. "The Colonel and Odessa are a little old-fashioned. Shirley would be more tolerant, I imagine. Being a gangster's moll probably gives one a less rigid outlook on certain matters."

"Don't count on it. Shirley would be as tough on me as the other two." Josh sipped his wine. His eyes gleamed.

Maggie felt herself growing more flushed. She started fiddling with her salad fork. "Look, don't worry about it, okay? You're in no danger of a shotgun wedding just because of a little fooling around on a sofa last night."

"I wasn't fooling around, Maggie. I was very serious."

She frowned, not sure how to take that. It seemed safest to try another topic. "Josh, why did you go down into the basement to watch Dwight work this morning?"

He grinned wickedly. "Do I make you nervous, Maggie? Is that why you're changing the subject?"

"Yes. Now answer my question."

"Okay. You're the client." He sat forward and folded his arms on the white tablecloth. The humor vanished from his gaze. "I wanted to see if Wilcox showed any surprise when he discovered that your basement wasn't flooded."

Maggie's eyes widened. "You suspected Dwight might have been the one who crawled through the basement window last night?"

"It was a possibility. He's slender enough to fit through that window and he knows his way around tools. Furthermore, as your handyman, he's had plenty of access to the manor. He could have sabotaged things like the chimneys and the refrigerator."

"Yes, but *Dwight?*" Maggie started to laugh. "I'll bet he showed absolutely no reaction whatsoever down in that basement. Am I right?"

"Right. The guy never missed a beat. Didn't even blink."

"That's our Dwight. Sorry to screw up your theory, but you really can't tell anything from Dwight's face. He's worn that same expression—or rather, lack of it—since the day I met him. I don't think Dwight would have shown any emotion if he'd walked down those basement steps and found an alligator that had crawled up from the sewer."

"Is that so?" Josh looked thoughtful.

Maggie smiled. "Look, forget Dwight. There's no way he could be behind the kinds of things that have been happening at the manor. He has his talents, but, to be honest, I don't think he's capable of the sort of devious cleverness that it would take to plot an entire series of harassing incidents. And what possible motive could he have, even if he were smart enough to dream up such a scheme? What made you suspect him?"

"Maggie, let me explain something here. You're my client. By definition, that makes everyone else a suspect. That's how I work."

She stared at him in amazement. "*Everyone* else?"

"Everyone else," he confirmed.

"Come on, Josh. Even the Colonel and Odessa and Shirley?"

"Yeah. Even them." Josh took another sip of wine and turned his head to look out into the darkness.

"You can't be serious? What possible motive would my three tenants have?"

Josh swung his gaze back to hers, his eyes cold and

intent. "You want some possibilities? I'll give you possibilities. We'll start with the Colonel. He's told everyone that he's a genius and that he's on the brink of perfecting a new and unlimited fuel for the world. What if, deep down, he knows his experiments are a joke and he's begun to fear he'll be found out?"

Maggie frowned. "You think he might be trying to destroy his own files before someone exposes him as a fraud?"

"A lot of the incidents you've described to me have originated in the basement of the manor where the Colonel keeps his papers. If he staged the destruction of his own files and made it look like the work of fuel-industry spies or malicious vandals, he could tell everyone that his experiments had been seriously set back, perhaps for years."

"You think the Colonel would risk destroying the manor just to protect his own illusions? I don't believe it," Maggie stated.

Josh smiled wryly. "That only goes to show how naive you are, Maggie."

"I am not naive. It's just that I've known the Colonel for years and I don't believe he would do anything potentially violent or harmful."

"He was a career military man," Josh reminded her gently. "He spent years studying and learning violent ways. For all we know, he was trained in sabotage. But if you don't like him for the bad guy, try Shirley."

"Shirley?"

"Uh-huh. She's been living with an illusion for years. She thinks the great love of her life, Ricky 'The Wrecker' Ring, abandoned her because he thought she ratted on him. Believing that he left her because

of that and not just because he found another girlfriend might be comforting for her. She might have
gone over the edge mentally and decided to stage the
incidents at the manor to convince her friends that
Ricky still cares enough to seek vengeance.''

"I see what you're saying. But I'm sorry, Josh. I
don't buy that one, either.''

He nodded obligingly. "Okay, try this one on for
size. Odessa wants you to sell the manor but she
knows that everyone else, including her lover, the
Colonel wants to hang on to it.''

"Her *lover?* The colonel?" Maggie was stunned.
"But they're just good friends.''

"You think people their age don't enjoy sex as
much as everyone else? Trust me, Maggie, they're
more than just good friends.''

"But they have different bedrooms. They don't
sleep together.'' Maggie was flustered.

"That generation still tends to be discreet. Especially in front of the younger generation.''

"Yes, but—''

"Never mind. My point is that it's possible, because of her feelings for the Colonel, that Odessa
doesn't want to openly encourage you to sell. But
maybe because she realizes they'd be financially better off if you did, she's staging the incidents, hoping
you'll eventually decide the manor's more trouble
than it's worth.''

Maggie groaned. "Now you're really clutching at
straws, Mr. Private Investigator.''

"I've got news for you, sweetheart. I've seen cases
where people have killed other people for far less
cause than any of the three motives I've just given
you.''

Maggie studied him for a moment. "I can understand how the business you're in would have a ten-
dency to turn a person extremely cynical," she said
gently. "No wonder your eyes look so cold sometimes. You *are* well named, aren't you?"

His eyes narrowed. "The business I'm in hasn't
made me cynical, Maggie. It's made me realistic. I've
seen enough of human nature to know that it's un-
reliable, untrustworthy and capable of incredible cru-
elty and greed."

"So you formed your motto based on experience,
is that it?"

He scowled at her. "What motto?"

"It Never Pays To Play Hero." Her mouth curved
faintly. "Poor Josh. It must be a constant battle for
you."

"What's a constant battle?"

"Trying not to play hero. Unfortunately for you, I
have a hunch the role is a natural one."

"The hell it is," he shot back. "I abandoned it long
ago."

"I'm not so sure about that." She leaned forward.
"You gave motives for everyone else at the manor,
but what about me?"

"I told you, you're the client," he growled.

"That doesn't make me innocent."

"I don't think you're behind the incidents, Maggie," Josh told her, sounding annoyed. "Let's change
the subject."

"All right. If that's what you want. There's a little
something I've been wondering about all day," she
said. "A professional question."

He gave her a hooded glance. "What's that?"

"Do you make love to all your female clients?"

"No, damn it. As a matter of fact, I have a strict policy against it. Extremely unprofessional. Getting emotionally involved with a client is about the stupidest thing a PI can do."

"I see." Maggie suddenly felt immensely more cheerful. Josh wasn't the kind of man who would break his own rules easily. The fact that he was breaking one of them with her warmed Maggie to her soul.

A MUTED MURMUR of voices from the study greeted Maggie and Josh when they walked back in the front door of the manor a few hours later. Josh swore softly but without any real heat.

"Hell. The television's on. Sounds like our three chaperons have waited up for us." He slipped Maggie's coat from her shoulders and hung it in the hall closet.

Laughter twinkled in her eyes. "How sweet. Just like you did the night Clay took me out to dinner. I don't know what I'd do without so many people looking out for my moral welfare."

Josh grinned ruefully. "We're just trying to keep you out of trouble, Maggie."

"I may have to sell the manor just to gain some privacy," she retorted as she started down the hall toward the study.

Josh followed, wondering exactly what she meant by that. Perhaps Maggie was telling him in her own obscure fashion that she wouldn't have minded coming home tonight and finding that her chaperons had all retired for the evening. That thought brightened his mood.

He watched Maggie come to a halt in the doorway of the study. She smiled at whatever she saw inside and turned to glance back over her shoulder. "The TV is on, but will you look at my three faithful guardians?"

Josh looked over her shoulder and saw that the Colonel, Odessa and Shirley were all sound asleep in front of the blaring television set. "So much for worrying about a shotgun wedding tonight."

"I told you not to panic about that."

"Yeah. You did." Josh went past Maggie into the study and switched off the television. Then he turned on the light. "All right, everyone, rise and shine."

"What's that? What's that?" The Colonel blinked and sat up. "Oh, it's you, January. Gave me a start."

Odessa stirred and opened her eyes. "Oh, dear. What time is it?" She smiled brightly at Maggie. "You're back. Did you have a good time, dear?"

"We had a lovely evening," Maggie assured her.

Shirley yawned and reached for her rhinestone-studded glasses. She put them on and peered closely at Josh. "'Bout time you two got home. Enjoy yourselves?"

"Had a great time right up until we walked in the front door a few minutes ago and realized you three had waited up for us." Josh lifted an eyebrow at Shirley. "It wasn't necessary. We're not exactly kids, you know."

Shirley harrumphed. "It was the Colonel's idea."

"I don't see what he was concerned about," Josh said smoothly. "I'm being paid to look after Maggie, remember?"

"Yeah, well the Colonel said that was a bit like paying the fox to watch the henhouse." Shirley yawned again. "But I guess we've done our duty. I say we all go to bed."

"Good idea." Odessa got to her feet and pulled her sweater more tightly around her. "Seems a bit chilly in here, doesn't it?"

"I'll check the thermostat," the Colonel offered. "Come along, my dear." He nodded at Josh. "You two will be right up, I imagine, won't you?"

"I'm not sure," Josh said. "Haven't quite decided what I'm going to do for the rest of the evening. I was considering the possibility of staying down here and ravishing Maggie in front of the television."

Odessa smiled fondly. "No, do stop teasing everyone, Josh. It's time we were all in bed." She started toward the door, making it quite clear that she expected everyone else to follow.

Josh watched her lead the small parade toward the stairs. Then he glanced at Maggie. He saw the laughter in her gaze; and beneath the laughter, he was sure he saw the promise. He stifled a groan. It was tempting, but he really was getting too old to engage in a lot of hot-and-heavy petting on a downstairs sofa.

He reached out a hand, caught hold of Maggie's and tugged her close. Then he steered her after the others, who were already halfway up the stairs. He held her back a few steps. When she turned her head to look at him with a question in her eyes, he smiled faintly and leaned down to whisper in her ear.

"The next time we get close, it's going to be in a bed," he whispered. He had the satisfaction of seeing her blush very nicely. Unfortunately, her response only served to make him hungrier for her.

A moment later Josh said a painfully gallant good-night to Maggie at her door under the discreetly watchful eyes of the Colonel, Odessa and Shirley. He saw her safely inside and then reluctantly went next door to his own room.

He closed the door behind himself, loosened his tie and eyed the computer sitting on the desk. It was clear he wasn't going to be able to sleep for a while. He would only succeed in thoroughly frustrating himself if he went to bed in his present, half-aroused condition.

The book was waiting.

So were a few questions that needed answering. And he was supposed to be doing a job around here. Josh glanced at his watch. It was nearly midnight, but McCray was something of a night owl.

Josh walked over to the phone and dialed his partner's home number. He sat down on the bed and propped his shoulders against the headboard.

The phone was answered on the other end at the first ring. "Yeah?" McCray sounded preoccupied.

"It's January."

"Not quite," McCray said. "My calendar says early December."

"McCray, when are you going to get tired of weather jokes?"

"Probably not as long as I've got a partner named January. Working a little late, aren't you?" McCray chuckled. "The doctor told you to take it easy. You're supposed to be getting lots of rest and relaxation. How are the ribs and the ankle?"

"Almost back to normal. How are things going at the office?" Josh cradled the phone between his shoulder and his ear while he unfastened the cuffs of his white dress shirt.

"That's right. First things first. Ask about the office. You know, January, you don't lead a balanced life. That's your problem. It's time you had a wife and kids, like me. Something to bring you home at night.''

"Just answer the question, okay? I'm not in the mood for one of your lectures.''

"No sweat, pal. Fact is—and I know it will come as something of a shock to you—but we're managing to scrape along here without you quite nicely. Finished the analysis for Coswell, and we've got a new client who wants us to set up a security system for his electronics firm. What can I say? Business is booming.''

"Glad to hear it. Listen, I've got a couple more questions for you.''

"Want me to check out a few more aging gangsters?''

"Forget the gangsters.'' Josh stripped off his tie and tossed it over the back of the nearest chair. "Try a guy named Dwight Wilcox. He's apparently lived in Peregrine Point for a couple of years. He's the regular handyman here at the manor. I doubt you'll find anything, but it's worth a shot.''

"Should be easy. I'll have Carol get on the computer for you tomorrow morning.''

"Right. Phone me as soon as you've got the report.''

"This case turning into something?'' McCray sounded interested.

Josh thought of the water-pipe incident. "Looks like it. Probably just a malicious-mischief situation. Any word on that Lucky, Inc. stock?''

"Company went bankrupt years ago. Looks like it was a scam from the beginning. The mine's a worthless pit.''

"So much for any possibility that someone's after Mrs. Hawkins's stock," Josh mused. "I was fairly certain that was a dead end. Just wanted to check it out. By the way, McCray?"

"Yeah?"

"There are a couple of things I want you to put into the mail for me tomorrow morning."

McCray listened as Josh told him what he wanted. Then McCray howled with laughter. "You're kidding. You want me to put together a file on you? What the hell for?"

"Just do it, okay?"

"You got it. I'll have it in the mail tomorrow morning. Should reach you in a day or two. Mind telling me why you want to know your own credit rating, blood type and marital status?"

"None of your damn business, McCray."

"Wait a second. Let me guess. You've fallen for the client, haven't you? Ever since you told me she wasn't exactly elderly, I've been suspicious. Well, I'll be damned. You want some advice, January?"

"No."

McCray ignored him. "If I were you, I'd give her flowers rather than a file on yourself. Much more romantic, you know? I've been meaning to talk to you about the way you deal with women. I hate to hurt your feelings, pal, but the bottom line is that you're not all that good with them. You don't understand how they think. As evidence, I submit the fact that you spend far too much time working."

"McCray, I urge you to keep in mind that I am the senior partner at BIS."

"Yes, *sir*." McCray was still chortling as he hung up the phone.

Josh replaced the receiver and sat quietly for a long moment. Then he got up and shrugged out of his dress shirt. He took off his shoes and trousers and padded barefoot across the room to the closet. He found his jeans, stepped into them, then went over to his portable computer. He opened the case and locked the screen into the upright position. Then he sat down and went to work.

As had been happening more and more frequently of late, Josh was soon lost in the story he was creating. The mystery flowed for him in a way that real life never did. He was in the process of having his lead character, Adam Carlisle, walk into a trap while checking out a suspect, when the knock came on the door.

"Josh?"

The sound of Maggie's voice, soft and tentative, brought Josh back to the real world as nothing else could have done at that moment. *Something was wrong.*

He got to his feet and crossed the room in two long strides that sent only a few twinges through his left ankle. He yanked open the door and found Maggie on the other side. She was dressed for bed and wearing the quilted robe she had worn that first night. She looked nervous but determined.

"What's wrong?" Josh demanded, automatically glancing down the hall behind her. All was quiet.

"Nothing's wrong. I just, well, I was wondering if you'd like to kiss me good-night. That's all." She smiled tremulously and clasped the lapels of her robe more tightly together.

Relief poured through him and with it a shot of

anger for the moment of alarm she had obliged him to endure.

"*Kiss you good-night?* Hell, lady, I thought something had happened. Don't ever do that to me again."

She winced and took a step back. "Look, if it's too much trouble, forget it. Damn, this is embarrassing. I was afraid it would be. I should have talked myself out of it." She gave him a bright, brittle little smile as she took another step back. "Sorry about this. I'll see you in the morning."

Josh scowled as Maggie turned and fairly leaped toward the door of her own room.

CHAPTER SEVEN

MAGGIE HAD HER HAND on the doorknob when Josh's fingers closed forcefully around her wrist.

"Hold it. Where do you think you're going?" His voice was very soft as he pulled her around to face him.

Her face aflame, Maggie turned reluctantly and saw that he was smiling now—a slow, sensually menacing smile that did wild and wicked things to Maggie's insides. The sight of him bare to the waist filled her with a pervasive longing. She wondered if she were actually melting somewhere deep in the pit of her stomach. The warmth was amazing.

"I didn't mean to scare you," she muttered, thoroughly embarrassed now, and wishing she hadn't given in to the impulse of a moment earlier.

"I was working." Josh tugged her closer. "When you knocked on the door my mind was on something else entirely and I overreacted. Ask me again."

She was very close to him now. The heat of his skin flooded her senses. She put her hands on his shoulders and luxuriated in the muscled strength she found there. "I can't ask you again. I used up all my nerve the first time."

His mouth curved as he tipped up her chin with his forefinger. "How about if I ask you?"

She smiled. "Okay."

"Will you kiss me good-night?"

"You really want me to?"

"I really want you to," he assured her.

She frowned worriedly. "You're not just saying that?"

"No."

"You're not just trying to make me feel less embarrassed?" she persisted.

"No."

"Because I wouldn't want you to do me any favors, you know. I mean, if you're not as interested in this as I am, just say so up front," she said firmly.

Josh swore softly. "At this rate we're going to waken the chaperons."

Obviously he just wanted her to get on with it, Maggie told herself. She took a deep breath, closed her eyes and stood on tiptoe. Then she raised her face to his.

Nothing happened.

"Josh?" She opened her eyes and found him studying her with laughter in his eyes.

"I'm waiting," he explained.

Annoyed, she braced herself with her hands on his shoulders and brushed her mouth quickly and rather awkwardly across his.

"You call that a kiss?" he asked with interest.

"It doesn't work if you don't cooperate," she muttered.

"Ah. So cooperation is what you want. Damn. You should have mentioned that earlier."

Before Maggie could think of resisting, he caught hold of her wrist and pulled her into his room. Then he shut the door and crowded her back against it. He loomed over her, his hands placed on either side of her head.

"Now, then, let's try this again." Josh brought his mouth very close to hers. "Kiss me."

Maggie swallowed a small, choked laugh that was part relief and part anxiety and put her arms around his neck. She gave herself up to the heat of his kiss with blissful enthusiasm. She could get addicted to Josh January's kisses, she thought. There was certainly nothing the least bit cold about the man in this department.

Josh moved in closer, sliding his bare foot between her slippered feet. She could feel the hard thrust of his leg all the way up the insides of her thighs. When he slipped his hand down her back and cupped her buttocks through the fabric of the robe, she sighed against his lips.

Her robe had parted and the movement of his leg caused her nightgown to ride up. With a thrilling shock, Maggie realized that she could feel the heat of his body burning hers. She clutched at him, feeling deliciously pagan.

"Maggie," Josh whispered thickly. "Maggie, sweetheart, you really want me, don't you?" He sounded dazed. "It took a lot of nerve for you to come here like this."

She turned her face into his shoulder. "Yes."

"It's okay, love. It's okay. Why are you shivering? It's all right. Everything's going to be all right. I want you, too. Very, very badly."

He swept her up into his arms and started toward the bed.

"*Josh.*" Maggie was horrified. "Your ribs. Your ankle. Put me down. You'll hurt yourself."

"We're not going far, Maggie. I think I can make it. Just remember to be gentle with me when we get there." There was sensual laughter in his voice as he carried her the few steps to the massive, canopied bed.

She studied him anxiously as he set her down on her feet and pulled back the covers. "You really shouldn't be lifting anything heavy in your condition. Are you sure you're all right?"

"You'll find out shortly, won't you?" Josh deftly loosened her fingers, which were clutching the edges of her robe again.

"Josh?"

He paused and looked into her eyes. "It's your choice, Maggie. If you'd rather wait, we'll wait. I'll understand. It's the way I had planned things in the first place. I don't want to rush you."

She took a breath and shook her head. "No. I don't want to wait."

"I'm glad," he said simply and slid the robe from her shoulders.

Maggie trembled when Josh started to lift the nightgown over her head.

"Relax, sweetheart. This is going to be very good. For both of us." Josh dropped the nightgown onto the floor and stood looking down at her. He plucked tenderly at first one budding nipple and then the other. "Don't be nervous."

"It's not that." She hugged herself, shielding her breasts from his inspection. "I'm cold. That's all."

"Then why don't you get under the covers?" Josh lifted the quilt, inviting her into the cozy warmth of the big bed. "I'll build a fire."

She tingled under the heat of his gaze as he watched her scramble into bed. She pulled the sheet up to her chin. Maggie wanted to be nonchalant about it but she knew her swift dive for cover only betrayed her tension. She wasn't accustomed to having a man warm her naked body with his eyes alone, the way Josh had done.

Safely ensconced under the covers at last, she watched as Josh went over to the stone fireplace, knelt down on one knee and expertly lit the kindling beneath the logs. Flames crackled to life.

Josh stared into the fire as it began to burn. "You're beautiful, Maggie," he said at last without turning his head. "Did I tell you that?"

"No." She was curiously touched. The sincerity in his voice was bone-deep. Josh was not one to hand out compliments lightly. "Thank you."

Josh got to his feet. "I just wanted you to know. Someone told me once that I wasn't very good with women. I'm not romantic enough, or something."

Maggie swallowed heavily. "I think you're the most romantic thing that's ever happened to me."

Josh studied her for a moment and then he smiled slowly. "You mean that?"

"Yes."

"I'm glad." He flipped off the wall switch, plunging the room into intimate shadow. The light from the fire bathed the bed in a soft, golden glow.

Silhouetted in the firelight, Josh unfastened his jeans and peeled them off. His gaze never left Maggie as he kicked off the briefs he wore underneath and walked to the bed.

Maggie looked up at him, transfixed by the evidence of his arousal. *He wants me,* she thought. The knowledge filled her with sensual assurance and a glorious feeling of her own power as a woman. She stopped clutching the sheet and held the covers back.

"I only came here for a good-night kiss." Maggie smiled at Josh as he slid in beside her.

"It's going to be one hell of a kiss." He put his hand on her bare shoulder and stroked slowly down her side to her hip.

Everywhere he touched her, Josh's fingers burned her skin. The fire pulsed through her, sending her senses spinning with a restless, excited energy.

But then Maggie relaxed completely as Josh pulled her close. The last of her tension and lingering uncertainty vanished, to be replaced by a growing passion.

This was right, she thought as her head fell back across his arm. This was what she had been waiting for all her life. Josh was the hero of her dreams.

She gazed up at him from beneath her lashes as he leaned over her. With questing fingertips she explored the muscular curve of his shoulder and the strong planes of his chest. She loved the feel of him, loved the power and the strength of him.

Maggie kissed Josh's throat and heard him groan in response. Then his leg was sliding between her thighs again and this time there was no denim to get in the way.

"So beautiful," Josh muttered, his lips on Maggie's breast. "So full of heat. I need your fire to warm me. Sometimes I think I've been cold forever." His hand slid down over her stomach and then lower still. His fingers threaded through the tight curls. "Open for me, sweetheart. Take me into your warmth."

A knock on the door came just as Maggie started to part her legs for Josh's touch.

"January? You in there, man?" the Colonel called softly.

"Hell." Josh groaned and rested his forehead on the hollow of Maggie's shoulder. "I don't believe this. Say it isn't so."

Still disoriented from the riot of excitement and passion that was singing through her, Maggie cradled Josh's head in her hands and stared up at the canopy. She tried to figure out what was happening.

The Colonel rapped softly once more. "January? Still awake?"

"Josh?" Maggie threaded her fingers urgently through his dark hair. "It's the Colonel. He's at the door."

"No one could be this unlucky," Josh growled as he reluctantly raised his head. "Not even me." He rolled to the side of the bed, got out and grabbed his jeans. He raised his voice to call out softly. "Hang on, Colonel. I'll be right there."

Maggie felt the laughter well up in her at the sight of Josh's grim face. She struggled to conceal her amusement but Josh saw it. He glowered down at her and then leaned over the bed, trapping her between his arms.

"You," he ordered very, very quietly, "are not to move. And don't you dare make a single sound. Not one peep. Got that?"

"Yes, sir." She grinned up at him from the pillow and reached out to tug playfully on his chest hair. She was feeling very bold.

Josh stifled another groan and straightened. Then he caught hold of a fistful of quilt and yanked it up over Maggie, covering her from head to toe.

Maggie lay curled in the pleasant warmth and listened intently as Josh crossed the room and opened the door.

"What's wrong, Colonel?"

"Believe the furnace is down," the Colonel announced briskly. "It's been getting colder and colder. When I got up to reset the thermostat a second time, I realized it wasn't functioning. Thought we'd better have a look. Could be a malfunction, but the last time this happened, we suspected sabotage, if you'll recall. Couldn't prove it, but we all knew someone had monkeyed with the damn thing."

"It was working fine after Wilcox serviced it. I watched him myself."

"Well, something's gone haywire. I'm going downstairs to have a look. Thought you might want to come with me. No need to awaken the ladies. They'd only worry."

"Right. I'll come with you," Josh replied.

Maggie waited until the door had closed and she could hear the sound of footsteps on the stairs. Then she pushed back the covers and sat up in bed. Her amusement faded rapidly as she contemplated the possibility that another "incident" had occurred.

She slid to the edge of the big bed and got to her feet; she found her quilted robe on the floor and pulled it on quickly. She would follow the men downstairs and see what was happening. The Colonel would think she had been in her own room all along and had simply been awakened by the cold.

Maggie walked over to pull the fire screen in front of the blaze Josh had built and saw the glow of the computer monitor. It was facing the far wall, which was why she hadn't noticed it when she'd entered earlier.

Josh had obviously been working late on the case, she thought. She was touched by his dedication to the job. She was certainly getting her money's worth.

Curious, Maggie stepped closer to read the text on the screen. She had always wondered how real-life private investigators worked....

I went down the darkened corridor, pausing briefly at each door to read the sign outside. The office building had been closed for hours. The guard was a creature of habit and would be doing his rounds on the third floor now. I figured I had maybe thirty minutes before he got to the twelfth floor.

I found Stallings's suite at the end of the hall. A quick check of the lock revealed that getting inside would be easy. Maybe dead easy. A man like Stallings, who was getting ready to steal millions and was prepared to cover up his theft with murder, didn't use cheap hardware-store stuff like this. I stroked the little lock as carefully as if it were a woman.

It was simple. Nothing to it. All in the wrist, you know. No doubt about it, I could be inside in fifteen seconds, max. The damn thing was practically an open invitation.

The last time I'd accepted this kind of invitation, though, I'd almost gotten killed. But what the hell. I was born to be socially flexible.

I went to work on the lock. I was wrong. It only took twelve seconds to open it. I spent the time wondering why Stallings was making it so easy for me to get into his private office.

Maggie sat down and stared at the screen, stunned by what she was reading. It looked as if Josh was writing a book!

Her work as a librarian had made her very familiar with computers. She frowned down at the keyboard and found the key that enable her to scroll through the text on the screen. She made her way back through the story until she found a chapter heading. It *was* a book. A mystery novel, from the looks of it.

She had been cheated! She hadn't gotten herself a private investigator—she had gotten a writer. No wonder Josh spent so much time up here in his room. His *free* room. And no wonder he was so insistent on having his home-cooked meals and his tea and scones. Unpublished writers were notorious mooches—always down-and-out and looking for a handout. Josh probably thought he'd landed in clover when he'd talked his way into this cushy job.

Maggie jumped to her feet, outraged by the way she'd been taken in. Josh wasn't even a published mystery writer, she reminded herself grimly. If he were, she would have heard of him. She'd read hundreds of mysteries.

She glanced around the room, her eyes narrowing. It was time she found out just what sort of man she was dealing with, she decided. She stalked over to the dressing table and started jerking open the drawers.

A collection of socks and briefs had been neatly arranged in the top drawer. There was nothing in the other two. Maggie stomped into the bathroom and surveyed the array of shaving gear on the counter.

She headed for the wardrobe next and flung open the doors to reveal several shirts, his one good-quality jacket, and a tie. The two suitcases she had laboriously brought up the stairs that first night were stacked on the floor. Maggie knelt down and pulled them out. They were both unlocked and empty.

Disgusted with the lack of clues as to Josh's true identity, Maggie closed the closet doors and considered the rest of the small room. Her gaze fell on the nightstand beside the bed.

She walked over and jerked open the drawer of the little table. A blush rose furiously in her cheeks when she saw a little foil packet lying inside next to a pen and notepad. The man obviously believed in being prepared. He'd probably been a Boy Scout. She slammed the drawer hurriedly and went back to the computer.

Slowly she sat down in front of the screen again and began to read.

"DAMN." Josh crouched in front of the furnace's guts, which had been revealed when he'd removed the access panel. He teased one wire out from the nest of control wiring and examined the neatly severed end. "Look at that sucker. Someone sliced right through it."

"Sabotage," the Colonel muttered. "I knew it."

Josh nodded. "Sure looks that way. No telling when it was cut, but it must have been done recently. Probably while Maggie and I were at dinner."

"You think someone got in while Odessa and Shirley and I were watching television?"

"It's possible." Josh remembered how he and Maggie had found all three asleep in front of the droning television set.

"Our hearing isn't what it used to be," the Colonel admitted. "And we had the television on loud. Someone could have gotten in here and cut that wire without us hearing him, I suppose.''

Josh put his left hand on the furnace housing and levered himself to his feet. He wished he'd thrown on a shirt before leaving the bedroom. The basement was cold. "The windows are both closed," he observed as he crossed the room to look up at them. "Closed and locked.''

"What do you think is going on here, January? You're the expert.''

"I think," said Josh, "that I'd better splice that cut wire so we can get some heat going in this place. The whole house will be freezing in another hour or so. Tomorrow morning I'll take a look around outside and see if I can find the point of entry.''

The Colonel nodded, looking suitably impressed. "Right. What about the ladies?''

Josh shot him a sidelong glance, wondering if the Colonel had any notion of where Maggie was at that moment. He didn't want her embarrassed in front of her three old-fashioned tenants. "We'll tell them everything in the morning. Like you said, there's no sense worrying them tonight.''

"Fine. I'll go on back to bed, then. Unless you need any help with that wiring.''

"No, it's just a simple splicing job. I can handle it. I've had a fair amount of experience with this kind of thing." Josh hunkered down in front of the exposed wiring.

"I suppose you use a lot of electronic equipment in your line of work, don't you?" the Colonel remarked, apparently pleased at the notion.

"Yeah, and you can't go calling in a service technician every time something goes wrong on the job.

You learn to make do." Josh used his pocketknife to strip the insulation back on the severed wire.

"Thought so. Well, then, see you at breakfast."

"Right." Josh relaxed as he realized the Colonel was oblivious to Maggie's present location. He concentrated on the task of splicing the control wire as the older man went back up the stairs.

A few minutes later Josh replaced the access panel, dusted his hands and took a last look around the basement. The ground-level windows were definitely locked and they could not have been relocked from the outside—not after the way he had rigged them this morning. That meant whoever had sabotaged the furnace must have entered the basement through the doorway at the top of the stairs.

Which meant that the intruder had let himself into the main part of the manor through a door or window upstairs while three of the residents were at home. It was the first time, as far as Josh could tell, that the vandal had taken such a daring risk. The bastard had walked straight down the front hall, as if he owned the place.

Josh frowned as he climbed the stairs to the first floor. He didn't like the idea that whoever was staging the "incidents" was apparently getting bolder. It was a sign that the sabotage and vandalism might soon grow more menacing. At the rate things were going, someone would eventually get hurt.

He had to put a stop to this now, before it got out of hand, Josh decided. He had hoped his presence in the house would discourage whoever was behind the incidents, but clearly that was not the case. And now the guy was getting desperate. Desperate men did dangerous things.

Josh walked through every room on the first floor, checking locks. Every window and door was securely fastened. *An inside job?* Josh wondered as he went up the stairs to his room. He thought of the list of suspects and motives he had given Maggie over dinner.

He doubted that Odessa or Shirley would have known how to disable the furnace. On the other hand, it didn't take a lot of mechanical aptitude to figure out that cutting a wire would cause trouble. But then, there was the water-pipe incident. Someone had definitely entered the house from outside to pull that one off. Or had someone inside merely wanted it to look that way?

Possibilities and motives clicked rapidly through Josh's brain as he reached the top of the stairs and opened the door of his room. The first thing he saw was Maggie sitting in front of the computer. The eerie blue glow of the screen bathed her face in a cold light. She looked up as he entered the room.

Josh saw the suspicion and anger in her gaze and his stomach clenched with despair. What a fool he had been! He'd forgotten all about the computer and the book when Maggie had come knocking on his door asking him to kiss her good-night. And now he was going to pay the price of his stupidity.

"Maggie, honey." Josh closed the door very softly and stood there, trying to think clearly. His brain, which had been in overdrive a minute earlier, suddenly seemed to have turned to cobwebs. He had to explain this, he told himself desperately. He had to make her understand. He took a deep breath and tried again. "I know you must be wondering about what you're seeing there on that screen."

She leaned back in the chair, crossed her legs under her robe and folded her arms. She gave him a disdainful look. "I suppose you're going to tell me that since you're posing as a writer, you wanted to have some props around in case anyone came snooping. I suppose you think I'll believe that you just selected some mystery novel at random and typed up a few chapters so anyone who came in here would believe you really are a writer."

Josh watched her carefully, aware that he wasn't quite certain of her mood. He felt as if he were walking on eggs. "I wrote that myself," he admitted.

"I know." She shot to her feet and strode over to the window. Her arms were still folded across her chest and her chin was tilted at a proud, defiant angle. "As soon as I'd read a few pages, I was sure of it."

"Maggie, I know what you're thinking."

"Do you?"

"Yes. You think you've been ripped off. That you ordered up a private investigator and got a con artist, instead."

"And did I?"

"No, damn it." Josh hooked his thumbs in the waistband of his jeans and braced his feet. He felt as if he were getting ready for battle—one of the most important of his life. The stakes, he suddenly realized, were higher than he had ever dreamed they could be. But then, he'd never wanted a woman the way he wanted Maggie Gladstone. "Give me a chance to explain, Maggie. You owe me that much."

She stood with her back to him and stared out the window. "Are you really Josh January?"

"Hell, yes. I told you to call that number I gave you, remember? I told you that if you had any questions, my partner would answer them. And send you the proof.''

"You're a genuine private investigator? Owner of Business Intelligence and Security?''

"Yes, damn it. I can show you my license. Listen, Maggie, this isn't what it seems. I'm doing what you hired me to do. I swear it.'' Josh felt desperate. He, of all people, knew you couldn't trust a man's word or any piece of paper he showed you unless you knew him very well. He could hardly expect Maggie to believe him. She had only known him a few days.

"Are you quite certain you aren't some aspiring writer, a friend of the real Josh January, perhaps? Maybe the real January had no more intention of taking me on as a client than any of the other investigators I contacted.''

"I am the real Josh January.''

Maggie ignored him. "Maybe not. Maybe you're just his friend. Maybe, because of that and because you're trying to write a mystery, he figured you could fake it out here for a month. After all, how hard can it be to pull the wool over the eyes of three aging retirees and one naive innkeeper?''

"Maggie, I'm telling you—''

She nodded thoughtfully. "I can see where it would have sounded like a neat arrangement. You're recovering from an accident. You've got some time on your hands and you want to write a book. What a deal! You get a free vacation and an opportunity to work on your manuscript. In addition, you even get to play private eye for real, for a few weeks. What fun.''

"Damn it, Maggie.''

"And, just to top things off in the fun-and-games

department, you decide to seduce the client. Is this how you big-city guys amuse yourselves?''

That did it. Josh stormed across the room, moving so quickly that he got a sharp warning twinge from his left foot. It was painful enough to make him wince, but he paid no attention to it. He had more important things on his mind.

When he reached Maggie, he put his hands on her shoulders and spun her around to face him. ''I *am* the real Josh January,'' he said through clenched teeth. ''I am the senior partner in BIS. I am investigating this case for you. *And I also happen to be trying to write a book.* I give you my personal guarantee that you are not getting stiffed. I'll find out whoever is behind these incidents. And I will find him real soon.''

''I'm getting what I'm paying for, is that it?''

''Yes, damn it. That's it. I'll admit I accepted this job initially because I was recovering from an accident. My doctor and partner talked me into getting away for a while. To be honest, this case looked like a cinch. I figured I could solve it for you within a month and at the same time do some work on my book.''

''What about the big seduction scenes?''

He groaned. ''Sweetheart, you're the first client I've ever tried to seduce. And so far, I haven't had much success, I might add. Maggie, our relationship has nothing to do with the case. I give you my word of honor.''

''You really do like me a little?''

He was shocked to see that she was smiling now. He could hardly believe his eyes. ''Maggie, it's a lot more than 'like.' I promise. I want you very much.

I've never met anyone I've wanted as much as I want you. Please believe me.''

"Hmm.''

He flexed his hands on her shoulders, willing her to give him a chance. "Look, honey, I can't give you any proof tonight. I don't expect you to take my word for everything. All I ask is that you wait until you can verify what I'm saying before you make any decisions.''

"I suppose we could do it that way,'' she agreed slowly.

Hope rose in him. "Tomorrow morning you can call that number I gave you or you can wait a day or two and I'll have something to show you. Something that will prove I am who I say I am.''

"Proof. That's all you can think about.'' Maggie wrinkled her nose in exasperation. "Oh, never mind, Josh. I believe you.''

"You do?'' He stared at her, dumbfounded. "Without proof?''

"Forget the proof. Nobody would make up a ridiculous story like the one you just gave me.'' Maggie ducked out from under his hands and took two steps to the bed. She hopped up on the step and sat down on the edge of the thick mattress. "So, are you coming to bed or not?''

"Maggie." He couldn't believe it. She was smiling at him in feminine welcome. She was willing to take his word for everything he had just said. Josh took a hesitant step closer to the bed. "Do you mean it? You want to spend the night here in my bed?''

She laughed softly. "The thing about you, Josh, is that you're exactly like that Adam Carlisle person in your book: You're one of the good guys.''

CHAPTER EIGHT

THE INSTANT Josh entered her he felt as if he had found a part of himself that he hadn't even realized was missing. Maggie's welcoming feminine heat consumed him and made him feel complete. For a split second of startling clarity, Josh recognized what was happening. *She's mine now,* he thought as her body tightened around him. *She was meant for me.*

In the next instant the crystal-clear understanding vanished amid the excitement that was sweeping over him. Sheer, glorious physical sensation took over. She felt so good...better than anything he had ever known. His thoughts were scattered as the intense, primal reality of their lovemaking swamped his senses. But the feeling of need and possessiveness remained lodged deep in his mind, even as Josh gave himself up to the sweet pleasure of the moment.

He was fiercely aware of Maggie's arms wrapped tightly around him as he surged deeply into her. He felt the tiny bite of her nails as they sank into his shoulders. He drank the small, soft cries from her lips as she surrendered to the passion they were sharing.

"Put your legs around me, sweetheart," he managed as he sensed her body begin to tense.

She did as he said, locking her legs around his hips, offering the very core of herself to him. Josh groaned as he felt himself slide a little farther into her.

"So deep," he muttered against her mouth. "I'm so far inside you, I feel as if I'm a part of you."

"You are," she said simply. Then her head moved restlessly against the pillow. "Oh, *Josh.*"

"Yes, love. Now. That's it. Let it happen *now.* I can't hold it any longer. *Yes!*" He drove into her one last time as he felt the first delicate ripples of her release.

The sensation was unbelievably erotic. She was literally caressing him in the most intimate manner possible. Josh's body threatened to explode and then it did explode. He captured Maggie's mouth with his own to drown his own hoarse shout of satisfaction as she breathed her exquisite cry of completion.

When it was over, Josh pulled her close and curled her body into his own. She fell asleep beside him, her relaxed body evidence of her trust.

Josh lay quietly for a long time. He stared up at the shadowed canopy and tried to comprehend what was happening to him. He felt different somehow. Something important in his world had changed. Maggie was at the heart of that change. She was very precious.

He would protect her, Josh told himself. At all costs, he would shield her and care for her.

He finally fell asleep himself on that thought.

MAGGIE AWAKENED feeling vaguely disoriented. She stretched languidly, wondering why the bed felt different. When her toe came in contact with a masculine leg, she froze in shock. And then memory came flooding back.

Josh had made love to her last night.

And it had been wonderful. The most wonderful experience of her life.

Maggie snuggled into the unfamiliar masculine warmth. Josh's arm curled around her, his hand coming to rest on her breast.

"Josh?"

"Yeah?" He sounded half asleep.

"Josh, are you awake?"

"No." He tightened his hold on her and his thumb began to glide slowly across her nipple. "Don't bother me. I'm dreaming."

"Well, in that case…" Smiling to herself, Maggie let her hand drift down across his broad chest. Her fingertips reached the tangled thatch of dark hair below his flat belly and she tugged gently.

"You're playing with fire, lady." Josh nibbled on her shoulder.

"Promises, promises. I— Oh, my goodness." Her fingers were suddenly filled with the heavy, thrusting warmth of him. "I *am* playing with fire, aren't I?"

"Told you so."

"I think I could get to like this game."

"You obviously have an aptitude for it. Maybe it's time I demonstrate a few of the finer nuances." Lazily, Josh stirred and started to inch his way down her body. His mouth was on her breast and he had one leg between her thighs when he abruptly stilled.

"Josh? What's wrong?"

"Damn." Josh raised his head and sat up, shoving aside the covers. He glanced at the clock beside the bed. "It's six-thirty."

"So what? We were up late last night." She reached for him, urging him back to bed.

His eyes narrowed as he looked down at her. "So

the Colonel, Odessa and Shirley will all be getting up soon. The last thing I want is for you to run into one of them out in the hall on your way back to your own room.''

"Don't worry about it, Josh." She smiled coaxingly up at him. "I'll be careful."

"Darn right, you're going to be careful. You're going to hop straight out of that bed, put on your robe and get your little tush back to your own room."

Maggie sat up slowly, a little surprised by his tone. She wrapped her arms around updrawn knees and tilted her head to one side to study him. "Are you really that concerned about the Colonel and the others finding out we spent the night together?"

"It would be embarrassing for you and for them." Josh got out of bed. He reached down to tug back the covers.

When he did so, Maggie was left sitting stark naked in the center of the white sheet. She smiled brilliantly up at him. "I think I can handle any embarrassment that I might experience."

Josh stared down at her, his eyes warm as he took in the sexy, inviting picture she made. "Well, you're not going to handle it as long as I have anything to say about it. It's my job to protect you, remember? Let's go, Maggie."

"I'm not a kid, Josh."

"Yeah. Well, you're not exactly an experienced woman of the world, either." He jerked on his jeans.

"I think I resent that remark. May I remind you that I was the one who took the initiative last night?" She fixed him with a proud grin. "If we'd waited for you to make a move I'd still be alone in my own room."

"We'll argue about who takes the initiative in this relationship some other time." He reached down to catch hold of her wrist and yanked her gently up off the bed. Maggie sighed and gave up the battle. She stood meekly while Josh tossed her nightgown over her head and fastened her robe.

"Are you always this grouchy in the mornings?" she asked as he tugged her toward the door.

"It varies." He turned, his hand on the doorknob, and kissed her soundly. "Sometimes I'm in a really terrific mood. Unfortunately, this morning isn't one of those days."

"Just my bad luck, I suppose."

"Right." He opened the door and gave her a little shove that sent her out into the hall.

The first person Maggie saw there was Odessa. The older woman was poised at the top of the stairs, preparing to descend. She was gazing straight at Josh's door as it opened.

"Good morning, dear," Odessa called in a cheery tone. She looked totally unfazed by the sight of Maggie emerging from Josh's room. "Sleep well?"

Maggie heard Josh groan on the other side of the door. In spite of her bold words to him a moment earlier, she felt herself blushing. She tried to plaster a nonchalant smile on her face.

"Good morning, Odessa. I slept quite well, thank you." The thing to do, Maggie decided, was to act as if nothing out of the ordinary was occurring. "How about you?"

"I got quite chilled in the middle of the night. The Colonel must have set the thermostat too low. But it's warm and cozy this morning, isn't it? And how is Josh today?"

"Josh," said Josh, emerging from the bedroom with a grimly determined expression, "is just fine this morning."

Odessa started to say something else but before she could speak, Shirley's door opened.

"Hi, everyone." Shirley pushed her rhinestone-studded glasses firmly onto her nose. She beamed at Maggie and Josh. "So you two have decided to take the big step, eh? Congratulations. Knew it was just a matter of time. We'll have to have an engagement party, won't we, Odessa?"

"Engagement party?" Maggie felt her stomach turn over. Behind her she was aware of Josh lounging in the doorway.

"Of course," Odessa responded. "I'm sure we have some champagne left down in the basement." She turned as the Colonel appeared from his bedroom. "Don't we have some champagne left, Colonel?"

"I expect we do. What are we celebrating?" The Colonel looked down the length of the hall and saw Maggie silhouetted in Josh's bedroom doorway. He gave a great start of surprise. "Ah. I think I get the picture now. I take it we have something important to announce here?"

"Don't they make a darling couple?" Shirley asked with a fond look. "Reminds me of my early days with Ricky."

"You know, dear," Odessa said lightly to Maggie, "I hate to say I told you so, but I did tell you that I thought you and Josh were made for each other. Didn't I say that, Colonel?"

The Colonel nodded, his eyes on Josh. "I believe you did say that, my dear."

Odessa smiled again. "And here they are engaged already. I think it's just lovely."

Maggie's initial embarrassment was giving way to a sense of panic. She realized she'd been waiting for Josh to take control of the situation, but he was making no move to do so. A quick sidelong glance out of the corner of her eye revealed that he was just hanging out there in the doorway, one shoulder propped against the wall, his arms folded across his chest. She wanted to yell at him, order him to stop the teasing before it got out of hand. But evidently he wasn't going to do a darn thing.

"All right," Maggie said, trying for an indulgent little laugh. "You've all had your fun. I think this has gone far enough. No more jokes, all right? It's too early in the morning for this kind of humor."

"Who's joking?" Shirley asked with perfect innocence. "We're all happy for you, honey. It's time you found yourself a real man. Nothing against that nice Clay O'Connor, mind you, but anyone could tell he wasn't for you."

The Colonel gave Josh a steely look. "Set a date yet?"

"No," replied Josh in an astonishingly calm voice. "But we'll get around to it one of these days."

The Colonel nodded again, looking satisfied. "Well, then, congratulations to you both. We'll see you at breakfast. Take your time. We can get things going without you for one morning. I used to make a fair cup of coffee in my military days. My fellow officers told me you could float horseshoes in it." He held out his arms to Shirley and Odessa. "Shall we go, ladies?"

"Yes, indeed." Odessa took his right arm. "I'm famished."

"So am I." Shirley took the Colonel's other arm with a flourish. Then she gave Maggie a teasing grin. "And I expect you two have worked up quite an appetite yourselves. See you in a few minutes."

Maggie stood rooted to the floor until her three tenants had vanished from sight. Then she whirled around to confront Josh. He cocked a brow when she pinned him with a frosty glare.

"Just what in the world do you think you're doing?" Maggie hissed. "They think we're engaged!"

"Yeah, I got that impression."

"Well, why did you let them *get* that impression?" she retorted. "Why didn't you say something? Why didn't you try to explain?"

"And just how the hell was I supposed to explain the fact that you were coming out of my room at six-thirty in the morning wearing your nightgown?"

"You didn't have to go along with the notion that we're engaged," Maggie wailed softly. She was feeling trapped. "Why are you standing there like a bump on a log? Doesn't this bother you just a teensy bit? Aren't you the least bit concerned by the fact that those three believe we're halfway to the altar?"

"What should I have said?" Josh asked softly. "Should I have told them I spent the night with you but my intentions weren't honorable? That would have been a little hard for them to handle, Maggie. They're from a different generation, remember."

"Since when do you worry about other people's approval?" Maggie's eyes widened as a thought struck her. "Josh, you're not really afraid of a shotgun wedding, are you? I know you joked about it, but you can't possibly think the Colonel would try anything like that. Not in this day and age.''

Josh glanced down at his folded arms and then back up to meet her anxious gaze. His own gray eyes had gone cold and unreadable. "Maybe I didn't feel like upsetting everyone, Maggie. I'm supposed to be doing a job here, remember? There's a little matter of professionalism involved. Lord knows my behavior has already crossed the line. I should never have let you into my room last night. But what's done is done, and I'd just as soon be able to complete this job without getting everyone hostile. It would complicate matters a whole lot. I need cooperation to solve this case.''

Maggie felt as though he had struck her. She instinctively retreated a step as she realized just what he was saying. "You're allowing them to think we're engaged just so you can complete this case?"

He frowned. "It's the best way. Maggie, I think I can wrap things up here in a few more days. I've got a couple of hunches I want to check out, and then I'm going to see about setting a trap for whoever is behind the incidents here at the manor.''

"I see." Maggie swallowed heavily. Josh would be leaving in a few days.

"In the meantime, I don't want to muddy the waters any more than I already have. I can't afford to send out any alarm signals to the person who's causing the trouble here. We've got to make everything look as normal as possible around the manor. Frankly, this isn't the worst thing that could have happened.''

"It's not?"

Josh thought. "No. In fact, the more I think about

it, the more I believe this just might be the right move."

"I don't understand." Maggie's mouth felt dry now. She wondered with horror if she were about to burst into tears.

"Yeah, I think this unfortunate little misunderstanding is going to work to our benefit," Josh stated. "Don't you see, Maggie? It's the perfect cover for the trap I'm going to set."

Maggie gazed at him, feeling sick. "I don't understand."

Josh straightened in the doorway and started back into his own room. "Don't worry about it, sweetheart. I'll explain the details later. In the meantime, just go alone with the engagement story, okay? I want everyone to believe it, including the Colonel, Odessa and Shirley."

"But, Josh—" Maggie broke off when Josh gently closed the door in her face.

She stood staring blankly at the door for a full minute before whirling around and dashing into her own bedroom. She would not cry, she vowed as she stripped off her robe and jerked off her nightgown. She hurled the nightclothes onto the bed as she strode toward the small bathroom. *She would not cry.*

But Josh's words about the "unfortunate misunderstanding" being a useful cover story proved too much for Maggie's bruised feelings. What had she expected? she asked herself forlornly. Of course, the man wasn't going to allow himself to be pushed into a real engagement. Nobody was *that* honorable, these days. In any case, the last thing she wanted to do was try to force him into doing "the right thing."

When she stepped under the shower, Maggie's

tears mingled with the spray of the water. It wasn't until she'd actually started to cry that she admitted to herself what had really happened to her during the past few days.

She had fallen in love with Josh January.

THE KITCHEN PHONE RANG just as Josh and the Colonel were telling everyone about the mysterious severed wire inside the furnace. Maggie jumped up to answer it. She plucked the receiver off the wall.

"Hello?"

"Josh January, please," said a crisp, male voice on the other end of the line.

"Just a moment." Maggie put her hand over the receiver and looked at Josh. "It's for you."

"Right." He got to his feet and took the phone out of her hand. "Yeah? Oh, it's you, McCray. No, you didn't interrupt anything except breakfast. Just give me what you've got and stop trying to get cute." There was a short pause. Josh's expression turned into a scowl. "McCray, that is not funny. None of your cold jokes are funny. When are you going to get that through your thick head? Just tell me what you've got on Wilcox."

Maggie and the others stopped talking at the mention of Dwight Wilcox's name. The Colonel assumed his pondering expression and Odessa looked disapproving. Shirley's eyes widened in fascination.

"He's investigating Dwight?" Odessa asked Maggie.

"I guess so." Maggie went back to her grapefruit. She was not in a chatty mood.

"Wilcox does know his way around our basement," the Colonel observed softly. "And he also knows how to handle tools."

"I don't know," Shirley murmured. "Somehow I can't picture that Dwight planning all those crazy incidents. My Ricky always used to say that it took real brains to be a successful criminal. The dumb ones got caught early."

Josh ignored the commentary going on around the breakfast table. He had taken a notepad out of a nearby kitchen drawer and was busily scribbling down information.

"Okay, McCray. It's not much, but it's information. Check something else for me this afternoon, will you? See if Johnny has the time to do some background work on the manor itself, will you? No, I don't know what I'm looking for at this point." Josh slid a glance across the four rapt faces around the table. "Old legends involving money or treasure...anything of interest. Yeah, right. That kind of thing. Call me back when you've got something. Take it easy."

"Well?" Maggie gave Josh a challenging look as he came back to the table and sat down. "What did that McCray person find out about Dwight?"

"Not much." Josh glanced down at the page on which he had written his notes. "Wilcox was in some trouble with the law a few years ago."

Shirley stared at him. "Our Dwight is a crook?"

"Not much of one, by all accounts." Josh tore out the sheet of paper, folded it in half and stuck it into his pocket. "He got picked up on a robbery charge. Did eighteen months. He's been clean ever since."

"Robbery?" Maggie put down her grapefruit spoon. "Are you sure?"

Josh nodded. "At this point it doesn't mean much. He was just a kid at the time and he didn't get away with it."

"Not surprising," Shirley muttered. "Told you he wasn't all that bright."

"Still, it may mean the young man has criminal tendencies," Odessa observed. She frowned at Maggie. "Perhaps we shouldn't have him do any more work around here, dear."

"Who else are we going to get?" Maggie picked up a piece of toast. "It's not like Peregrine Point is full of handymen."

"Nevertheless, perhaps we should start advertising for someone else," Odessa stated.

Maggie put down her toast. "Aunt Agatha hired him, didn't she?"

The Colonel nodded solemnly. "That's right. About two years ago. Shortly after he moved to town. She was always quite satisfied with his work."

Josh held up a hand. "Look, there's no point discussing what you're going to do about Dwight Wilcox right now. I don't want Maggie making any changes in the way things are run around here yet. It would alert whoever is behind the incidents that we suspect they are more than just incidents."

The Colonel nodded again. "Quite right, January. We must all continue to give the impression that we think we've suffered from nothing more than bad luck around here."

"Bad luck is right." Maggie got to her feet and started toward the sink. She thought about the horrendous dose of bad luck she had experienced earlier that morning when she'd walked out of Josh's room and ran straight into Odessa. "There certainly has been a lot of it around here lately, hasn't there?"

"Nothing we can't handle," Josh responded dryly.

THAT AFTERNOON Maggie found herself sitting beside Josh in his black Toyota. She hadn't asked for an escort into town. Indeed, she had done her level best to try to talk Josh out of accompanying her. But he had been in one of his insistent moods. Maggie was learning that when Josh decided to do something, it was extremely difficult to deflect him from his chosen course.

"I don't need help picking up the groceries, Josh. I could have handled the shopping on my own." Maggie stared out the window at the gray ocean. A new storm was coming in fast. She could see the rain sweeping over the sea. It would hit land in another half hour.

"No problem." Josh's hands were relaxed and competent on the wheel of the Toyota. "I need to pick up a few personal items myself."

"I could have bought shaving cream or blades for you," she muttered.

"Yeah, but I felt like the outing." Josh slanted her a glance. "How come you're sulking today?"

"I am not sulking."

"Bull. You've been in this mood since you ran into Odessa and the others outside my room this morning. Hey, you're not still worried about our phony engagement, are you?"

"What if I am?"

"Maggie, I've told you, everything's going to work out just fine. Leave it to me, okay?"

"I left it to you and look what happened." Maggie

turned her head to glower at him. "This is all your fault, Josh. Some private investigator, you are. You could have at least checked to see that the coast was clear this morning before you shoved me out the door. But, oh, no. You couldn't wait to get me out of your bedroom."

"You really are mad, aren't you?" Josh threw her a surprised look.

"Yes, I am. I do not like this, Josh. I do not like any of it."

"Take it easy, Maggie. In a few days, I'll have this thing sorted out."

"Oh, that's just ducky. Then what happens? What am I supposed to tell the Colonel and Odessa and Shirley when you leave town?" Maggie wailed. "They'll think I've been abandoned. They'll feel sorry for me."

Josh studied the road ahead. "Tell them you changed your mind and decided to call off the engagement. They'll understand."

"They will not understand. They'll think that what happened between you and me was nothing more than a one-night stand, and they'll be right."

"So don't call off the engagement."

She stared at him in disbelief. "Are you crazy? What am I supposed to do after you leave? Pretend we're still engaged? How do you expect me to carry that off?"

"I'd be willing to help," Josh said quietly. "We can string our engagement out for a few months and then say we've changed our minds."

"Oh, sure. And just how are we going to string out our engagement when you're in Seattle and I'm here in Peregrine Point?"

"I could come out for a while on the weekends. You could come into the city. Let's be honest here, Maggie. We're attracted to each other. Last night was very good. You know that as well as I do. Why shouldn't we go on seeing each other?"

Maggie closed her eyes. "I wish you would stop being so damn reasonable about the whole thing. You're missing the point here. Don't you understand what I'm trying to say? I don't want a fake engagement."

"Not even for the sake of solving this case?" Josh asked.

Maggie groaned and turned her attention back to the heavy gray rain that was moving in from the sea. "I feel trapped," she whispered.

"Don't worry about it," Josh said lightly. "You've got me around to rescue you, remember? I'll figure something out."

"You're the one who's always saying that it never pays to play hero."

"I'm not playing hero this time. I got you into the engagement. I'll find a way to get you out of it without embarrassing you any more than you already are."

"I'm not embarrassed," Maggie retorted fiercely. "It's just awkward, that's all. The Colonel and the others are all so old-fashioned and protective."

"Tell me the truth, Maggie. You were embarrassed as hell when you walked out that door this morning and saw Odessa, weren't you?"

She sighed. "Yes."

"The engagement was the only way to handle the thing," Josh continued relentlessly.

"And so convenient," Maggie shot back under her

breath. "You'd worked it into your cover story before I could count to three."

Josh was silent for a long moment. "Is that what's really bothering you?" he asked at last. "You're angry because I'm using our phony engagement as part of my cover?"

"I don't want to talk about it anymore," Maggie declared. They were in town now and Josh was slowing to turn into the small supermarket parking lot. "The damage is done, so we'll just have to hope some good comes out of it."

"Trust me, Maggie. You did last night."

"Well, I learned my lesson this morning, didn't I?"

CHAPTER NINE

MAGGIE WAS LOADING grocery sacks into the back of Josh's car when Clay O'Connor hailed her from across the street.

"Maggie," he called out as he emerged from his office. "I thought that was you."

Maggie straightened and turned to wave. Downtown Peregrine Point consisted of a mere two blocks of shops. O'Connor Real Estate was located directly across from the grocery store. Clay had obviously spotted her from his office window.

Maggie watched as Clay checked for oncoming cars and then quickly crossed the street without bothering to go to the corner. He was dressed for the crisp cold day in a handsome, chunky-knit sweater and a pair of wool trousers. His hair was styled in a full, curving line that could only have been achieved with the aid of mousse. The diamond in his heavy gold ring flashed briefly when he moved his hand. He looked as if he had stepped right out of a men's fashion magazine.

The sight of Clay, with his cheerful, open face and dazzling smile made Maggie vividly aware of the contrast between him and Josh. It was like the contrast between day and night. With Clay, one got what one saw. But instead of the reassurance that fact should have provided, it only made him seem bland

and shallow to Maggie. Josh, on the other hand, brought to mind the old adage about still waters running deep. He made her think of hidden depths and disturbing passions. Deep water was frequently dangerous, Maggie reminded herself.

"I almost didn't see you," Clay complained lightly as he reached her. "Didn't recognize the car. Who does it belong to? That writer fellow?"

Maggie felt herself blushing. It dawned on her how monumentally awkward the phony engagement was going to get. She had to try to keep it contained, she told herself. She didn't want it spread all over Peregrine Point. But even as she frantically tried to figure out a way to control something as uncontrollable as gossip in a small town, she knew her efforts were futile.

"Hello, Clay. Yes, the car belongs to Josh. He had to come into town for some things so he gave me a lift." Maggie hoisted another sack into the vehicle. Mentally she toyed with the notion of telling Clay the truth.

"You know, Maggie, I've been thinking about that guy." Clay's handsome features shaped themselves into serious lines. "I don't want to alarm you or anything, but does it strike you as a little strange that he showed up when he did?"

Startled, Maggie straightened quickly. She frowned as she turned to face Clay. "Strange?"

Clay shrugged and braced one hand against the roof of the Toyota. "Well, here you are, closed for the winter and all, and then he lands on your doorstep for a month. I bring you home from a date and he's waiting at the front door. The next thing I know the two of you are seen having dinner in town. And now he's shopping with you. Seems to me he's really made himself a part of the family in a hurry.''

Maggie chewed on her lower lip. ''You know how it is, Clay. He's the only guest at the manor these days, so we've just sort of made him a part of our household for the month. Most of the time we don't see all that much of him. He's always upstairs working on that book of his.'' That statement certainly had the ring of truth about it now, Maggie reflected grimly.

Clay eyed her thoughtfully. ''Have you ever actually seen any evidence of that book?''

''Yes, as a matter of fact, I have.'' Maggie was relieved to be able to tell the full truth for once. Lately there had been far too many half-truths and downright fabrications. ''It's a mystery novel. Very exciting, from what I saw of it.''

''Hmm.''

''What is it, Clay?''

He gave her his charming, crooked little smile. ''Hell, don't pay any attention to me, Maggie. Sheer jealousy motivating me, that's all.''

Maggie felt wretched. And slightly guilty. ''Clay, I'm sorry if you feel I, well, if you think I implied that my feelings were stronger toward you than they actually are. I mean, I've enjoyed your company very much but I wouldn't want you to think that I...''

Clay's charming smile turned wistful. He touched her mouth with his fingertips, gently silencing her. ''Hey, don't worry about it, Maggie. I'm a big boy. I know that for you our relationship has been casual so far, but I plan to change all that. In the meantime, I can handle a little competition.''

Maggie began to seethe with annoyance. This was

so awkward. "Clay, it isn't exactly competition. I wouldn't want you to think I'm trying to play games. Josh and I, well, we've become quite friendly since he moved into the manor. That's all."

Clay's smile widened into a grin. "I'm not worried. I figure I've got the edge. After all, January will be gone in a couple of weeks and I'll still be here, won't I?"

"Clay, that's very sweet of you—really, it is."

"Remember that I'm a sweet guy by nature," he advised ruefully. Then his expression sobered. "Maggie, I meant what I said earlier. You really don't know all that much about January. If he says or does anything that makes you nervous, promise you'll call me immediately."

"But, Clay—"

"Just promise, honey. I want to know you'll feel free to call me if anything happens at the manor."

"Like what?" Josh asked in an icy drawl as he materialized from between two parked cars.

Maggie jumped at the unexpected sound of his voice. She turned her head and saw that he was carrying a small, white paper sack in his hand. It bore the logo of the Peregrine Point Pharmacy. "Oh, Josh, there you are," she said weakly. "I was wondering what had happened to you." She made a show of glancing at her watch. "Good heavens, just look at the time. We'd better hurry. It's starting to rain."

Josh ignored her. He absently dangled the little white bag while he smiled at Clay with faint challenge. "Did I hear you say you were worried about something going on at the manor?"

Clay took his hand off the Toyota's roof and shoved it deep into his pocket. "Maggie and I were just having a friendly little chat. We've been friends for several months now, haven't we, Maggie?''

"Uh, yes. Yes, we have, Clay." Maggie wanted to crawl into a hole and hide. Never in her life had she been the subject of conflict between two grown men. It was terribly embarrassing. "Listen, we have really got to be on our way. I'll see you later, Clay. Josh, will you please hurry? I've got things to do back at the manor."

"Sure thing, sweetheart." Josh turned his back on Clay and sauntered over to the passenger door of the Toyota. He opened it with a cool possessiveness and ushered Maggie inside. Then he went around to the driver's side and got in behind the wheel. "See you, O'Connor."

Maggie waved at Clay as Josh swung the Toyota out of the parking lot. "Honestly, Josh, that was extremely rude."

"What was rude?"

"The way you behaved toward Clay. And don't you dare act as if nothing happened back there. You were very uncivil and you know it."

"The guy was trying to warn you off me, wasn't he?"

Maggie tilted her chin. "He was merely pointing out that I know very little about you and that it was rather odd the way you turned up at the manor when you did."

"I turned up at the manor because you hired me," Josh growled. "And don't you forget it."

"I could hardly tell Clay that, could I?"

"Not as long as you want me to do my job," Josh agreed coolly. "So what did you tell him?"

Maggie sighed. "Not much. Just that you'd sort of become a part of the household lately."

Josh gave a roar of laughter. "Just an old friend of the family, huh? O'Connor will have to be a hell of a lot dumber than he looks to believe that."

"There's no need to talk about Clay like that. He is not dumb. He's a very nice man—which is more than I can say about some people around here."

"Is that right?" Josh abruptly slowed the Toyota. He turned off the road and pulled into a secluded parking area. A thick stand of fir shielded the car from the view of passing drivers.

"What are you doing?" Maggie glowered across the seat at him.

"I want to talk to you and it's hard to do it at the manor. Too many people around." Josh switched off the ignition and sat for a long moment, his brooding gaze on the rain-spangled sea.

Maggie sensed that their conversation was about to change significantly. "Josh? Is something wrong?"

"What did you think of it, Maggie?"

"What did I think of the way you talked to Clay? I told you what I thought of it. I thought it was rude. It was pure *machismo* in action. And it didn't make me feel especially valuable, either. I know for a fact I'm one of the few single women under the age of fifty here in Peregrine Point. It's not as if the two of you chose me out of a crowd and decided I was worth squabbling over."

"Forget the scene with O'Connor." Josh rested his hands on the steering wheel. "What did you think of the book?"

Maggie studied his harsh profile. "The book?"

"You're the only one who's read any of it, so far.

Last night while I was downstairs messing around with that furnace you had time to read quite a bit of it. How far did you get?''

"Josh, I'm sorry I read what you had written. It was very wrong of me to pry like that. But you have to realize that I was afraid I'd been conned.''

"How far did you get?'' Josh repeated, spacing each word out carefully for emphasis.

"A couple of chapters,'' she admitted.

"So what did you think?''

Maggie smiled slightly. "I thought it was terrific, Josh.''

His head came around quickly, his eyes intense. "I want the truth.''

"The truth is that I have read an enormous number of mysteries and I can assure you that what I saw of yours is as good as the best,'' she said quietly.

He exhaled deeply. "You really think so?''

"I really think so. Your main character, Adam Carlisle, is wonderful. He tries to go through life with a protective coat of cynicism, but underneath he's a born hero. That's very appealing. He's the good guy. The one who will fight for the weak and the innocent, even while he's grumbling about how being a hero doesn't pay. He's a lot like you, isn't he, Josh?''

"Hell, no. He's just a figment of my imagination.''

"I think he's more than that,'' Maggie replied. "He's your alter ego. He gets to solve the kind of clear-cut cases you got into the business to handle— the kind where there's an innocent victim and a real villain. The kind where there's no question about right and wrong. He gets to do battle against genuine evil and win.''

"It's always so simple with Adam Carlisle's

cases," Josh agreed softly. "And he gets to step over the line occasionally to make certain justice gets done."

"He gets to play hero. Deep down, readers love real heroes and they love it when justice is done. More than that, I think readers *need* those kinds of stories. They satisfy something deep inside. You're writing straight to the heart of that market, Josh. You're going to be a success."

"You're not just saying that?"

"Josh, I can't believe you've actually got any doubts. You're always so sure of yourself."

His hand moved in a small gesture of dismissal. "Like I said, so far, yours is the only opinion I've had—besides my own, of course."

"Tell me something. Is Adam Carlisle going to have a girlfriend who gets to help him solve the cases? I love mysteries that feature a strong relationship between the main character and someone else. I hate it when there's only a single male protagonist who goes around sleeping with all his female clients. I mean, that just really bugs me."

Josh turned to her, a gleam of amusement in his eyes. He unbuckled her seat belt and wrapped a hand around the nape of her neck. He pulled her close. "You said I was a lot like Adam Carlisle. In some ways you may be right. He does not sleep around with his female clients any more than I do." He brushed his mouth tantalizingly across hers.

"Glad to hear it," Maggie breathed tremulously.

"I believe I will think seriously about giving him a permanent female companion." Josh tugged her closer. The white paper sack from the pharmacy crackled beneath his weight.

"What was that?" Maggie asked, glancing down.

"Nothing." Josh urged her back into his arms.

"Hang on. We're liable to crush whatever you've got in there." Maggie picked up the paper bag and started to set it on the floor. It slipped from her hand. "Oops."

"I'll get it." Josh moved swiftly to scoop up the contents of the sack—but not swiftly enough.

Maggie saw the brightly colored box of condoms that had fallen out. "Josh. You *didn't*. Tell me you didn't just buy those in the Peregrine Point Pharmacy. How could you?"

"It was easy. I just opened my wallet and took out some cash. Next thing you know, the entire box was mine." Josh shoved the offending box into the sack and tossed it into the back seat. "What's the big deal? We *are* sleeping together, remember?"

"One time." Maggie's head came up sharply. "We slept together one time, Josh."

"So?"

"So now everyone in Peregrine Point will know," she shouted. "How many times do I have to tell you this is a very small town? How could you do this to me?"

"I thought it added credence to the cover story," Josh said innocently.

"Cover story?" Maggie's mouth fell open. Fury welled up inside her. She reached for his throat with both hands.

Josh caught her wrists and chuckled softly. "Maggie, Maggie, take it easy. I was just teasing you."

"This is my reputation you're playing with. I don't consider it a fit subject for teasing," she snapped.

He smiled soothingly. "Sweetheart, in a day or two

everyone will hear we're engaged, and that should take care of the gossip.''

''But we're not engaged. Not really.'' She squeezed her hands into small fists. Frustration burned within her. ''Damn, this is getting so complicated.''

''Maggie, will you stop worrying? I've told you I'll take care of everything.''

''Oh, sure. I've got news for you, Josh. Your big plan to pretend we're actually engaged for a while and then just fade off into the sunset isn't going to work.'' Maggie grabbed her purse, opened it and jerked out a tissue. She blew her nose, furious at the tears that were threatening to fall. She wouldn't cry a second time, she vowed silently.

Without a word Josh pulled her close against his chest. He said nothing as she began to cry in earnest.

''This is so humiliating.'' Maggie sniffed and wiped her eyes on Josh's shirt. ''I don't know why I'm acting like this. I think I've been under too much stress lately.''

''Probably.'' Josh continued to hold her close. He didn't seem to mind the fact that she was dampening his shirt. ''Maggie, it doesn't have to be a fake engagement.''

''What?'' She stirred against him, finding comfort in the warmth and strength of his arms.

''I said, it doesn't have to be a fake engagement. We could make it a real one.''

Maggie went still. Then she slowly lifted her head to stare at him. ''A real one?''

He smiled slightly and caught her chin in his hand. His thumb slid over her lower lip. ''Why not? It seems to me we've got a lot going for us. We're attracted to each other. Why don't we try? I think we could make it work."

She drew back slowly, struggling to comprehend what he was saying. "My God. You're playing hero again, aren't you?"

He frowned. "What the hell does this have to do with playing hero?"

"You *are*." Maggie scrambled back to her side of the car. "You're playing hero. You're offering to make the engagement a real one because you're beginning to realize how much the fake one is upsetting me. You feel responsible. Well, I won't have it, Josh."

"You won't?"

Maggie straightened her shoulders and rebuckled her seat belt. "Absolutely not. I've got my pride, you know." She finished drying her eyes and dropped the crumpled tissue into her purse. "I don't need rescuing that badly. I am not some weak, innocent, helpless victim, you know. I can take care of myself. I've been doing it just fine, so far."

Josh leaned back into his corner and studied her from beneath half-lowered lashes. "You think I'm made of such sturdy stuff that I'd actually commit myself to marriage just to play hero? Better think again, Maggie. I've told you before, my days of playing hero were over long ago."

She heard the cold anger in his voice and shuddered. Warily, she glanced at him and saw that he was not in a good mood. In fact, he looked extremely dangerous. "Then why did you suggest we make the engagement something more than a cover story for this case?"

"I told you why. I think we've got enough going

for us to make a marriage work. Hell, I'm nearly forty. It's time I settled down. You're almost thirty, and so far, you haven't encountered any real-life hero who's going to sweep you off your feet and put a ring on your finger.''

''I do have some possibilities,'' she flared. ''I'm not a lost cause. There's Clay, for example.''

''Come on, Maggie. You can't be serious. You were already getting bored with O'Connor when I arrived on the scene.''

''How do you know that?'' she demanded, furious.

''It was pretty damn obvious when you came back from that date with him,'' Josh retorted. ''You were grateful to me for getting rid of him.''

''I never said that.''

''You didn't have to say it. I'm a private investigator, remember? I pick up clues real good when they're right in front of my eyes.''

''Is that so? Well, here's a clue for you, Mr. Private Investigator. When I finally decide to get engaged for real, it will be because I'm in love and because the man involved loves me. It will not be because the romance happens to be a useful cover story. Nor will it be because the guy has an overdeveloped sense of responsibility or because he thinks he should settle down and he's not going to do any better. Do you hear me?''

''I hear you.'' Josh tapped one finger against the steering wheel.

A long, heavy silence fell inside the vehicle. The rain had reached the shore now and was drumming relentlessly on the roof of the Toyota.

Maggie began to fidget nervously. She wished she hadn't gotten so emotional about the whole thing. She wished she were a more devil-may-care sort of person. She wished she could simply enjoy the romance and passion and adventure that had so unexpectedly come her way. She wished last night had not seemed so monumentally significant.

She wished for a lot of things; but most of all Maggie wished she hadn't fallen in love with Josh January.

"So," Josh went on after several minutes of apparent contemplation of the problem, "do you think you might be able to fall in love with me one of these days?"

Maggie considered the two alternative responses to that question. She could either scream and sob hysterically at the injustice of a universe that had created such an insensitive species as the human male, or she could compose herself and react in a mature, sophisticated manner. With a great effort of will, she chose the latter.

"Who knows? I've got so many other things on my mind at the moment, I haven't had time to consider it." Maggie managed a bright little saccharine smile and glanced at her watch. "Don't you think we'd better be on our way? It really is getting rather late."

Josh regarded her in acute silence for another long moment and then, without a word, he switched on the Toyota's ignition with a decidedly savage twist of the wrist.

MUCH LATER THAT NIGHT Josh sat alone in his room and put the finishing touches on his plan to trap the Peregrine Manor intruder. His scheme was simple, as was the case with most such schemes. If his suspicions were correct, he wasn't dealing with a criminal genius. No point in getting fancy.

Another consideration was Josh's own gut-level feeling that he had to move quickly to put an end to the harassment. He had sensed the escalating level of danger after the incident with the furnace. Whoever was coming and going in the basement was either getting bolder or more desperate. He had to be stopped.

When he was eventually satisfied with his plan, Josh made the decision to put it into effect the following day.

That left him with nothing of particular interest to do tonight. Maggie had already gone to bed and showed no signs of sneaking across the hall to his room a second time. And he didn't feel like working on the book.

But it was a cinch he wasn't going to get to sleep easily—not after that conversation with Maggie in the Toyota this afternoon. Not after the way Clay O'Connor had tried to warn Maggie about getting chummy with strangers. Not after the way Maggie had blithely refused to admit she was falling in love.

Josh chewed on all three annoying occurrences for a while and then got to his feet. He went over to the window and stood looking out at the night-shrouded sea.

Why was Maggie fighting her feelings for him? Josh wondered. He'd been asking himself that same question since early that morning. He'd been so sure of her last night. She had given herself to him in wholehearted, loving surrender. A woman like Maggie couldn't fake that kind of sweet passion. Besides, she respected herself too much to get involved in short-term affairs, Josh was certain.

But when he had calmly agreed to the engagement under the watchful eye of the Colonel, Maggie had been furious. Josh had been forced to fall back on the excuse that an engagement would be useful cover for him while on this case. That gambit had apparently only enraged her further.

What Josh couldn't understand was why she had been so upset in the first place. If he had read the signals right, she was head-over-heels in love with him. And she was a woman who believed in commitment. So why had she gotten so riled up over the idea of being engaged to him, he wondered bleakly.

Josh moved restlessly away from the window. Maybe McCray was right. Maybe he wasn't very good at dealing with women. Maybe he lacked a sense of romance, or something.

Josh gave up that depressing line of thought in favor of something more practical. He would do another tour of the house. He had already checked all the locks on the windows and doors once tonight, but doing it a second time wouldn't hurt.

He let himself quietly out of the room and went down the stairs. His ankle no longer twinged very much when he walked and his ribs only protested when he rolled over in bed. It was a relief to feel almost normal again.

Josh went through each first-floor room and then double-checked the small basement windows. When he had stalled as long as he could, he went slowly back up the stairs to the second floor.

He came to a halt outside Maggie's room. Unable

to resist, he cautiously tested the knob. To his surprise, the door opened easily.

"Maggie? Don't be afraid. It's me."

She sat up in bed. "I heard you walking around." She sounded wary but not frightened. "Checking locks?"

"Yeah." He closed the door and stood watching her in the shadows. "Everything's fine downstairs."

"Good."

"Maggie?"

"What is it, Josh?"

He tried to think of a way to introduce the topic of their relationship. Words failed him. But he couldn't bring himself to leave her bedroom just yet. He struggled with another approach, another reason to stay for a while.

She looked so inviting there in bed with her hair loose and soft around her shoulders. There was just enough pale moonlight filtering in through the window to enable Josh to see her. The sight made him ache with need. He wanted her so much it hurt.

"I, uh, I've made the plans for the trap I'm going to set," Josh finally said. He began wandering around the room, examining things in the shadows. He touched the perfume bottle on the dresser and ran his fingers along the spines of some books. *Mysteries, no doubt,* Josh thought, unable to read the titles in the darkened room. Maybe one day his book would be on her shelf. She liked what she had seen so far of it. It had been an enormous relief to hear that this afternoon.

"Tell me about your plans," Maggie urged softly.

He went over to the bed and stood looking down at her. "I'm going to need your cooperation."

"How?"

"I want to make it look as though the two of us have left town for a few days. I want people to think we've gone off together. Seattle or Portland. Anywhere. It's important that everyone thinks we're out of the area."

"I see." She sounded thoughtful and distant. "I suppose this is what you meant when you said a phony engagement would be a useful cover story?"

He forced himself not to react to that. "Let's not talk about the engagement. Just tell me if you'll help me make it look as though we've taken off for a few days."

"All right. I might as well. My reputation is in shreds, anyway. What does it matter if everyone in Peregrine Point thinks I'm off having a wild weekend. Heck, it may do wonders for my image around here. What happens after we take off for a passion-filled holiday?"

"I come back here at night and set up a stakeout."

"A *stakeout!*" Now she sounded genuinely interested. "A real stakeout? Just like in a mystery novel?"

"A real stakeout," he confirmed, amused by her enthusiasm.

"You think the intruder will strike when we're out of town?"

"I think it's a good possibility. I think the guy is getting desperate and frustrated. I think he'll make a move with a bit of encouragement from us."

"This is exciting," Maggie said. "I'll help you bait the trap, Josh, on one condition."

"What condition?"

"That you let me come with you on the stakeout."

He winced. "Stakeouts are not a lot of fun, Maggie. They're incredibly boring, for one thing. And I'll be doing it in a car. There are certain, uh, physical needs that have to be attended to from time to time. It's easier for a man to handle a stakeout like this, if you see what I mean."

"Nonsense! I used to go camping when I was a kid. I can use the bushes when I have to."

Josh sought for a stronger argument. "I'm hoping to catch the guy, Maggie. If he shows up, I'm going to try to grab him. At the very least, I plan to get close enough to ID him. Things could get rough."

"Then you'll need a partner along to cover your back," she declared. "You can't talk me out of this, Josh. I'm the client, remember? I'm giving the orders around here. If you're planning a stakeout, I insist on being allowed to help."

He eyed her narrowly. "You promise you'll follow orders?"

"I promise," she said eagerly.

"I mean it, Maggie. If you come with me, you'll do exactly as you're told and you won't take any risks. Understood?"

"Sure."

Josh swore softly. "All right, you can come along."

"Oh, Josh." Maggie leaped out of bed and threw her arms around him. "Thank you, thank you, thank you. I can't tell you how much this means to me." She hugged him fiercely. "A real stakeout."

The feel of her soft breasts pushing gently against his chest was enough to turn the smoldering need in Josh into a raging fire. After his first startled reaction to her hug, he recovered instantly and started to pull her closer.

But Maggie was already dancing out of reach. "You'd better get some sleep, Josh. Sounds like we might be up all night tomorrow. We'll both need plenty of rest. See you in the morning."

She was right. That was the hell of it. "Yeah. Sure. See you in the morning." It took an astounding amount of willpower to let himself back out the door and into the hallway.

It was better this way, Josh told himself as he stalked back to his own room. At least she was feeling enthusiastic and friendly again. If he was careful, he could recover the territory he seemed to have lost this morning with his brilliant notion of a phony engagement.

A thought struck him then that made him smile. Stakeouts were usually very long and extremely dull. A man and a woman trapped for hours together in the front seat of a car had to do something to pass the time.

Josh was feeling much more cheerful—even optimistic—when he finally undressed and got into bed. He fell asleep at once.

CHAPTER TEN

JOSH WAS WAITING a discreet distance down the hall from Odessa's bedroom door the next morning at five. He cleared his throat politely and glanced pointedly at his watch when the Colonel emerged in a bathrobe and slippers.

"Right on time, Colonel."

The Colonel looked up, alarmed. Then he scowled ferociously, his mustache twitching. "What the devil do you think you're doing, young man?" he demanded in a soft growl.

"I wanted to talk to you privately," Josh murmured. "I figured this would be the best time to catch you. Besides, I figure after that little stunt the three of you pulled on Maggie yesterday morning, a little rough justice was in order."

"Stunt?"

"The timing was a little too perfect to be sheer coincidence. All three of you emerged from your rooms simultaneously. It was a neat little ambush, Colonel, and you might as well admit it. I decided to set my own this morning."

The Colonel sighed. "Odessa and I have always been so discreet. How did you find out?"

"I'm an early riser. And I've got real good hearing." Josh grinned. "Hey, I know just how you feel. Come on downstairs. I've already got the coffee going. Heck, I'll even fry us a couple of eggs. Me, I've been sleeping the sleep of your typical chaste and gallant gentleman, but I'll bet you've worked up quite an appetite.''

''No respect for your elders. That's what's wrong with your generation. If you'd served under me, I'd have straightened you out in that department.'' The Colonel tightened the tie on his bathrobe and followed Josh toward the stairs. ''You won't, uh, mention this to Maggie, will you?''

''Why? You afraid she might demand that you do the right thing?'' Josh shot the Colonel a dry look.

The older man had the grace to blush. ''I suppose I did rather put you on the spot yesterday morning, didn't I?''

''You sure as hell did. And I don't mind telling you it was lousy timing, Colonel. Because of your little surprise foray, I damn near lost the war.''

The Colonel eyed him sharply. ''What do you mean by that?''

''I mean,'' Josh said, ''that the business of playing the heavy-handed patriarch outside my bedroom door has made Maggie skittish. She's spent the past twenty-four hours thinking up reasons why she can't marry me. You'd be amazed at her creativity.''

''Can't marry you?'' The Colonel glared at him as they reached the bottom step and headed for the kitchen. ''Why can't she marry you? See here, you haven't already got a wife and half a dozen kids stashed away somewhere, have you? Because if so, sir, I can personally assure you that I will not tolerate this behavior of yours.''

''No wife and no kids.'' Josh went into the kitchen, which was already smelling nicely of freshly brewed coffee. He grabbed the pot and filled two mugs. "But you rushed things yesterday morning. Maggie's nervous now. I've got a job ahead of me, undoing the damage you did."

"Nonsense." The Colonel accepted his mug and sat down at the small table. "She'll come around. You just see to it you do what's right and proper by her. She's a small-town girl at heart. Kind of old-fashioned in a lot of ways. And don't you forget it."

"My intentions are honorable," Josh drawled. He sipped his coffee and watched the Colonel carefully. "They have been from the start. Which is more than I can say about yours, isn't it?"

The Colonel's head came up proudly and his eyes flashed. "What the devil is that supposed to mean? Now see here, if you're talking about my intentions toward Odessa, you can apologize at once. My intentions toward her always have been and always will be honorable."

"Then why haven't you married the lady?" Josh asked calmly.

The Colonel heaved a sigh. "It's that damn gold-mining stock of hers. I'm afraid she'll think I'm marrying her to get my hands on it. I've got my pride, sir."

"Have you considered going to a lawyer and getting a prenuptial contract that would protect her assets?"

"I raised the subject once. Delicately, you understand. But my Odessa is a romantic at heart. She doesn't care for the notion of prenuptial agreements."

Josh decided to take a chance. "How about if I told you that Odessa's stock isn't worth the paper it's printed on?"

The Colonel looked shocked. "Are you certain of that, sir?"

"I had someone research it back at the office. I wanted to check out Odessa's theory that her nephews were after the stock. The mining company she bought twenty years ago went bankrupt nineteen years ago. The mine was never worth a damn thing."

"I've always wondered about that stock. She never seemed to get any income from it as far as I could tell. But a man hesitates to inquire into a woman's finances. Extremely bad form, you know."

"Private investigators do it all the time," Josh explained wearily. "A lot of investigations boil down to money."

"An interesting thought." The Colonel brightened. "Are you saying this one is going to boil down to money, too?"

"That's my hunch. I've ruled out all the other motives. It's either money or a psycho case. Frankly, I'd prefer money. I like nice clean motives when I can get them. The nut cases make me nervous."

"Yes, I can understand that." The Colonel leaned back in his chair and peered at Josh. "So, what's the plan? You do have a plan, don't you? I assume that's why I found you waiting for me outside Odessa's door this morning?"

"Yes, sir, I've got a plan. But I could use some backup help here inside the house. I want someone to take care of Odessa and Shirley just in case things go wrong. It'll mean staying awake most of the night."

The Colonel looked pleased. "Be honored to assist you, sir. I'm still capable of doing sentry duty. And I've still got my old service revolver upstairs, you know. Been a while since I used it, of course, but I reckon there are some things you don't forget."

"If everything goes as planned, you won't have to use it. But I'll feel better knowing you're awake and armed upstairs tonight."

"Certainly."

Josh folded his arms on the table. "Now, here's how it's going to go down, Colonel. Maggie and I are going to leave town on an overnight trip to Seattle. As soon as we're out of the house, I want you to call Dwight Wilcox and tell him you're worried about the furnace. Tell him it gave you some trouble again and you want him to double-check it. Make sure he knows that Maggie and I are out of town."

The Colonel narrowed his gaze. "You really think Wilcox is the one behind these incidents?"

"I think he's the one who's been staging them, yes."

"Don't suppose the oil companies are paying him, do you?"

"Uh, no. No, in all truth, I don't think anyone's after your research, sir."

The Colonel nodded. "Well, it was just a theory, of course. Hate to say it, but Odessa's right. That boy just doesn't seem bright enough to plan this kind of thing without getting caught."

Josh smiled grimly. "That's the whole point, Colonel. He is going to get caught. Tonight."

AT FIVE MINUTES TO eleven that night, Maggie got up on her knees in the front seat of the rental car Josh had chosen for the stakeout. He had told her his black Toyota was too well-known in the area. She reached into the back seat for another bag of potato chips.

"Only one more large bag left," she reported.

Josh wistfully eyed the sweet curve of her bottom, which was nicely outlined in a pair of snug-fitting jeans. "That's okay. We've still got the cheese crackers and the jalapeño dip. And we haven't even started on the chocolate bars."

"Do you always eat like this on a stakeout? I've never seen such a collection of junk food." Maggie turned around and dropped back onto the front seat.

"I told you surveillance is boring. I like to reward myself." Josh took a swallow from the can of cola in his hand. He leaned back into the corner of the seat and turned his gaze toward the manor.

The big house was visible through the stand of trees where he had parked the nondescript rental car two hours ago. The manor looked like a Gothic castle in the pale, watery moonlight. Its fanciful architectural embellishments made Josh think of pictures he had seen in old children's books.

From amid the trees, he could keep an eye on the kitchen door and the small ground-level windows of the basement. He could also watch the only approach to the old house, which was from the main road.

"You think he'll just drive right up to the manor, hop out and do his dirty work?" Maggie asked as she popped a potato chip into her mouth.

"Well, he sure as hell isn't going to make his approach from the other side of the house. The beach is too dangerous this evening because of the high tide and the storm that's on its way in. Even if he made it as far as the manor from that direction, he'd still have to find the cliff path at night and climb it. Too tricky. My hunch is that Wilcox will take the easy way."

Maggie slid him a sidelong glance. "I suppose you operate on hunches a lot in this business, don't you?"

"Uh-huh." Josh reached into the bag on her lap for a potato chip.

"Josh?"

"Yeah?" He munched on the chip.

"I was just wondering. Do you plan to stay in this business for the rest of your life?"

The question startled him. He turned his head to find her watching him intently in the shadows. "What?"

"I was just wondering if you would want to keep running Business Intelligence and Security, Inc. after you've sold your book."

"Selling the book is not a sure thing, Maggie."

"I think you will sell it."

Her confidence gave him a quiet thrill. Josh stretched his shoulders and resettled himself in the seat. He studied the approach to the manor while he thought about her question. "I don't know what I'll do if I sell the book."

"Do you still like your work?"

"What's liking it got to do with anything? It's a job. I'm good at it. It's a living. A fairly good one, to be perfectly honest."

"Yes, but does it give you any real satisfaction?" Maggie persisted gently.

Josh slanted her a curious glance. "What are you trying to say?"

She crunched another potato chip. "Nothing."

"Maggie, don't give me that. You're after something. What is it?"

She stirred uneasily. "It's just that I've had this feeling for several days now that you're kind of burned-out. I was wondering if maybe that's the real reason you came over here to the coast for a month.''

Josh groaned. ''You and McCray. A couple of amateur psychologists.''

''It's true, isn't it? You're here because you burned out back in Seattle.''

He exhaled slowly. ''Yeah. It's true.''

''What really happened in that 'accident' that had you on crutches when you first arrived?'' she asked softly.

''A kidnapping case went sour. Things got a little rough when I went in after the jerk who had taken the girl. He was trying to use her as a shield.''

Maggie looked suitably horrified. ''What happened?''

''The girl is safe. The jerk's back in jail.''

''My God, Josh, you could have been killed!'' Maggie frowned. ''You were playing hero again, weren't you?''

''I told you, it never pays. The kid I rescued was only seventeen. She didn't even thank me. In fact, she hated me for saving her. The guy who had her was her boyfriend, you see. She thought they were going to run off together and live happily ever after. She didn't believe me or her father when we told her she was in love with a two-bit ex-con who planned to take the ransom money and run. Last I heard, she now blames me for ruining her entire life.''

''Little twit. I don't suppose it's any consolation to know that in a couple of years she'll be thanking you.''

''I don't need her thanks. I was just doing her father a favor. Good public relations. He's head of a large corporation that uses BIS services. He came to me after he got the ransom note because he didn't want any publicity. I should never have agreed to help. Jobs like that are always messy.''

"What's going to happen when you go back?''

"What do you think will happen? I'll go back to work.''

"What about the book?''

"I'll work on it when I can.''

"Josh, maybe you need more than a month off,'' Maggie said hesitantly. "You know, when you think about it, you really haven't even had the month off you had planned to take, anyway, have you? Here you are, back at work. This is just another job.''

"Believe me,'' Josh growled, "this is not just another job.''

"Well, you can hardly call it a vacation.''

He thought about that. He had gotten a good start on his novel, he had found the woman with whom he wanted to spend the rest of his life and he was on a stakeout, waiting to catch Dwight Wilcox in the act of breaking and entering. "You're right. It hasn't exactly been a vacation. But it has been interesting.''

She coughed delicately and stuffed another potato chip into her mouth. "So maybe you should take an extra month or so here at the coast after you wrap up this case.''

Josh went still as it finally dawned on him she was trying to say something very important. "Here? You think I should spend the extra month hanging around Peregrine Point?''

"You said yourself it would be a good place to write your book. And you fit in very well at the manor. You've been extremely helpful, to tell you the truth. If you're about to catch Dwight Wilcox in the act of staging some mischief tonight, then it strikes me that I'll be in the market for a new handyman tomorrow morning."

Josh nearly choked on his cola. He finally managed to swallow the laughter and the soft drink. "Maggie, are you by any chance offering me a two-month job as handyman here at the manor?"

"It wouldn't be much of a job because I can't afford to pay very much. Room and board is all it would amount to, I'm afraid. At least until I get the manor back on its feet financially."

"I see."

"Think of it as sort of a change of pace," she continued eagerly. "It might do wonders for your burned-out condition if you spent a couple of months doing something entirely different for a while. And you'd have plenty of opportunity to work on your book. Who knows? You might even get to like it out here. Look at me. I love it here."

Josh finished the cola and carefully set the can on the floor of the car. He said very softly, "So do I."

Maggie stopped munching potato chips. Her eyes widened in the shadows. "You do?"

"Your offer is tempting, Maggie."

"It is?" She watched him anxiously.

"Yeah. But there's only one way I can accept it."

"What's that?" she demanded instantly.

He turned his head finally to look at her. His stomach was clenched with anticipation. Josh was afraid that he was moving too fast again. But he reminded himself that she had been the one to start this crazy conversation. He also reminded himself that opportunity didn't always knock twice. All his instincts were clamoring for him to make the move; and he had always been inclined to follow his instincts.

"The only way I could accept your offer, Maggie, is if you agreed to let our engagement story stand while I'm living at the manor."

She looked stunned. "But, Josh—"

"I'm serious, Maggie. I'm too old to play games. If I stay, I'm going to be spending the nights in your bed. And I won't have the Colonel, Odessa, and Shirley—as well as everyone in Peregrine Point—think we're just having an affair. I've got my pride and so do you. This is a small town. People will talk."

"Oh, Josh, I understand." She threw herself against him, her arms curving tightly around his neck. Her eyes were wide and searching in the shadows. "You want to protect me from the gossip. It's the gallant side of your nature. It's really very sweet of you."

Josh grinned slowly. "I've got news for you, Maggie. I am not sweet. I've told you I want to give the engagement a chance. That's my price for staying on around here as your handyman."

Maggie was quiet for a long moment. He could tell she was torn between doubt and desire. Josh knew she wanted him but she was still trying to wade in the shadows of their relationship. She was wary of going deeper because she still didn't know him very well. She needed time. He understood that.

Maggie took a deep breath. "All right, Josh. All right, I'll do it. We'll give our engagement a chance while you're here."

Josh felt a wave of relief wash over him. He had two months to work on her now, he thought in triumph. In two months' time, surely she would get to know him well enough to feel secure about his intentions.

"You've just hired yourself a new handyman," Josh said. He lowered his head and began to kiss her slowly, letting her feel the depth of his need.

Her response was instantaneous. Maggie's desire for him was a heady thing; it set a match to his own passion.

Josh groaned and twisted slightly in the seat so that he could ease Maggie's slender, supple body between his thighs. She smiled at him in the moonlight and crowded close. Josh could feel the warmth and the softness of her against his hardening body, and the sensation sent shudders of desire through him.

"Maggie—" Josh froze as he glimpsed a shadowy movement from the corner of his eye.

"Josh?"

"Bingo."

Maggie tensed. "What's wrong?"

"It's Wilcox. He's here. Early, too. Must have decided that as long as you and I were gone, it would be safe. He's figuring that the Colonel and the others will be in bed by now."

Maggie sat up quickly, peering into the darkness. "Are you sure? I don't see anything."

"He didn't drive up to the manor. He walked. Must have parked his car farther down the road. I caught a glimpse of something under his arm. Tools, probably. Damn it to hell." Josh disentangled himself from Maggie and opened the car door. He had disconnected the interior lights of the vehicle earlier.

"Josh? Be careful. Please."

"I will. You stay put, understand?"

"Maybe I should follow you," Maggie suggested

helpfully. "In the mysteries I've read, the hero always gets into trouble when he doesn't have backup."

Josh moved to squelch that idea at once. "No. You're not going to follow me. I don't want you anywhere near the house." He shut the door with a firm *thunk* and started through the trees toward the manor. He didn't look back. He was afraid Maggie might view that as an indication that he was having second thoughts about allowing her to accompany him.

He wanted her safe.

The shadowy figure of Wilcox moved steadily toward the manor. It was easy to keep track of him through the trees. Wilcox didn't once check behind to see if anyone was tracking him. He was intent on his goal; a man on a mission.

Josh edged closer, using the deep shadows of the trees for concealment just in case Wilcox got smart at the last minute and took a good look around.

Wilcox walked along the side of the manor and went right up to the kitchen door. Josh shook his head in amazement at the man's boldness. He watched as Wilcox set down the parcel he was carrying and slipped a key into the kitchen-door lock.

It had undoubtedly been very easy for the handyman to get a key to the back door, Josh reflected. Much too easy. Josh decided he would institute some new security precautions around the place when this was all over.

It struck him quite forcibly that he was already thinking of Peregrine Manor as his home.

Josh waited until Wilcox had let himself into the darkened kitchen before he followed. He paused on the back-door step and listened as Wilcox clomped across the tile floor. When he was certain Wilcox was in the hall and heading for the basement, Josh silently let himself into the kitchen.

He moved out into the hall when he heard Wilcox's big boots on the stairs that led down to the basement. This was good enough, Josh decided. He had Wilcox neatly trapped. All that was necessary now was to close the basement door and lock it from this side and call the sheriff to report an intruder. While waiting for the sheriff to arrive, Josh would make certain Wilcox didn't wriggle out through one of the ground-level windows.

Piece of cake.

A snap.

Like shooting fish in a barrel.

No heroics required.

This was the way a job was supposed to go—simple and neat.

Josh caught the unmistakable whiff of kerosene just as he was about to shut the basement door.

And suddenly he realized what had been in the parcel under Wilcox's arm. Not tools for staging another act of mischief—*kerosene.*

Wilcox had gotten desperate, all right. He was planning to set fire to the manor. The fact that the odor of the highly flammable liquid was strong on the stairs meant the handyman was already going to work.

So much for simply locking the door and calling the sheriff. The kerosene would do untold damage to the Colonel's files, besides which the least little spark would start a blaze that could burn down the manor.

"Hold it right there, you bastard!" Josh flicked on the light switch as he leaped down the steps.

The lights came on, revealing Wilcox caught in the

act of pouring a thin stream of kerosene across the concrete floor. He was working his way slowly and methodically toward the Colonel's filing cabinets.

Wilcox looked up, startled. At least Josh assumed the handyman was startled. His expression was barely altered. Maggie had been right. Wilcox had all the animation of a banana.

Dwight set the kerosene can down at his feet. "Stay back, January. It's too late." He dug into his hip pocket and came up with a cigarette lighter.

Josh swore but wasted no more breath trying to talk the fool out of what he obviously intended. He reached the bottom step and threw himself forward in a long, flat dive just as Wilcox flicked the lighter and touched the flame to the thin rivulet of kerosene.

The trajectory of his dive brought Josh down on Wilcox like a ton of bricks, carrying both men heavily to the floor. But even as he rolled on the concrete, struggling to pin the other man, Josh heard the terrifying whoosh of fire.

There was a shout from the top of the stairs.

"Josh!"

It was Maggie. Josh heard her racing down into the basement. He could smell the kerosene burning and he wanted to yell at her, order her to get out of the firetrap.

He forced himself to ignore everything but the job at hand. First things first. He could do nothing about the fire until he had Wilcox under control.

And Wilcox had somehow managed to produce a knife in his right fist. *The man was good with tools.*

Josh slammed a body blow into his opponent and started to roll to his feet. Wilcox lashed out with a series of blade thrusts. Already off balance, Josh threw himself out of the range of the blade, stumbled…and came down far too heavily on his weak left ankle. Pain tore through him. So did rage.

"You son of a bitch!" Josh kicked out with his left foot, ignoring the agony. He had no choice; he was going to have to use his right foot to anchor himself.

The bone-shattering blow connected with Wilcox's forearm. It sent the knife flying and it caused Wilcox to crumple. The last of the fight went out of him. He lay in a helpless heap on the floor.

An instant later, foam from a fire extinguisher cascaded over everything in sight.

Josh closed his eyes as the white stuff splattered across his face and covered his shirt. "Point it toward the fire, Maggie."

"I'm trying. It's heavy."

Josh wiped off the foam and opened his eyes. Maggie was, indeed, struggling with the big, unwieldy extinguisher. But she had managed to douse the flames.

She set the extinguisher down and looked at him triumphantly. "We did it. We saved the manor."

Josh looked at her and then looked at the can of kerosene that was sitting a short distance away. He felt a little sick as his imagination conjured up horrifying possibilities and might-have-been scenarios. He wanted to shake Maggie for the risk she had just taken.

"I told you to wait in the car. That thing could have gone up like a bomb," Josh said evenly, exerting an incredible amount of effort to control his temper.

"But it didn't," she replied cheerfully. "I got to the fire in time and you got Wilcox. We make a great team, don't we, January? What do think about ditch-ing your friend McCray and taking on a new partner? Peregrine Point doesn't have an investigation agency.''

Before Josh could think of a response to that there was another shout from the top of the stairs. The Colonel lumbered down the steps, a huge, old revolver in his fist. Odessa and Shirley were right behind him, clutching at their robes.

''Oho!'' yelled the Colonel exultantly. ''You got him. Always knew you were a martial-arts man. Said it the first time I saw you, if you remember, January.''

Josh took a deep breath and got a grip on his temper. He turned toward Wilcox. It was time for some answers.

''All right, Wilcox. Who paid you to do this little job?''

There was a stunned silence behind him as everyone in the basement absorbed the implications of the question. Josh knew he needed to act swiftly if he was going to get to the bottom of the thing. If Wilcox had time to recover from the shock and the pain he was in right now, he might think twice about talking.

''He didn't pay me nothin','' Wilcox muttered. ''Said he'd tell everyone in town I had a record if I didn't do what he said. I'd never have gotten any more work. Don't ya see? I had to do it. He forced me. It was blackmail, that's what it was. And he kept complainin' 'cause nothin' ever worked.''

''Good grief,'' Maggie breathed.

Wilcox turned his head toward her and regarded her with something that might have been hurt reproach. ''You was supposed to sell after the first couple of incidents. You was too stubborn. That was the problem. It weren't my fault. I told him that.''

"Did you?" Maggie asked quietly. "What did he say?"

"He said I had to go back and try somethin' else." Wilcox cradled his broken wrist. "So I did. And look what happened."

"Yeah," said Josh. "Life's tough sometimes. But the way I see it, there's no need for you to take the rap for this all by yourself."

Wilcox peered intently up at him. "You can't touch him. He'll have covered his tracks. He's real clever. Not dumb like me. It'll be my word against his."

"No." Josh shook his head. "I can nail him. All I need is a little information. I can nail anyone if I have the right information."

"I'd like to see that." Wilcox grimaced. "I'd like to see you nail him, all right. Made my life hell, he has."

"Tell me who set you up, Dwight," Josh urged gently. "And I'll set him up for you."

Wilcox stared at him with what might have been eagerness. "Yeah?"

"Yeah."

"Like to see that." Dwight nodded. "Yeah, I'd really like to see that. Bastard. He deserves it."

Maggie frowned. "Who deserves it, Dwight?"

"That fancy real-estate man. You know. The guy with the pinkie ring. O'Connor," said Dwight.

CHAPTER ELEVEN

JOSH STOOD MOTIONLESS in the darkest shadows of the O'Connor Real Estate office. He had been there nearly three hours. It was two in the morning. Not a single car had moved down the main street of Peregrine Point for the past hour.

One of the hardest things about this kind of work, Josh reflected, was the waiting. Of course, now that he was changing jobs, he wouldn't be spending many more nights like this one. He planned to spend his evenings curled up in bed with his new boss.

He wondered when he should tell Maggie that he planned to stay at Peregrine Manor permanently—not just a month or two.

Josh reached down absently to massage his aching ankle. Maggie had wanted to put an ice pack on it but he had told her there was no time for first aid. He didn't know how long O'Connor would wait for Dwight Wilcox to report, but Josh figured it wouldn't be long. When Wilcox didn't show, O'Connor would get nervous. And when he got nervous, he would most likely want to destroy anything that could be used as evidence.

Josh had already amused himself going through the files with a tiny penlight. He could have done the search without the light if it had been necessary—

there was enough of a neon glow filtering in through the windows to illuminate much of the office interior.

He had found what he was looking for inside a small, locked drawer. He had the file in his hand.

Josh heard the soft purr of the Mercedes engine from a block away. His body responded with the adrenaline rush that always went through him at times like this.

O'Connor parked the silver Mercedes outside the office and got out. Josh watched as Clay glanced quickly around and then dug his keys out of the pocket of his expensively styled trench coat. He was so nervous he dropped them on the sidewalk.

His head ducked deep into his upturned collar, Clay hurried to the front door of the office and shoved a key into the lock. He didn't bother to turn on the lights.

Josh watched from the shadows as Clay headed unerringly across the room to the small, locked drawer. He waited until he heard O'Connor's sharply indrawn breath.

"Looking for this?" Josh reached out and switched on the light. He idly slapped the file of papers he was holding against his leg.

"*January!*" Clay stared at the file, his mouth working. "What the hell are you doing here? You're trespassing. I'll have you arrested."

"Will you?" Josh strolled over to the desk and sat down behind it. He opened the file folder and glanced at the incriminating paperwork in front of him. "Not exactly a routine multiple listing, is it, O'Connor? But, then, Maggie had no intentions of selling in the first place. So you tried to convince her."

"What the hell are you talking about?" Clay's face

was turning an ugly shade of red. He was sputtering. "That file is private property."

"This file," Josh said coldly, "is an agreement to sell Peregrine Manor quite cheaply to a New York development firm."

"There's nothing wrong with an offer like that. Real-estate people are always soliciting clients. It's the way we make our living."

"Yeah. Except that the manor isn't for sale. And you knew it." Josh flipped through the paperwork. "Hell of a commission for you in this, isn't there, O'Connor? Not the usual six percent."

"It's a finder's fee," O'Connor raged. "Perfectly legitimate."

"Only if the manor was actually for sale. And only if you had informed the seller of the true value of the property. Which you did not, did you?" Josh slanted O'Connor an interested look. "You didn't tell any-one, including Maggie, what the New York firm was really willing to pay for that stretch of land, did you? When did the New Yorkers first put out feelers?"

"They expressed an interest shortly after Agatha Gladstone died," Clay replied stiffly. "Nothing out of the ordinary about that."

"Except that you forget to mention their interest to Maggie. Instead, you decided to see if you could in-terest the New York crowd in a real steal of a deal. You'd get the land for them dirt cheap and in exchange they would pay you a fat finder's fee. Nice work if you can get it."

A speculative gleam appeared in O'Connor's eyes. Josh could read the look on the other man's face, even in the dim light. He had seen it often enough before on the faces of people who had been caught red-handed.

Their first assumption was that the person who had caught them might be interested in making a deal. The theory was that everyone else had the same kind of morals as they did. *Just good business.*

"They want to put in a world-class resort and spa here on the coast," Clay eagerly explained. "Big development companies like the ones behind this deal have to keep a low profile when they go into a new area to pick up land. If people know they're buying, the prices start shooting up in a hurry. Keeping quiet is just good business. That's all."

"Just good business." Josh closed the file, wondering how often he had heard that excuse over the years. "But in this case there wasn't going to be any business at all, was there? Because you couldn't talk Maggie into selling. And you sure as hell didn't want to tell her how much the manor was really worth. If you couldn't get it cheap, you couldn't do a deal with the New Yorkers."

"The manor is worthless to them. It's just an old house. What they want is the land."

"So you decided on a plan. You'd drive Maggie into selling by making it appear that the manor was falling apart around her. If you could convince her that it was too expensive to keep it going and that business was going to fall off, she'd have to let it go. But Maggie can be stubborn, can't she?"

"Damn stubborn. You don't know what I went through trying to get her to sell. I had to pretend I was falling for her. I was willing to take her to bed, if necessary. What the hell. No big deal. It probably would have been mildly amusing. She's kind of cute—if you like the sweet, innocent type.''

Josh jumped out of his chair in a flash. He barely noticed the pain in his ankle as he whipped around the corner of the desk and grabbed a startled O'Connor by the collar.

''What the hell...?'' O'Connor's eyes flared wide with fear and anger.

''You got desperate tonight, didn't you?'' Josh slammed O'Connor up against the wall. He leaned in close. ''You decided to take drastic action. Any idea what the penalty is for arson in this state, O'Connor?''

''*Arson?* I don't know what you're talking about. I told Wilcox to stick to mechanical stuff.''

''Yeah, well, he didn't. Apparently you pushed him a little too hard. Tonight he tried to torch the manor.''

O'Connor looked genuinely astounded. Then he looked ill. ''My God! What happened?''

''Nobody got hurt, if that's what you mean. You won't be facing murder charges.''

''Murder.'' O'Connor looked more nauseated than ever. He started to crumple. He licked his lips. ''Look, you said everybody's okay. Nobody got hurt. So why don't we cut our losses and make a deal? Huh? Where's the harm? I'll split the finder's fee with you if we can convince Maggie to sell. Come on, January. You're sleeping with her. Everybody in town knows it. Surely you can talk her into selling.''

''Forget it,'' Josh said. ''Your problem, O'Connor, is that once in a while when I'm real bored, I like to play good guys and bad guys. Guess who gets to be the good guy tonight?''

SHORTLY BEFORE DAWN Josh let himself into his room. The manor was silent. Everyone else had apparently retired while he was busy talking to the local sheriff.

He didn't bother to turn on the lights. Instead he stripped off his clothes in the darkness, yawned, and pulled back the quilt on the big, canopied bed.

"Hi," said Maggie in a soft, sleepy voice. "I was wondering when you'd get home. Lot of paperwork in your business, I guess."

Josh smiled slowly as he looked down at her. A sense of deep happiness and satisfaction welled up inside him. "I'd have finished the paperwork a lot faster if I'd known you were going to be here in my bed waiting for me."

"Where else would I be?" Maggie opened her arms and smiled. Love glowed in her eyes. "Welcome home, hero."

Home, thought Josh as he gathered her close. That was where he was now. Home.

He lost himself in Maggie's sweet warmth. Nothing had ever felt so right.

"I JUST CAN'T BELIEVE IT," Odessa declared for what must have been the hundredth time the next morning. "He seemed like such a nice young man."

"I never did like him," Shirley announced. "Always said O'Connor was soft around the edges."

"Dwight's the one I feel sorry for," Maggie said, carrying a plate of crumpets and honey over to the kitchen table. "He was virtually blackmailed into doing what he did. I wonder how Clay found out about his past?"

"Wilcox let something slip once when he was doing a small job for O'Connor.'' Josh slathered honey on a crumpet. "O'Connor did a little research after he got in touch with the New Yorkers. He realized he could use someone like Wilcox to help him push Maggie into selling.''

"Well, it's all over now,'' the Colonel added with satisfaction. "We can open the manor after the first of the year and it should be in good financial shape by early spring. We didn't lose much time, thanks to our man January, here. You did a fine job, sir. A fine job.''

"Thank you,'' Josh acknowledged humbly. "I like to think I give an honest day's work for an honest day's pay.''

Maggie's eyes sparkled with laughter as she bit into a crumpet. "You get what you pay for. That's what I always say.''

"And sometimes a little more than you expected, hmm?'' Josh took a large bite out of his own crumpet.

The Colonel cleared his throat portentously. "Speaking of the unexpected, Odessa and I would like to make an announcement. We are officially engaged as of this morning and we will be getting married as soon as possible.''

Odessa blushed becomingly. "We're so excited.''

Maggie put down her crumpet. "*Married?* You two? Why, that's wonderful. Congratulations. I'm thrilled for you. But why the sudden decision?''

"Yeah,'' Shirley said bluntly. "How come, after all this time?''

"I guess it's just in the air,'' Odessa answered brightly. "The Colonel surprised me by popping the question this morning and I said yes before he could change his mind. Apparently he's had some foolish notion that I would think he was marrying me to get control of my mining stock. But I told him I trust him completely. Always have. He's a perfect gentleman.'' She gave Josh an expectant look. ''Have you two set the date yet?''

''No,'' Maggie replied quickly before Josh could answer. ''But we do have some news. Josh is going to be staying on around here for a month or two. He's thinking about making a career change, you see, and he wants to test the waters. If everything works out, he may opt to stay in Peregrine Point permanently.''

The Colonel frowned. ''Sounds a bit unsettled, if you ask me. What's the matter with you, January? Can't you make up your mind?''

''*My* mind's made up,'' Josh told them. ''I'm waiting for Maggie to make up hers.''

''Why the delay, Maggie?'' Shirley peered at her. ''Take it from me, in this world a gal's gotta grab her opportunities.''

Maggie felt herself turning a vivid pink. Everyone at the table, including Josh, was watching her. ''There's no point trying to intimidate me. I refuse to be rushed. Josh needs time, in spite of what he says. I want him to be certain about what he's doing.''

''I'm certain,'' Josh countered.

''No, you're not,'' Maggie shot back.

''You're the one who's still got questions.'' Josh licked honey from his fingers and stood. ''But I think the mail has arrived, so maybe we can get started on helping Maggie make up her mind.''

Maggie glared at his broad back as Josh left the kitchen. She saw that he was limping again this morning. Her glare turned into a look of concern.

"Don't fret, Maggie." Shirley chuckled. "Josh is tough. He'll do just fine."

"I suppose. But I wish he hadn't reinjured that ankle."

"Give him a few days and he'll be as good as new," the Colonel said.

"Right," Josh agreed, limping back into the kitchen with a small stack of mail in his hand. "Good as new in a few days. No sweat." He shuffled briskly through the letters. "Ah, here we go." He selected a white manila envelope from the pile and tossed it onto Maggie's lap.

"What's this?" She picked up the envelope, frowning.

"Answers." Josh sat down and started applying honey to another crumpet.

Maggie tore open the envelope and dumped the contents on the table. For a moment she couldn't make sense of the assortment of official-looking forms, licenses, and records that lay in front of her.

Then she saw that every one of the formal-looking pieces of paper in front of her bore the name and description of one Joshua January. She jerked her head up to meet Josh's watchful gaze.

"This is a file on you, isn't it?"

He nodded. "Anything you want to know about me should be in there somewhere, Maggie."

"Is that so?" Anger shot through her. She flattened her hands on the table and pushed herself to her feet. "Will it tell me if you love me, Josh? Will it tell me that? Because that's the only question that you haven't answered for me. I already know everything else I need to know about you."

"Maggie…" Josh started to get to his feet, obviously taken aback by her reaction.

"I don't need *data* on you, Josh." Maggie picked up the pile of forms and papers and hurled them into the air. "I just need to know if you can love me as much as I love you, damn it! A real simple question, Josh."

"You love me?" Josh stared at her, a slow smile warming his cold eyes. "You love me, Maggie Gladstone?"

Maggie was battling tears now. She wiped them away with the back of her hand. "Of course I love you, you big idiot."

"I was sure you did, sweetheart, but you never said it. You kept saying you needed time."

"I said *you* needed time. Time to figure out that you loved me. You kept giving me all sorts of stupid reasons for letting our engagement stand. You said it was a good cover story. And then you said you thought maybe things would work between us, so we might as well give the engagement a chance. And then you agreed to stay on here for another month or two while you recuperated from burnout. But you never once said you loved me."

"Maybe that's because I've never said those words to anyone else in my life and I wasn't sure how to say them to you."

"Oh, Josh." She wiped her eyes again.

"I love you, Maggie." Josh shoved his chair back and moved around the table to take her into his arms. He folded her close, heedless of the smiles on the faces of the Colonel, Odessa and Shirley. "I fell in love with you that first night when you opened the door and told me I didn't look like what you'd ordered up in the way of a private investigator.''

"Josh."

"I'll be staying on for a lot longer than a month or two, sweetheart. I've decided I need more than a vacation. I need a career change.''

"Oh, Josh.'' Maggie wrapped her arms tightly around his waist and squeezed.

Josh sucked in his breath. "Easy, honey. The ribs took a beating last night when I was rolling around on the basement floor.''

"Oh, dear. I knew you should have stayed in bed today.'' Maggie stepped back and examined him from head to toe. "I really think we should take you to the Peregrine Point Clinic for a thorough check, Josh.''

"No. I am not going to another doctor,'' he stated. "All I need is plenty of rest and relaxation. I came out here to recuperate—if you will recall. So far, I've had very little opportunity to do so, but I intend to start working on it immediately. I'd like to be in reasonably good shape for my wedding.''

Maggie raised her head, smiling brilliantly. "When is that?''

"How about the end of the month?'' Josh suggested.

"The end of the month?'' Maggie was instantly horrified. "I can't possibly get ready for a wedding by the end of the month.''

"I think we can manage.'' Josh grinned at the faces of the three people who were still sitting at the table. "We'll have lots of help.''

"Might as well make it a double wedding,'' the Colonel announced cheerfully. He beamed at Odessa.

"No sense going to all the expense of two receptions in a short period of time."

"You're right," Josh agreed. "We're going to have to watch the budget around here until the manor is taking paying guests again."

"Spoken like a born innkeeper," Maggie said. "I think you'll go far in the business, Josh."

IN SPITE OF the short notice, most of Peregrine Point showed up for the double wedding celebration at the manor. The cars filled the small parking lot and stretched in a line all the way down the driveway to the road. The guests swarmed through the first floor of the big house, filling the beautiful rooms with laughter and chatter.

Midway through the reception, Josh finally found himself alone for a moment. He stepped out onto the front porch and glanced down at his watch. He frowned. McCray was rarely late.

Just as that thought flickered through his mind, Josh heard the sound of a car coming up the driveway. He grasped the porch railing and leaned forward to watch as a familiar blue Oldsmobile came to a halt in front of the manor. There were two men in the front seat. McCray got out first and came around the hood of the car.

"Well, hell, January. Don't you look spiffy." McCray cast a perusing eye over Josh's black-and-white formal attire. "Congratulations, pal. Are we in time for the party?"

"There's still plenty of champagne left." Josh glanced at McCray's passenger, who was just getting out of the car.

The man looked to be in his late sixties. Obviously

still hale and hearty, he was built like a mountain. The gray trench coat he wore was stretched across shoulders that appeared to be a yard wide.

"That's him?" Josh asked quietly.

"That's him. Sorry we're late. Took me a while to find him. He was in the middle of one of his literacy classes. But when I told him who was waiting for him, he dropped everything and got into the car."

The big man lumbered up the steps and stuck out a hand. "You're January?"

"I'm January." Josh shook the beefy hand. "Thanks for showing up here today."

"I don't mind telling you, I'm a little nervous. After all these years…"

A high-pitched feminine shriek interrupted the big man's words.

"Ricky!"

Josh turned to see Shirley standing frozen in the doorway. She was resplendent tonight, having chosen to wear nearly every rhinestone in her extensive collection. Her eyes were filled with shock as she took in the sight of the huge man in front of her.

"Hello, Shirley." Ricky "The Wrecker" Ring stood uncertainly in the porch light. "Been a long time, honey. You're just as pretty as I remembered."

"Ricky, it *is* you. I ain't dreamin'?"

"I figure I'm the one who's dreamin'," Ricky said in a hoarse voice. "Thought you'd have found someone else a long time ago. Someone worthy of you, Shirley. I couldn't believe it when this here McCray showed up telling me you were living on the coast and had never married."

Shirley took a hesitant step forward. "I thought you

hated me. I thought you believed I was the one that ratted on you all those years ago.''

Ricky looked genuinely startled. ''Hell, no, honey. You'd never turn rat. I knew that. You were always loyal and true-blue. It was the feds who nailed me. They used wires and tapes. All that new-fangled technology. I never stood a chance. I was always an old-fashioned kind of guy. I realized the day they put me away that when I got out, I was going to have to find a new line of work. I'm not cut out for carrying on the old business under modern conditions, if you know what I mean.''

''Ricky, are you sayin' you've gone straight?'' Shirley was obviously overjoyed.

''Straight as an arrow, honey. Record's clean from the day I got out of prison. I know I'm not what you deserve. I knew it back in the old days, too. I didn't contact you after they sent me up 'cause I didn't want to mess up your life again. Told myself you deserved a chance to start fresh. But these guys say that as long as I'm clean, you might be interested in takin' me back.''

''In a hot minute, Ricky.'' Shirley hurled herself into his arms, her rhinestones flying. ''Lord, I missed you, lover. You were the best there ever was. I never stopped thinkin' about you. Not once.''

''I never stopped dreamin' about you, honey.'' Ricky's arms closed around her.

''I think we ought to leave these two alone,'' Josh murmured to McCray. He opened the front door of the manor.

''Yeah, kind of makes you misty-eyed, doesn't it?'' McCray glanced inside at the crowd of people milling about. ''So, what do you say you introduce me to your bride? I'd like to meet the lady who is about to make me sole owner of BIS.''

Josh smiled as Maggie materialized from a throng of well-wishers. She came toward him, looking glorious in yards and yards of white lace and satin. He thought he had never seen anything half as beautiful in his entire life. She was everything he'd been searching for all his life. She was his future.

"There you are, Josh. I've been looking for you. It's time to cut the cake." She tilted her head to look at McCray. "Are you his ex-partner?"

"I'm McCray. And I just want to say, Miss Gladstone—"

"Mrs. January," Josh corrected dryly.

McCray chuckled. "I just want to say, Mrs. January, that I am very impressed with you. Never thought any woman would be able to take the chill out of this guy. All I can say is that you must be some kind of female."

"Heavens, Josh is not the least bit cold," Maggie said, laughing gently. "He just likes to hide his true nature behind that tough-guy image."

"Is that so?" McCray arched an ironic brow at Josh who smiled blandly back.

"Yes, indeed. You only have to get to know him to realize—" Maggie broke off as she caught sight of the couple out on the porch. "Who on earth is that with Shirley? She's kissing him."

"Ricky Ring," Josh explained. "I had McCray check him out. He's been clean for years. Turns out he never forgot Shirley. Just figured he wasn't good enough for her. That's why he hasn't contacted her."

Maggie's eyes widened in astonished delight. "So you arranged to bring him here to be reunited with

Shirley? Josh, that was wonderful of you. You are so sweet. Isn't he sweet, McCray?''

"Sweet enough to give you cavities," McCray agreed. "Would somebody mind pointing me in the direction of the champagne?"

"Straight down the hall," Josh advised. "The other groom is pouring. You can't miss him. He's wearing the same kind of funny suit I've got on. You can call him Colonel."

"I'll find him." McCray slapped Josh on the shoulder and ambled off to find the Colonel.

Maggie turned to Josh. "Shirley looks so happy out there. It really was nice of you to go to the trouble of tracking down Ricky Ring. Do you suppose she'll be leaving us to go live in Portland, now?"

"Wouldn't surprise me. I think we'd better go cut that wedding cake. Odessa and the Colonel will be waiting." Josh took Maggie's arm, aware of a satisfying sense of possession. *She's Mrs. Joshua January now,* he reminded himself. She was his wife. Life couldn't get any better than this.

"You know, Josh, I've been thinking."

"About what?"

"About our partnership," Maggie said. "It's got so many possibilities."

"Yeah, I think the inn is going to do just fine." Josh already had a lot of plans for the place. McCray was buying him out of BIS, and Josh planned to invest some of the cash in Peregrine Manor.

Maggie looked up at him, her eyes bright. "I wasn't talking about the manor. I was talking about opening Peregrine Point's first private-investigation agency."

Josh came to an abrupt halt. "What the hell are you talking about?"

"Josh, I'm sure I've mentioned this before."

"No, I don't believe you did," Josh said grimly.

"Well, why not?" Maggie smiled enthusiastically. "We can give you an office right here in the manor. You can work on your Adam Carlisle mysteries when you aren't working on a case—which will be most of the time, because there won't be many cases to work on here in Peregrine Point."

"Try zero cases."

"Oh, I expect we'll get the odd job now and again. Human nature is the same in small towns as it is in big cities. And once in a while you're going to feel the urge to play hero. It's your nature."

"Maggie…"

"I was thinking we could call the agency January Investigations. When I'm not busy running the manor, I'll give you a hand on your cases."

"Gosh, thanks."

"I'm really looking forward to learning the ropes of the private-investigation business, Josh."

Josh couldn't help it. He started to laugh. He was still grinning a few minutes later when Maggie cut into the wedding cake and found the little box hidden inside.

The look on her face when she opened it and discovered Agatha Gladstone's emerald brooch was priceless.

"*Josh!*" Maggie's eyes were shining as she looked up at him. "You found it. You found Aunt Agatha's brooch. How on earth did you do it?"

"I keep telling you, I'm a trained investigator. I'm real good at spotting clues."

She threw her arms around his neck as the crowd of reception guests cheered. "You're a perfect hero," she whispered against his throat as she hugged him tightly.

"Yeah. Well, I've learned that once in a while it pays."

KEEGAN'S BLUFF
Dani Sinclair

CHAPTER ONE

THIS WAS WHERE Rio worked? Maybe she had the wrong place. The directions that had sounded so clear and simple in Trueblood, were a lot harder at night when a person was on foot.

Gillian O'Malley fingered the crumpled picture she carried in the pocket over her breast. Rio Cardonza. Her young cousin would be very surprised to see her, that was for sure. When she thought of what he must have gone through, thinking there was no one to turn to all this time, it broke her heart. Her uncle had a lot to answer for, but at least he had confessed to his own guilt and attested to his son's innocence before his death. That was something, anyhow. She never had believed that Rio was the one who held up that gas station and shot the clerk.

She moved cautiously, carefully, limping slightly. The looming outline of the barn was her destination. She would find a place inside to curl up before the rain came. Judging by the scent in the air, it wouldn't be long now. In the morning when Rio came in to saddle his horse, he'd find her waiting. She had to convince him to come back with her.

Fortunately, she discovered that they didn't lock barn doors out here in the middle of nowhere. They hadn't even closed this door. Lucky for Cade Mc-Govern, the ranch's owner, she didn't have larceny in mind. She stepped inside, her nose wrinkling at the pungent animal smell. A horse snorted restlessly somewhere inside the black maw. No one responded to the animal's restlessness. Good. She was too tired for long explanations right now. Thankfully, the ranch didn't seem to have dogs. That would have been the capper to a perfect day. On the other hand, how much more trouble could she be in?

Something brushed against her pant leg in the dark.

Fear rooted her quaking body.

"Mrrow?"

Shaking from head to toe, she closed her eyes. A cat? It had only been a cat? She exhaled deeply. A cat was good. If there was a cat, there weren't likely to be rats, right? The animal brushed her leg again. She reached down and let it sniff her hand before stroking the silky head. Yep. Definitely a cat. A friendly one at that.

"How about standing guard while I sleep?" she whispered to the animal. The horse stirred, *whuffling* at the sound of her voice. She couldn't see in the dark, but she guessed he was several stalls down from where she stood.

Horse, singular? That couldn't be right. Lily Garrett had told her this was a busy working ranch. She strained her eyes trying to see. She wanted to save the batteries that were left in her flashlight until she really needed them. On the other hand maybe she needed them right now. The barn had an empty feeling. Her nervousness increased. Where were the rest of the animals?

Being a city girl, Gillian knew little about ranching beyond what she'd seen in a couple of old movies. Still, something about this barn didn't feel right.

Standing still, she strained to listen. In the distance came a sound that might have been thunder. Otherwise, there was nothing to hear. Maybe this wasn't the Circle M, after all. God knew she could have wandered anywhere by now. It seemed as if she'd been walking forever since her rental car broke down. Why did Rio have to go to ground in the middle of absolute nowhere? Couldn't he have picked a city? Cities were at least familiar territory.

Adrenaline spurted through her bloodstream at an unexpected noise behind her. She reached for her weakened flashlight too late. Something came at her out of the dark. It slammed into her, hard and terrifying, carrying her to the hard-packed dirt floor.

THE PROWLER STRUGGLED like a wildcat, nails ripping a slice of skin down the side of his face before Keegan was able to grab both hands and force them to the ground.

He hadn't realized it was a woman when he charged the intruder. He'd been getting undressed to take a shower before the storm hit when he spotted someone slipping inside the busted barn door. He hadn't taken time to dress. He hadn't even remembered to grab his gun. He'd just pelted over to the barn, intent on protecting Bristol. If anything happened to his horse he'd be stranded here. Besides, Rio had told him a bunch of stories about cattle rustling and other problems that the Circle M had encountered long before he signed on. Still, the ranch should have been deserted. He figured everyone would be pleased if he nabbed someone in the act of some new sort of trouble.

Only, the feel of this slender body bucking beneath

his had a shocking effect. One that she obviously recognized, as well. Suddenly she went completely still beneath him.

"I'm not going to hurt you," he promised.

"You've got that right, you bastard," she breathed.

She renewed her efforts, nearly breaking free. It was like trying to hold a supercharged eel.

"Calm down!"

"Never," she spat at him.

Keegan had no choice. He used the full weight of his 180 pounds to pin her down until her struggles waned and finally stopped. By then he was fully aroused and completely embarrassed. It had been a while since he'd had a woman under him, but his body hadn't forgotten what to do. Since all he wore was a pair of briefs, she knew exactly how much she was affecting him.

"Damn." He shifted a little, wishing he wore boxers.

"Same to you."

An unexpected smile curved his lips. While she'd stopped fighting him physically, he suspected she was simply conserving her strength before renewing her attack once more. The woman had spunk, he'd give her that.

"I'm sorry."

She snorted. "Get off me."

Her breath smelled of wintergreen candy. Strands of dark silky hair had fallen across one eye and her cheek. He had a ridiculous urge to brush it away—or bury his face in the clean fresh scent that probably came from her shampoo. Man, he really had it bad. He hadn't remembered how good a woman could smell. Or how soft she could feel.

"I said, get off me!"

Or how sharp her tongue could be.

"I can't breathe!"

"Oh." She was breathing okay. Far too okay for his peace of mind. Her breasts rose and fell against his naked chest. The thin material of her blouse wasn't much of a barrier between them.

In a sudden flash of lightning, he saw her eyes grow wide and wary. Did she think he was planning to rape her? The knowledge of her fear was more effective than a cold shower.

"I'm going to get up," he told her quickly. "But I'm warning you right now, if you try to run I'll bring you down again. Do you understand?"

"Yes."

Her quiet voice quaked with relief making him feel like a heel. Keegan rolled away, releasing her hands and getting to his feet in one quick motion. The woman didn't jump up right away as he'd expected. She rose slowly, hands adjusting her clothing. He realized what she was doing a second before the gun appeared, pointed straight at his chest.

CHAPTER TWO

"I DON'T SUPPOSE we can talk about this."

Gillian tried to control her shaking. "Don't come near me."

"Wouldn't think of it."

Lightning flared again. For an instant his body was revealed by a blinding light. All he wore was a pair of dark briefs. Very brief briefs considering. And that was a ludicrous thought, even if it would be a long time before she forgot the feel of that nicely muscled body resting against her own. Gillian swallowed hard. The gun trembled in her hand, heavy and awkward. Thunder rumbled, moving closer.

"Who are you?" she demanded. She glimpsed the flash of his smile.

"I think that should be my question."

"I'm the one with the gun."

"Good point. The name's Keegan. Keegan West."

"Keegan?"

"Hey, it's a good Irish name." He lowered his voice conspiratorially. "It means small and passionate."

And she nearly blurted that his parents had only got it half right. She blushed at the memory of his potent arousal. Fortunately, he wouldn't see that in the dark.

"Your turn," he said.

"What?" How had he come to be standing so much closer? She hadn't noticed him move. He appeared totally relaxed despite the gusty breeze that sent the temperature plunging rapidly.

"Your name?" he prompted.

"Gillian. O'Malley." And why was she answering him?

"Nice."

His voice was a soft rumble that stroked her fluttery nerve endings adding to her complete awareness of him as a potent male.

"Looks like we have a few things in common, Gillian O'Malley."

She shook her head. He was much too close. This man was dangerous. "Stay where you are. We don't have anything in common."

"Sure we do."

With shocking ease he took the gun from her hand so fast she didn't have time to react.

"We share an English-Irish heritage and we're desperately attracted to one another."

"We are not! Give me back my gun."

"I don't think so. Amateurs holding guns scare me."

Every nerve in her body seemed attuned to him. The sudden clash of thunder made her jump. "What makes you think I'm an amateur?"

The flash of his teeth came again as he smiled. "For starters, you had the safety on. Now what do you say we make a run for the bunkhouse before that storm gets any closer. In case you hadn't noticed, it's getting colder. I don't fancy getting wet."

She was going to protest, but he took her hand in

a warm, firm grip as another blast of cold, damp air swept in through the open door.

"Let's go!"

Going anywhere with this man was a bad idea, but when he started running, so did she. Her ankle gave out on the first uneven patch of ground. She would have fallen if he hadn't caught her.

"What did you do to your leg? Never mind."

He swung her up in his arms and started running again. Her heart began pounding louder than the growl of thunder overhead. Or maybe it was his heart; it was hard to tell. Wind lashed them with bits of dirt. Lightning illuminated their way. The heavens rumbled in ominous warning. By the time they reached the porch of the bunkhouse, fat drops of rain mixed with hail were smacking the ground.

Keegan set her down as if she was made of spun glass. For a moment, she'd had the heart-stopping feeling he'd been going to carry her over the threshold! She needed to get a grip here. Even if it had been a long day, she had to stop feeling so dazed and start thinking again.

"Lean on me," he offered after he opened the door.

"I can make it."

"I don't doubt it for a minute. I've got a feeling you can do anything you set your mind to."

She couldn't find anything to say to that. With a smile, he reached past her to flip on the light switch giving her her first view of the inside.

"Oh, no!"

"Well, I admit no one would give it a four-star rating, but it's not that bad," Keegan protested. "What did you expect to see?"

Wide chocolate eyes stared at him in consternation. "I thought this was the Circle M!"

She tossed back her shoulder-length brown hair. The bits of straw gave it a nicely mussed, tousled look that was wildly appealing. She wasn't beautiful in the classic sense, but she had...something.

"What makes you think it isn't the Circle M?" he asked, rubbing at the scratch she'd inflicted. It wasn't bleeding, but it stung.

"There's nothing here! This room is practically empty. Lily said this was a working ranch."

"And Lily would be?"

"Lily Garrett. Over in Trueblood."

He watched Gillian limp forward, taking in the remnants of furniture Cade had left behind when he'd moved everything to the new spread he'd built for his bride. Admittedly the furniture in here was scarred and in need of repair, but considering this former bunkhouse was now serving as a line shack, he had no complaints.

"I've never heard of Lily Garrett."

"She's the detective I hired."

His gut tightened. *Detective* was practically synonymous with *police*. Just thinking the word was enough to give him cold chills all over. Being a wanted man was something he didn't think he'd ever get used to.

He walked across the room to where he'd tossed his jeans. Setting her gun on the table he took his time stepping into his jeans, trying to calm his thudding heart. Wind rattled the windowpanes, howling around the corners of the wooden structure.

Keegan tried to keep his voice bland. "Now why would a nice girl like you want to hire a detective?"

Her eyes fastened on his hand as he zipped his pants. He could all but feel that gaze like a lover's caress as it traced the path of dark hair that ran up his chest. Their eyes clashed and held. The flash of desire was unmistakable. Something about this woman stirred emotions he hadn't experienced in a long time.

Color bathed her skin as her gaze slid hastily away, stopping on his cheek.

She raised her hand tentatively as if to touch him. "I scratched you."

"Don't worry about it."

Her hand fell to her side and she inhaled sharply. No doubt she'd just noticed the newly healed scar that ran from his left shoulder to his breastbone. Her lips parted.

"The last lady came at me with a knife instead of a gun," he explained tersely. And he wished he could call back the words the moment they were uttered. "What did you do to your ankle?" he asked quickly to divert her attention. "Did I hurt you when I knocked you over?"

"No. I tripped over a gopher hole or something. Are you serious?"

"About the knife? Oh, yeah," he said grimly.

"I see." She tucked several strands of hair behind her ear. "Well, your bedroom approach could stand a little refining, you know." The back of her hand pressed her mouth shut in dismay. "I didn't mean to say that."

Laughter spilled from his throat. He couldn't help it. The sound was practically foreign to him, but the more she tried to apologize, the funnier it seemed. She limped to the table and sat down, putting her face in her hands. He got control then. "Sorry. It's been a long time since I found anything to laugh about."

Red-faced, she lifted her head. "Glad I could help."

That only set him off again. This time as she waited, her features softened. Her lips curved in a smile that caught him unprepared. He wouldn't have said she was beautiful—until she smiled.

"You have a nice laugh," she told him seriously. "You should do it more often."

Disturbed by his unexpected reaction, Keegan reached for his shirt, pulling it on. Rain slammed into the building in wind-driven waves. "Always happy to oblige a beautiful lady."

"I'll bet. Look—"

"Shh."

Headlights, not lightning, winked off beneath the stand of trees that lined the driveway. In the next flash of lightning, he got a view of the truck. It didn't belong to Cade or any of his people. A local would have pulled up into the yard. He could only think of one reason for someone to stop there and kill his lights. The driver didn't want to be seen.

"You expecting company?" he demanded.

She shook her head.

"Then I think we may have a problem."

CHAPTER THREE

KEEGAN MOVED with the grace and speed of a predator. He was suddenly across the room, pulling on boots over his bare feet.

"What do you mean we have a problem? What kind of problem?"

"Ever fire a gun before?"

Saliva fled, leaving Gillian's mouth bone-dry. His sense of urgency sent blood racing past her pulse points. "No."

"Okay, crash course. You point this end toward the middle of the body and squeeze. Don't rush your shot. Take time to get the muzzle centered. Then, keep firing until the gun stops. Got it?" He thumbed the safety off the small nine-millimeter.

"I can't shoot anyone," she breathed.

"Trust me. You'd be amazed at what you can do when your life is on the line."

"Why would my life be on the line?"

"Because a couple of guys want to see me dead and there's a chance they may be in that truck out there. I knew I was pushing my luck staying in one place this long."

"Why do I think you aren't kidding?"

"I'm not." He grabbed his jacket off the back of the chair. "If I'm right, these guys aren't going to leave any witnesses behind. Let's go!"

Gillian gaped at him. "Go? Go where?"

"I'll explain later. I don't need your death on my conscience, too."

Too? This was all happening too fast. She rose to her feet as he crossed the room and threw open a window. Wind drove needle-sharp beads of cold rain across the floor.

"Are you crazy?"

"I'll lift you over the sill. Run for the trees."

"We can't run under a tree in a storm like this!"

"Gillian, get that sweet ass of yours over here right now. In a few seconds it's going to be raining bullets in here. Personally, I'd rather take my chances with the trees."

"You *are* crazy!"

"So they tell me."

He wasn't some muscle-bound weight lifter, yet he scooped her up once more as if she weighed nothing at all. She knew better, yet she didn't even have time to squawk a protest. She was soaked to the skin before her feet touched the ground. Wind tore at her sodden clothing. Keegan followed her out and thrust the gun in her hand.

"Run!"

Obviously, he'd forgotten about her ankle. She suspected this wasn't a good time to remind him. His grim expression didn't bode well for comments or questions. Gillian ignored the pain searing a path up her leg with each jarring step as she tried to follow him. She was pretty sure the ankle was only sprained, but this couldn't be conducive to healing.

The storm had moved right over top of them, but at least it masked the sounds of her flight. Keegan moved like a panther. The pounding rain and din of the storm didn't seem to faze him. She followed, biting her bottom lip to keep from crying out. Following him had to be the dumbest thing she'd ever done in her life, but she kept wondering whose death he already had on his conscience.

The gun was a cold scary weight in her hand. Despite his crash course, Gillian was pretty sure she could never actually fire the weapon at a person. Heck, she wasn't even sure it was loaded. Now probably wasn't a good time to mention that fact, either.

It was hard not to cringe at each clap of thunder. The lightning hurt her eyes and the thunder deafened her. No wonder someone wanted to kill him. She shared the sentiment. This was more insane than coming down here in the first place. The minute the Finders Keepers Detective Agency located her cousin, she should have told someone instead of taking it upon herself to try to reunite the broken family. She might die and she didn't even know why!

They ran behind the main house. Obviously, Keegan had no intention of going inside. He seemed to have a plan, but that didn't mean she had to go along.

Gillian stopped. Keegan turned back.

"What's wrong?"

Her scalp began to prickle. Keegan launched himself at her without warning, shoving her down onto the sodden ground.

The tree came down a few yards behind them with a thunderous crash. If the lightning had struck a little closer, or if the tree had fallen toward them instead of the corner of the house, they would have been killed. Protecting her from a pair of cold-blooded killers, only to have her die in the storm was not what Keegan intended. He hauled Gillian to her feet.

"Come on."

She appeared to be in shock. He'd feel bad about that later. *If they had a later.* The storm was racing past them, but the rain wasn't slowing enough to matter. They needed to reach the truck before the men who'd been inside realized he intended to take it. She was limping badly when he finally glimpsed it up ahead.

"Wait here."

Gillian didn't answer, but she did stop moving. Her hair and clothing were plastered to her body and she was visibly shivering. He had to get her away from here.

Keegan discovered the bastards had locked the doors. Lightning lit the scene, confirming his worst fears. On the back seat sat a duffel bag and a pair of crumpled uniforms, both plainly marked. Somehow, the killers had traced him to Darwin Crossing. He reached for the gun tucked in his waistband. Bristol's sudden whinny of protest carried over the storm's fury. They were herding the truculent horse out of the barn.

"Damn!"

They had the same idea—strand him here until after the storm. Only, they didn't know Bristol. The horse hated storms, but he'd been very well trained.

Keegan motioned Gillian to stay put as Bristol tore off across the field at a full gallop. The men were carrying Keegan's gear and heading toward the truck. There was no time to move back under the trees with Gillian. He flattened himself in the shallow ditch beside the road. If they bothered to look around, they'd spot him. Fortunately, the men apparently didn't like getting wet either. They were swearing volubly as they dumped his saddle and gear in the truck bed.

The engine coughed to life. Lightning offered him a clear view of the passenger, not that he'd needed further confirmation. Swearing under his breath, Keegan squirmed backward until he reached the nearest bush. Standing in a half crouch, he tried to melt back into the line of trees. There was no need to work his way back to where he'd left Gillian. She stood deep in the shadows nearby. Her gun was aimed past his shoulder at the truck and its passengers. This time, he noticed, her hand was rock steady.

Something inside him lightened. She was acting as his backup? She didn't even understand what was happening here, yet she was prepared to defend him. The woman was incredible.

She motioned him to stop. Too late, he heard the truck come to a halt. Doors opened. Powerful flashlights cut a swath through the darkness.

Keegan pressed against the bole of the nearest tree. The beam swept the ground scant inches from his position. Wind carried away their words, but he could tell they were arguing. Finally, they returned to the truck. Keegan didn't so much as twitch. The engine started again, but they didn't drive away. They drove right up to the house. They must have realized the ranch was abandoned.

"Has anyone ever told you you're a moron?" Gillian whispered fiercely.

"Wha—"

"You had them covered before they got to the truck. We could have told them to put their hands up and made a citizen's arrest."

The image nearly made him smile. "It wouldn't

have worked, Gillian. They would have started shooting at us.''

''You would have had time to shoot them in the legs or something.''

He wiped at the rain streaming down his face with the back of his hand. ''I never would have taken you for such a blood-thirsty little thing.''

''You said they came here to kill us! We have a right to defend ourselves.''

''True, but there's a problem with that. It would be our word against theirs, and they're both cops.''

CHAPTER FOUR

GILLIAN FOLLOWED Keegan numbly toward the main road, stunned by his revelation.

"It's been my experience," he continued calmly, "that when it comes down to being believed, cops always have the advantage."

Gillian wiped water from her eyes and tried to make sense of his words. "You're running from the police? You said they were going to kill you."

"You've heard of good cop, bad cop? They're the bad cops."

"You're completely insane," she whispered.

"Don't worry. It isn't contagious."

Keegan looked back and Gillian did the same. The men were on the porch.

"What are they doing?"

"Breaking inside, at a guess."

"Why do they want to kill you?"

"Because I can testify against them."

Why did she believe him? "What are we going to do?" She was so cold her teeth were chattering.

"Get you out of the rain before you freeze to death."

"Great."

So insanity was contagious. How else could she explain why she was letting him guide her through the trees? When she thought about how ready she'd been to pull the trigger to protect this man…this complete stranger…

"Oh, God." She jerked to a stop, forcing him to do the same. "Are you wanted by the police? I mean, besides those two men?"

"In a manner of speaking. Could we have this discussion later?"

It was too much. Her tired brain couldn't cope. "I just came here to do a good deed. How could it backfire so completely?"

"Good deed, huh? I wondered what you were doing here. Ah, there he is! I didn't think he'd go far." Keegan uttered a shrill whistle.

A large shadow moved. Lifting its head, the enormous beast shook rain from his mane impatiently, and whinnied before trotting toward them.

"Taxi's waiting," Keegan told her.

Gillian didn't move. She'd never had so much as a pet goldfish. A horse was lots bigger than a goldfish. She took an uneven step back even as Keegan went forward. To her utter amazement and horror, Keegan grabbed a handful of its mane and swung himself onto the animal's bare back.

"Gillian?" He reached a hand toward her.

He thought she was getting up there?

"Oh, no."

"No? Don't tell me you're afraid of horses."

"Okay, I won't." The massive head swung in her direction, Gillian took another hasty step back and nearly fell when her ankle screamed in protest.

"How can you live in Texas and not know how to ride?"

"I'm equestrian challenged. We don't keep horses in apartments in Dallas."

Keegan muttered under his breath. "Bristol won't hurt you."

"He certainly won't. I don't intend getting close enough to let him."

"You can't stand out here in the rain all night."

"Sure I can. Or maybe I'll just go and throw myself on the mercy of the policemen."

Keegan slid off the horse, who pranced sideways nervously. Keegan grabbed her wrist before she could move away. His expression was as fierce as his grip. "Those bastards are working for J. D. Crowe, the mob boss."

"He's in jail!"

"That hasn't kept him from running his organization. Trust me."

"Trust you? I don't even *know* you."

Yet for some ridiculous reason she couldn't explain even to herself, she did trust him. She felt connected to Keegan.

His expression turned bleak. "Funny. I feel like I've known you for…" He shook his head and released her. The storm left a cold light drizzle in its wake. "I understand. You've got no reason to believe me."

It was the sadness she glimpsed in his eyes that got to her. Maybe she was a fool, but she did believe him. She was about to tell him so when his voice turned grim.

"I'm sorry, Gillian. You aren't leaving me any choice."

Keegan grabbed Gillian around the waist and lifted her onto Bristol's back. He'd expected her to fight him, but Gillian perched there rigidly, those impossibly wide eyes simply staring at him.

"I'm sorry," he said again, swinging up behind her. Bristol *whuffled* and turned his head at the unaccustomed feel of the two bodies on his bare back. Keegan reached around her to stroke the animal's neck, crooning to them both softly. "It's okay. Easy, boy. Take it easy."

A shot whistled out of the darkness.

"Lean forward and hold on to his mane." Pushing her face into Bristol's neck to minimize her exposure, he leaned over Gillian's back and urged the animal into a full gallop.

He hadn't ridden bareback since he was a kid. If Bristol hadn't been so well trained this would have been a nightmare. As it was, he had to make sure Gillian didn't fall off. The men wouldn't drive across wet fields even if the rain had almost stopped. Once they were out of range, he slowed Bristol to a walk.

"You okay?"

For an answer, Gillian shivered.

"Lean back against me so we can share body heat."

She resisted a second before letting him pull her back against his body. A mistake, Keegan realized instantly. What was it about this woman that got to him so fast?

Hell. Hadn't he learned anything from Alice? His former lover had fooled him completely—right up until she'd tried to kill him so he couldn't testify against one of J. D. Crowe's hired hit men. He was drawn to Gillian by more than mere physical attraction, but was she really so different from Alice? Or did he just want to believe that? What if she wasn't as innocent as she seemed?

"You're a long way from Dallas," he said against

her wet hair. "What were you doing out here on foot in the middle of the night?"

Her breasts rose and fell above the arm he held around her small waist. Keegan curbed a desire to shift that arm just a bit.

She shrugged. "I got lost. By the time I figured out my mistake, the stupid rental car was acting up. I thought I could make it to the nearest town. Who knew there was no such thing out here? Doesn't anyone *live* in this part of Texas? There're no houses, no cities, no pay phones...."

Keegan chuckled as she turned her face to his, looking aggrieved. Gillian was *nothing* like Alice.

"No cell phone?" he asked mildly.

"My battery wasn't charged."

Maybe not, but the hormones flying between them sure were. She held his stare. For a moment he was tempted to taste those tempting lips, but she turned away, breathing fast.

"Go ahead and laugh, cowboy," she said breathlessly. "For you all this empty space is normal. My idea of roughing it is a hotel without room service."

"What would you say if I told you I'm really an investment counselor from Dallas?"

"Ha!"

"Succinctly put." He admired her sense of humor. "I wish I'd known about your car sooner. Maybe I could have gotten it running again."

"Forget it. You'd have wasted a bullet if you'd shot it to put it out of my misery. I'm pretty sure the transmission went. My aunt's car sounded the same way. *Rattle, rattle, ka-klunk.* Then nothing. Deader than my cell phone."

He smiled, inhaling the sent that still lingered in

her hair. "You said a good deed brought you to the Circle M?"

She eased her death grip on Bristol's mane. "Mama always said no good deed goes unpunished. Only, for crying out loud, it wasn't *this* good a deed." She waved her arm to indicate their situation.

Keegan chuckled out loud.

"Go ahead and laugh," she told him. "I hired the Finders Keepers Detective Agency because they specialize in finding missing persons. My cousin ran away at 15."

For a moment he wondered if Gillian meant Cade's pretty new wife, Jayne. But Jayne was no runaway. Everyone knew she was H. L. Bateman's daughter. The highly respected breeder had been raising expensive, well-trained cutting horses for years. Buying Bristol had cinched Keegan's job when he'd ridden to the Circle M looking for work. The finicky breeder didn't sell to just anyone.

"What's your cousin's name?" Keegan asked, trying to think of another woman connected with the Circle M that Gillian could be looking for.

"Rio Cardonza."

"Hell. That's impossible!"

Gillian glared at Keegan over her shoulder, then remembered where she was and gripped the animal's mane a little harder. "Why is Rio's being my cousin impossible?"

"Well, for one thing, you don't look anything alike. For another, *Cardonza* is an ocean away from *O'Malley*."

"Our mothers were sisters," she explained. "Aunt Lara married Paulo Cardonza. My mother married Quillen O'Malley."

"Quillen? And you thought Keegan was odd?"

"Not odd, different. So why do the police want to kill you?"

His hand tightened across her rib cage. She was too conscious of that arm and the hard, lean body pressed against hers in an almost sensual embrace. Of course, that kept her mind off the jarring gait of the beast underneath them.

"We're talking about you, not me," Keegan said.

"Not anymore. I think I have a right to know what's going on, don't you?"

He was silent so long she didn't think he was going to answer. Suddenly, he expelled a long breath against her hair.

"They say I killed a police officer."

CHAPTER FIVE

GILLIAN DECIDED a flying saucer could land in front of them without shocking her any further. "Did you?"

"No."

"So tell them what really happened."

"I can't. I don't know what really happened." He expelled another breath in frustration. "I was more than half-asleep when she came at me with a knife."

"A female police officer made that scar on your chest?"

"Yeah. Fortunately, she'd never killed anyone before. She was nervous and her aim was off. Plus I wasn't asleep like she'd thought. I got the knife away from her, but in the struggle she fell and hit her head. She was alive! Conscious and everything."

The words tangled with some deep, painful emotion. Gillian sensed his grief and it made no sense.

"She started crying. Said she had no choice. Crowe's people had some sort of evidence against her. They offered to trade it with a fee if she killed me."

His pain was as tangible as the ache in her ankle.

"This woman meant something to you, didn't she?"

The pause was longer this time. "I'd thought about asking her to marry me."

Gillian ignored a feeling she didn't want to define right then.

"Alice dressed better than most cops. She drove an expensive car, lived in a pricey condominium. I knew, but it never occurred to me to wonder how she could afford it on a cop's salary. I surprised a murderer in her parking garage one night. Alice had been paid to look the other way and give a false report, but my presence screwed things up completely."

Pain underscored each word. Gillian decided against offering him a useless platitude.

"So what's the going rate for murder?"

His answer was slow to come, but she was relieved when it contained a hint of humor.

"Planning to kill anyone I know?"

"You're safe for the moment. Why didn't you tell the police what she'd said?"

"I did. They arrived minutes after I called for help. Turned out, they were waiting for the call downstairs. They were supposed to back up her story after she killed me. I got lucky and got away."

Gillian shook her head. "Is the entire force on the take?"

"Good question. I was trying to decide who to call when I heard I was wanted for Alice's murder."

"But—"

He nodded against her neck. "They must have killed her. She wasn't hurt that badly. But blaming me bought them time."

"And makes your testimony against the real murderer questionable."

"Exactly."

"And I thought Dallas had problems," she muttered. "So what are you going to do now?"

"Gillian, I lived in… Whoa, boy!"

Bristol stopped. Ahead of them stretched a rushing river.

"There must be a bridge," Gillian said.

Keegan shook his head. "This is normally a stream." Something large and half-submerged rushed past them.

"Not anymore."

He felt dog-tired, and she sounded exhausted. He turned Bristol around.

"We'll go back."

"To the ranch we just left?"

He squeezed her waist reassuringly. "It's the closest place. Don't worry, they'll be gone by now."

"And if they aren't?"

"I'll shoot them," he offered, only partly teasing.

"Okay."

He smiled at her easy acceptance. She really was tired. "Lean back, close your eyes, and try to rest."

"You have to be joking. We're on a horse!"

But after a few minutes, she did settle back more comfortably against his body. Funny how important it was that she believed him. Not one of the "friends" he'd tried to contact had. On the other hand, he hadn't told Gillian everything. She didn't know about the public and private fights he and Alice used to have. Alice liked making him jealous and her temper tantrums were legendary. Looking back, it was hard to understand what he'd ever seen in her—besides the obvious.

He'd been so tired of the whole dating scene by the time they met. She was great in bed, and they shared several common interests. She also looked

good on his arm. Men always gave Alice a second look.

But she had never once made him laugh.

Approaching the ranch from a different direction,
Keegan studied the scene carefully. As expected, the
truck was gone. The men weren't likely to split up.
Not only were they in unfamiliar territory, but if he
wasn't mistaken, another storm was coming in behind
the first one.

Gillian was more asleep than awake as he swung
her down inside the barn. Taking a flashlight from the
wall near the open door, he hunted around, discovering several old blankets in the tack room. They
smelled faintly of horse and leather, but they were
dry. Even he was shivering now.

He handed Gillian the blankets and tended to Bristol. The bastards had taken his gear, but Cade had
deliberately left equipment behind. Keegan settled
Bristol in his stall and came out to find Gillian tightly
curled in a ball on some sacks of grain. The blankets
covered all but a bit of her face.

He was about to wake her when his heart thudded
to a stop and then started racing. Her wet clothing
hung over a stall to dry. He'd planned on going to
the main house to bed down, but watching her sleep
so peacefully, he didn't have the heart to wake her
again. Besides, staying in here was probably safer.

Keegan stripped down to his briefs and followed
Gillian's example, hanging his clothes over a different
stall. The clothes wouldn't have time to dry, but
they'd sleep better and stay warmer without the wet
garments. Spreading out the remaining blankets he lay
down beside her. Thunder grumbled in the distance.
Keegan wished he hadn't been right about the second

storm, but the spring weather had been weird and un-predictable lately.

He pulled Gillian against his body and used the other blankets to cover both of them. She mumbled in her sleep and spooned tightly, fitting as if she'd been made just for him. He shoved that thought into a "do not go there" place in his mind and tried not to think about Gillian naked in his arms. Going to sleep was not going to be easy.

Something tugged him from the deep well of dreams where erotic images were playing havoc. A cat mewed in his ear. As he came fully awake he realized two things. Despite his best intentions it was past dawn, and Gillian was wrapped around him like a lover....

CHAPTER SIX

GILLIAN STARED sleepily into Keegan's eyes, watching them darken in desire. Her erotic dream mingled with reality as she lightly fingered the rough bristles that shadowed his face. He stirred and her stomach fluttered in reaction. The tip of her tongue sought to moisten suddenly dry lips.

Keegan inhaled sharply. "You're playing with fire," he warned.

His arousal pulsed against the bare thigh she had thrown over him at some point. The blankets lay tangled about them. Her nipples strained against the material of her thin bra while liquid heat pooled deep inside. Dream or reality?

"I'm cold. Fire sounds good," she whispered. Boldly, she traced his lips, shocked by the fine tremor of her fingers.

"Ah, hell."

He claimed her mouth.

Incredible sensations raced for dominance. She'd been kissed many times before, but never like this. The wanting was primal, insistent. Raw need clawed at her. Her lips willingly surrendered to his insistent demand for more. His hands tightened, drawing her firmly against his taut body. Anticipation hardened her nipples. They strained against the lace of her bra, sliding over the hard planes of his chest.

It wasn't enough—not nearly enough.

His mouth fused over hers, tongues mating, teeth nibbling lightly. Gillian moaned her pleasure. She felt his smile against her skin. He chased butterfly kisses over her face and chin. The scratchy beard added a shocking dimension of excitement, especially when he kissed the sensitive skin of her neck.

"Keegan!"

Her lips throbbed from his kiss. She felt, as much as heard, his rumble of satisfaction at the sound of his name, even as his lips found her ear. Electrified by the unexpected sensation, she couldn't prevent the small sounds of pleasure tumbling past her lips. Her hands had taken on a life of their own tracing patterns across his chest and playing with the fine hairs sprinkled there. He inhaled sharply when she found the small nubs of his nipples. Lightly she stroked one, testing his reaction. He made a startled sound when she bent her face to lick one and then the other. Pleased by his reaction, her fingers delved lower, tracing his outline through those sexy briefs.

"Gillian! Stop."

"No."

He gathered her wrists in one hand, raising her arms over her head even as he rolled her beneath him. She felt deliciously exposed and helplessly pinned all at the same time.

His eyes glittered fiercely. "You're making me crazy."

"Good."

Laughter crinkled the lines around his eyes. He kissed her until she couldn't breathe. His fingers deftly parted the front clasp of her bra and he parted the material, gazing his fill. Gillian had never felt so wanton—or so wanted. His eyes gleamed, hot with pleasure. He watched her as he lowered his mouth with excruciating slowness, deliberately prolonging the teasing.

She burned with desire, straining to allow him better access as his mouth claimed first one breast and then the other. He made a thorough job of it, sucking strongly.

"Keegan!"

"Do you like that?" Watching her, he let his teeth scrape her nipple.

A cry of desperate need wrenched from her throat.

"I see that you do."

She bucked, trying to force a more intimate contact. "Keegan, please!"

"I plan to, darlin'."

And he chuckled sensually, before claiming her mouth once more and freeing her hands. Instantly, she tugged at his briefs, releasing him so she could explore every velvety hard inch of him with insistent fingers. Now he was the one breathing hard. But when she would have lowered her head to taste him, he stopped her.

"I'm too close," he warned.

"So am I."

His hand slipped inside her panties. The contact was electrifying. Stomach muscles contracted and fluttered. Her body quickened, dampening with matching excitement as he cupped her there, testing the evidence of her desire.

She wanted him, right here, right now. Yet he was a stranger. A man she had just met. She didn't do things like this. So why did this feel so right?

Their gazes locked....

Keegan sensed her hesitation. Common sense reasserted itself. What was he doing? He was on the brink of losing control completely. The last thing he needed in his life right now was another complication. Gillian spelled COMPLICATION in all caps. This wasn't a woman he could have sex with and walk away from. This was Gillian.

And then she smiled, a siren's smile that rippled right down his body.

"Don't stop," she pleaded, her voice thick with desire.

To emphasize, she rubbed his nipple, pinching lightly. Coherent thought fled. He couldn't stop. Nothing else mattered but this woman. The need to possess her was compellingly primitive but he wanted more. He yearned for something he couldn't put a name to.

"Keegan!"

It took incredible control to temper his raging need now, but her pleasure heightened his own. The desire to please her as no one else had ever done kept him from completing their union. He held himself rigid, testing, teasing, loving her until neither could take any more. Then he entered slowly, still resisting the urge to rush. He relished the feel of each muscular contraction inside her snug, slick passage. She breathed his name in intense satisfaction as he sheathed himself completely.

That gentle spur coaxed him to move. Nothing had ever felt like this. He began to move faster, harder, yielding to her insistent demands. The natural rhythm swept them in a passionate current that could have only one outcome. Gillian climaxed beneath him, crying out his name. Keegan abandoned all restraint and followed her over the edge of the world.

Utterly spent, more satisfied than he'd ever been in his life, Keegan lay there savoring the incredible sensations. This emotional closeness he felt between them was something new. He didn't mind. He didn't want this moment to end.

Gillian stirred and he kissed her lightly, rolling to his back and pulling her along with him. She murmured something and snuggled against his side.

Nearby, Bristol stirred in his stall. Keegan opened his eyes, startled to see a surprisingly large barn cat sitting a few feet away. It stared at him in regal reproach.

"We have an audience," he told Gillian softly.

"What?" She rolled half on top of him to look. Her breast mashed against his chest. "Oh, the cat. We met the other night. It's okay—he's friendly."

"And a voyeur."

Gillian giggled. The light, happy sound made him smile.

"It is his barn. Maybe he was taking notes."

Disgusted, the animal stood and stretched, turning its back.

"I think we offended him."

"Then he shouldn't have been staring. And as much as I hate to say this, we'd better get dressed."

The mood shattered. Her body tensed. "Do you really think they'll come back here?"

"They might if they think I'll come back for my belongings. Why else would they take them?"

Reluctantly, he rose, skimming her body with his eyes. She made no effort to hide from his gaze, watching him with an unreadable expression. Keegan noted the marks made by his morning stubble and the puffiness of her lips. Some perverse part of him was glad he had branded her for all to see. Why hadn't he realized how beautiful she was?

Only the fierce need to protect her kept him from lowering himself back down beside her. Instead, he looked around for his briefs. He retrieved them as Gillian reached for her panties. Funny. He couldn't even remember pulling them off.

"I'd suggest going to the bunkhouse for a shower, but—"

"We should go."

"Yes."

Gillian grimaced, struggling into her still-damp slacks. "Wish we had a dryer."

"There's one in the bunkhouse."

She smoothed a tangle of hair behind her ear. Her rumpled clothing and delicate color reinforced the sensual image of a woman coming from her lover's bed.

"You couldn't have mentioned the dryer last night?"

"I didn't think of it last night. Besides, you fell asleep, remember?"

They whirled as one at the sound of gravel crunching beneath a vehicle's tires....

"Keegan, it's a police car!"

A gun appeared in his hand.

"You can't shoot a police officer in cold blood!"

CHAPTER SEVEN

KEEGAN LOWERED THE GUN, his grin crooked. "I've got no reason to shoot *him* at all. That's the local sheriff. As far as I know, he's one of the good guys."

"Then tell him about the others!"

"He'd only have my word and *I'm* wanted for murder. He'd have to arrest me. If that happens, I won't live to testify. Let's go see what he wants."

Frightened for him, Gillian grabbed his arm. "What if *you're* what he wants? Let me go talk to him."

He looked surprised. After what had just happened between them, didn't he expect her to take his side?

"Gillian, wait."

But the sheriff had already seen movement inside the barn. His hand was reaching toward his weapon. Gillian hurried forward, limping even more this morning as pain moved up her leg. "Hello."

The hand stilled. "Mornin'. Would you be Gillian O'Malley?"

"How did you know?"

"Found your car a mile or so up the road."

"Well, I hope you impounded it for impersonating a motor vehicle. Piece of junk," she grumbled.

His lips curved, but never quite made it to a smile as his gaze darted past her. "Keegan West, isn't it?"

"Sheriff," Keegan acknowledged.

The sheriff looked from one to the other. So what if he realized what they'd been doing in the barn? Gillian squared her shoulders and mentally dared him to say a word.

"Cade McGovern asked me to keep an eye out for you, Mr. West. He figured you might hole up here after the creek flooded."

"We're glad to see you," Gillian interrupted. "Two prowlers broke into the house and the barn last night and stole Keegan's gear."

"City types," Keegan affirmed after a moment's hesitation, his voice dangerously soft.

Gillian could tell he was angry. She doubted the sheriff would realize the anger was directed at her.

"That how you got the scratch down your face?" he asked.

"I did that," she admitted hastily. "It was an accident."

"We haven't been in the house," Keegan said, ignoring the question and her answer. "After the tree came down I wasn't sure it was safe. Not much inside worth taking." He rattled off a terse description of the men right down to the make of truck and the license number. "They were armed so Gillian and I stayed out of their way."

"Smart thinking. I'll call it in."

Instead of using the radio on his shoulder, the sheriff walked back to his car. Keegan's features were unreadable. She rested her hand on his arm. "I'm on your side."

"Then let me handle this."

She snorted. "You haven't done a great job so far."

His lips parted in surprise. Gillian forced back the

memory of how those lips had explored so much of her. She jammed a finger against the wall of his chest. "Let me tell you something, mister, I've never done that before in my life."

"You were a virgin?"

Another time she might have laughed at his shock. "Of course not, but I don't sleep with perfect strangers."

He looked from her face to her finger still buried in his shirt. Tension drained from him. "I'm hardly perfect."

"Cute. I'm trying to help you here."

"Getting me arrested won't do that."

She dropped her hand to her side. "No, but getting *them* arrested might."

"They have badges."

"Bet the sheriff's badge is bigger."

Unwilling humor skated over his face, replaced by speculation. "Why?"

Gillian didn't pretend to misunderstand. "I believe you."

"Because the sex was good?"

"Actually, the sex was fantastic, but if I hadn't believed you last night, there wouldn't have been any sex to rate."

His lips twitched. "Fantastic?"

"Skip the swelled head routine."

The twitch became a full grin. "That isn't what's swelling."

He caught her looking to his zipper. Gillian laughed out loud.

"Hold that thought, cowboy. Right now we need a game plan."

He kept underestimating her, but then Keegan had

never met anyone like Gillian before. He doubted there was anyone else like her in the world. "Gillian—"

"Sorry to interrupt," the sheriff said, striding over, "but the storm's left a mess. If you'll grab your belongings I'll give you a ride to Darwin Crossing."

"I've got a horse inside." Keegan wasn't about to leave Bristol behind.

"But no saddle," Gillian said.

"He's well-trained. I'll follow you."

"And if those men come back?"

Her concern warmed him. Why couldn't he have met her instead of Alice? Ignoring the sheriff, he stroked her bottom lip with his thumb, feeling her tremble. He wanted to pull her into his arms and take her back inside and make love to her all over again. Instead he managed a smile, "Bristol and I can go where no vehicle dares to follow."

"You sure?" Sheriff Beaufort asked. "I can't spare anyone to watch the place right now."

"I'm sure. I'll meet you at Doc Zimmerman's place. She twisted her ankle," he explained. "It should be checked."

Beaufort nodded. "All right. I'll need to fill out a report on the break-in."

"No problem."

Meeting Gillian's concerned look, Keegan realized running was no longer an option. As if to emphasize that thought, she drew his head down and kissed him full on the mouth. It was not an innocent peck. Forgetting their audience, Keegan pulled her against his body and let the rush of desire stir to life once more as he returned her kiss.

When he released her, Gillian stepped back breathlessly, eyes half-shut. "Maybe we should go for stupendous next time," she whispered.

She limped to the police car leaving him standing there awkwardly beside the sheriff.

"Better tell Doc Zimmerman to keep an eye on her," Keegan warned. "She attracts trouble faster than a lightning rod."

The sheriff smiled. "I'll catch up with you later."

"I won't be hard to find," he promised.

He'd never planned to run in the first place. Things had simply worked out that way. Maybe Gillian was right. He had a feeling she often was. Darwin Crossing was a long way from Dallas. The sheriff had a good reputation. Maybe he could help.

Keegan had plenty of time to think on the ride to town. He wondered if Gillian would be shocked or pleased by some of those thoughts.

At the doctor's place he took a few liberties, making use of a clean stall inside the barn. After seeing to Bristol, Keegan headed for the part of the house where the doctor had his office. Several cars were parked in the dusty lot—including one marked Sheriff. Inside the door of the crowded waiting room a deputy took up a great deal of space. Keegan looked past him for a glimpse of Gillian.

"Keegan West?"

He met the deputy's hard stare. Tension knotted his muscles. Getting past the man would take more luck than skill. Keegan suspected he didn't have enough left of either one to make it back out the door in one piece. Where was Gillian? Surely they hadn't arrested her, too. "I'm West."

"Deputy Gooding. Sheriff Beaufort would like to see you."

"All right. Let me find Gillian—"

"Keegan?"

His relieved gaze swept her as she came down the corridor. She looked fantastic—until he noticed the crutches and the bandage swathing her ankle.

"It's a sprain," she hurried to assure him.

Only slightly relieved he took in the breezy print skirt, cinched by a wide gold belt that emphasized her slender waist, and the boldly colored blouse. The sheriff must have stopped at her rental car for her suitcase, but he doubted Gillian had changed clothing, fixed her hair, and applied lipstick for Doc Zimmerman's sake. That she'd done it for him made him smile.

"What's going on, Keegan?"

"The sheriff wants to see me."

"Why?"

Conversation in the waiting room died as people listened with unabashed interest....

CHAPTER EIGHT

"WE'D LIKE Mr. West to see if he can identify a truck," the deputy said reluctantly.

"You caught the prowlers already?" Gillian asked eagerly. "Great. Let's go."

"Begging your pardon, ma'am, but Sheriff Beaufort didn't say anything about bringing you."

"We're together," she stated boldly, daring either man to contradict her. Their frowns were nearly identical but Keegan's features quickly softened. Looking ruefully amused, he gave the deputy a "what can we do" sort of shrug.

"The receptionist has my suitcase at the front desk," she told the deputy crisply. Pivoting on the crutches the way she'd been shown, Gillian headed for the main door as if there was no question of them agreeing. Her gambit paid off. The deputy muttered something about letting the sheriff handle her and went for her case.

The door burst open before Gillian reached it. Two wet, mud-covered cowboys staggered inside. The younger one was bleeding profusely from a gash on his head. Keegan rushed forward to support the injured man. "What happened, Zed?"

"His horse went down in the mud. Tossed him against that stone retaining wall."

"I'm okay," the younger man protested.

"Sure you are," Keegan agreed. "It would take more than a stone wall to dent that stubborn head of yours, Rio."

"Rio?" Gillian gasped. "Rio Cardonza?"

The young man lifted his pockmarked face to stare at her through dazed eyes. "Do I know you?" Fear suddenly crossed his features.

"How could you? You aren't Rio Cardonza."

If Keegan and the other cowboy hadn't been holding him, she felt sure the younger man would have bolted.

"What are you talking about, Gillian?"

"Who are you?" the man called Zed demanded.

"He's not Rio," she told Keegan.

"Rio Cardonza is her cousin," Keegan told the cowboy.

A young nurse bustled forward. "I don't care who any of you are. Get this man back in treatment room two right now. He's bleeding all over the floor."

Deputy Gooding set Gillian's suitcase down. As the men hurried to obey the nurse, the deputy turned to Gillian. "Rio Cardonza has worked on the Circle M for several years, ma'am."

Gillian shook her head. "You have it wrong, Deputy. A man *calling* himself Rio Cardonza has worked there for several years. He may even resemble my cousin a little, but I promise you, that man is not Rio Cardonza. I want to know what that imposter's done to my cousin."

Keegan and the cowboy called Zed reappeared.

"Now, what's goin' on?" Zed demanded.

"Gillian is trying to locate her missing cousin," Keegan told him.

"Okay. So she found the wrong Rio Cardonza. It happens."

"Then why is Rio so scared?"

Gillian pulled out a worn, badly creased photograph and handed it to the deputy. Zed crowded his shoulder as the two men studied the image.

"This could be Rio," Zed said dubiously.

"You did say he ran away at age 15, Gillian," Keegan reminded her.

"That man isn't Rio." She turned to the deputy. "If you don't stop him, he's going to run, and we'll never find out what happened to my cousin."

"You don't know that anything's happened to your cousin," the officer said, looking from Zed to Keegan.

"Rio's scared about something," Zed admitted reluctantly.

"Okay, wait here," the deputy ordered. "I need to check with Sheriff Beaufort."

Keegan introduced Zed to Gillian. "Would you both excuse me for a minute? I need to use the radio in the truck to let Cade know what's happening. I'll be right back."

The nurse reappeared before either of the men returned. She glared at them, visibly annoyed. "Ms. O'Malley, Mr. Cardonza insists on talking to you. He has a concussion. He needs to rest. And you shouldn't be on that ankle. You can have three minutes."

CHAPTER NINE

RIO STRUGGLED to sit up on the examination table when Keegan and Gillian stepped inside the small room. Keegan held him down. The white tape covering his forehead nearly blended with his complexion.

"Take it easy," Keegan said.

"Are they going to arrest me?"

Gillian came forward awkwardly on the crutches.

"That all depends on what you did to my cousin."

"Nothin'. I swear it! He was fine, last I saw him."

"When was that?" Gillian demanded.

"Three, maybe four weeks ago."

"Four weeks ago!" Relief swept her features and Keegan realized she'd thought Rio was dead.

"We didn't figure anybody'd come looking for us after all this time."

"Where is he? I need to see him."

The young man clamped his lips together in a firm line. "I can't tell you."

"What do you mean?"

Keegan laid a restraining hand on her shoulder. "Why can't you tell her, Rio?" he asked gently.

"I promised."

"I'm his cousin!"

The man Keegan knew as Rio stubbornly set his

jaw. Pushing him would get them nowhere. "Can you tell us how you ended up with his name?"

His shoulders lifted and fell. "We switched identities on the bus to San Antonio. He said it would confuse things if anyone ever came looking for me."

"You ran away, too?"

He studied Keegan, looked at Gillian, and sighed. "When my gramps died, the court wanted to make me a ward of the state. I didn't like the idea. I figured I could just disappear, you know? Gramps taught me about ranching. I figured I could get a job if I was older, like Rio."

"How old are you?" Keegan said gently.

"Almost 19, but I look older, don't I?"

Keegan smiled at him. "Definitely," he agreed. "And your gramps would be proud. He taught you well. Zed and Cade depend on you."

Rio relaxed. "Are you gonna tell them?"

"None of my business," Keegan said.

Rio's gaze shifted to Gillian. "Your cousin doesn't want to be found."

"I know," she said sadly. "He thinks he's wanted for armed robbery."

Keegan gaped at her.

"His father was an alcoholic," she explained. "He never held a job for long. Rio and Uncle Paulo had a fight one night and Uncle Paulo went to meet a couple of buddies. Rio snuck out to meet his own friends. Uncle Paulo stopped at a gas station on his way home. It had started raining, so he put on a jacket that was in the car."

"Rio's jacket?" Keegan surmised.

Gillian nodded. "A young man was working there by himself. His brother was a friend of Rio's, so the youth recognized the jacket. My uncle wore a mask, so the boy thought he was dealing with Rio. He refused to hand over the money. Uncle Paulo claimed he didn't know the gun was loaded, but it went off and the boy was shot.''

"Did he die?'' the fake Rio asked. "Rio always wondered.''

Gillian shook her head. "He survived, but he identified Rio as his assailant. The police found the gun in Uncle Paulo's car, but couldn't get any usable prints from it. Rio's friends swore he was with them. Rio and his father had a terrible fight and he disappeared. My uncle was later arrested for another armed robbery and confessed. Please, he needs to know what happened, and his mother really needs to see him again. Can you get in touch with Rio?''

"Maybe.''

Keegan rested a comforting hand on her shoulder.

"Tell him I'm here. Just to talk,'' she added quickly.

"Will we go to jail?''

Gillian flashed a questioning look at Keegan, who shook his head. "Not unless one of you broke a law. It's not illegal to change your name, and you're too old to be a ward of the state now.''

Rio perked up. "Hey, that's right. I didn't think about that. I wonder if Rio will let me keep using his name?''

The door opened. "Time's up,'' the nurse said. "Deputy Gooding wants to see you both outside.''

"I'll call,'' the youth offered, "but I won't tell you where he is if he doesn't want to see you.''

As they stepped into the hall, Gillian jerked Keegan to a stop. "Go out the back. I'll stall the deputy.''

"Not this time. I think Sheriff Beaufort will listen.''

"But what if he can't help?"

He kissed the tip of her nose. "Then we won't get to try for stupendous."

IN DAYLIGHT, the swollen stream looked more like a river than ever. A cluster of men stood on the bank watching a tow truck pull a dark red pickup truck from the water, where it was jammed on its side between a dead tree and a large rock.

Gillian waited in the deputy's car since she couldn't maneuver crutches over the saturated ground. Unfortunately, she had a clear view as the body of the driver was revealed, wedged behind the crumpled steering wheel.

"Musta' got caught in the flash flood," she heard the deputy say.

"Is this the truck?" the sheriff asked Keegan.

"You can see my saddle still in the truck bed. There were two men, Sheriff."

"We're searching for the second body."

The deputy walked forward and peered inside. "Sheriff, you'd better have a look at this." The mood changed in an instant. The sheriff walked back to them with a grim expression. "You want to tell me why a Dallas police officer would steal your gear and saddle?"

Gillian's heart began pounding as Keegan shrugged. "I'm guessing they hoped to use my belongings to draw me out."

"Now why would they want to do that?"

"So they could kill me and say I was resisting arrest."

The sheriff looked from Keegan to where Gillian sat in the car. "I think we'd better go to my office for a chat."

CHAPTER TEN

FEAR SETTLED like concrete in Gillian's stomach. She'd pushed Keegan to do exactly what he was doing, but what if she'd made a mistake? What if the sheriff didn't believe him? What if the sheriff wouldn't help? Keegan might be killed and it would be her fault.

"You know I'm going to have to check your story out."

Keegan nodded. "I was hoping you'd know of someone we could trust."

"You're in luck. I used to work for Zach Logan."

"Isn't he the chief of detectives?" Gillian asked.

"I'd trust him with my life."

Keegan frowned. "Yeah, well, you're trusting him with mine."

The sheriff had no choice about arresting him since there was a murder warrant out, but he did offer Gillian the name of several local lawyers and helped her find a place to stay for the night.

Time inched forward. For such a small place, the sheriff's office was a beehive of activity. When the deputy brought Keegan a meal from the diner across the street, Gillian pleaded to go back and talk to Keegan. She couldn't stand the thought that he might believe she'd simply left him to his fate.

The deputy was reluctant, but the sheriff agreed,

probably to keep her from pestering him any further. "Five minutes," the deputy said, ushering Gillian inside the locked cell area.

"What happens if I go over?" she snapped, her patience breaking. "Do I get a parking ticket?"

Keegan grinned. "You do like tempting fate, don't you?"

"I'm not the one locked behind bars."

"Touché."

He'd been lying on the cot and his hair was mussed as if he'd been running his hands through it. Gillian had never believed in love at first sight before, but she thought she could make an exception in Keegan's case. Even rumpled and behind bars, Keegan was incredibly appealing.

"Keep looking at me like that and I'm going to find the strength to pull these bars apart with my bare hands."

"How about if I punch the deputy so they'll lock me in the cell with you?"

"I like the way your mind works, but there're two cells."

"Figures. Two prison cells, but I've got to go to the next town over just to find a place to stay."

"City girl."

Her smile faded. "I know. That's going to present us with a problem, isn't it?"

The door clanged open again before he could answer....

"It hasn't been anything like five minutes yet," Gillian protested, then stopped when Sheriff Beaufort strode inside.

"No, ma'am, but I thought you'd both appreciate a little good news for a change. I just got off the telephone with the Dallas police department. It appears all three police officers, including the dead woman, were already under investigation for suspected mob connections at the time of the shooting.''

Relief surged through Keegan. As grateful as he was for Gillian's unquestioning belief in him, it was nice to finally have something more concrete than that in his corner.

"Does this mean you can release Keegan now?'' she demanded.

"I'm afraid not. They're sending a couple of officers here to escort him back to Dallas.''

"Oh, no. How do we know they won't try to kill him, too?''

"Zach assures me the men were handpicked, Ms. O'Malley.''

"It's okay, Gillian, I have to trust someone,'' Keegan told her, but he couldn't suppress his own mistrust after what had happened.

"I wouldn't worry too much. If anything short of an act of God happens to Mr. West at this point, the paperwork would take a lifetime to fill out.''

Keegan found himself sharing a grin with the sheriff, but Gillian looked less than amused.

"Besides,'' the sheriff continued. "There isn't much point in killing Mr. West now. The man he was supposed to testify against committed suicide last week.''

Something cold ran down Keegan's spine. "No way,'' he protested.

The sheriff smiled without humor this time. "Zach agrees with you. That death is under investigation, as well.''

"If this is supposed to make us feel better, it isn't

working," Gillian told him. "You're saying everyone involved in this situation is dead?"

"Does this mean you found the missing body?" Keegan demanded.

The sheriff held out his hands. "I understand your concerns here, but this is a good thing from the standpoint of Mr. West's safety. It appears someone is tidying up loose ends."

"And you don't think I qualify?" Keegan asked.

"Yes and no. From an organized crime point of view, you no longer matter because there isn't anyone you can hurt, which means no one is left who can point a finger at the people behind the initial event."

"Except the missing policeman," Keegan pointed out.

"It's only a matter of time before we find his body, given the situation. The water has started to recede, so we should have a report on its location by morning. And in the meantime, I've found someone willing to give you a ride over to the boardinghouse, Ms. O'Malley."

Gillian scowled. "Does this mean I don't even get my five minutes?"

The two men shared a look. Amused, the sheriff's lips quirked. "I'm pretty sure my neighbor won't mind waiting for five minutes."

"Thank you so much."

The door opened and the deputy stuck his head inside. "Telephone, Sheriff."

"I give up," Gillian said in exasperation. "There's no such thing as privacy around here."

Keegan laughed out loud. It felt good. Better than good. He was almost afraid to get his hopes up too high, but for the first time in a long time, he could see some light at the end of this tunnel he'd felt trapped inside.

"This is a jail, Gillian," he told her.

"Yeah? Whose side are you on?"

She took his hands through the bars. Her unreserved support lifted away the last of his depression.

"Forget the five minutes," she said. "I'll settle for a kiss."

"Well, I won't."

Kissing her through the bars was a challenge, but he managed to make a reasonably thorough job of the process. Of course, he'd probably be left staring at the ceiling all night, wishing for a cold shower, but Gillian was worth it. He had a feeling she was worth just about anything....

CHAPTER ELEVEN

GILLIAN LEANED on her crutches, staring at the deputy. "What do you mean Keegan's gone? Gone where?"

"Dallas police flew him out early this morning."

Terrifying what-if scenarios filled her with fear, but there was no point mentioning them to the hapless deputy. "Did he leave me a message?"

"Uh, not that I know of."

"Nothing at all?" She couldn't believe it. She *didn't* believe it. "Where's Sheriff Beaufort?"

"Hopefully, getting some sleep. He was up all night."

Defeated, Gillian left. She could wait for the sheriff to arrive, but it would be better to return to the boardinghouse since the owner's car was still parked at the gas station. She hoped she could catch a lift back, because until the rental car company showed up with a replacement this afternoon, she was at the mercy of strangers. Neither of these tiny towns ran to civilized things like taxis.

Morning turned to afternoon. Keegan didn't call. Neither did anyone else. Gillian wondered if the fake Rio had talked with her cousin yet. The real Rio probably thought the family believed his guilt when the truth was, none of them had even known about the situation. Aunt Mary hadn't told her sister anything at all until her husband was arrested and confessed.

The new car arrived midafternoon. Gillian decided her sprain wouldn't interfere with driving. Besides, she couldn't stand sitting still any longer.

"Ms. O'Malley? You have a telephone call."

If it hadn't been for the crutches she would have run to the phone. She fumbled for the receiver with indecent haste.

"Gilly?"

Not Keegan. The voice was unfamiliar, yet it teased a distant memory that finally clicked into place. "Rio? Is that you?"

"Can we meet?"

"Of course! Where and when?"

Gillian heard a gruff voice in the background ordering him to hurry.

"Look. I have to go. Meet me outside the post office in Trueblood. Six o'clock."

"Wait! Rio?"

He'd hung up. Gillian stared at the wall while something cold worked its way down her spine.

"Is everything all right Ms. O'Malley?"

She brought the owner into focus. "I'm not sure. Can you give me *simple* directions to Trueblood from here?"

THE PLANE WAS DELAYED in Dallas. The officers were treating Keegan as a material witness instead of a suspect, so his personal effects had been returned and they didn't cuff him, but he still felt as if he were under arrest. His escorts had little to say as they stashed him in a secluded office at the airport. He hoped the sheriff had given Gillian his hastily scrawled message since they wouldn't let him use a telephone.

"Uh, fellows, I need to use the rest room. Your bladders might not have limits, but three cups of coffee is definitely mine."

"We'll have to go across the hall," the string bean said. Though Keegan had been given their names, he'd taken to thinking of them as String Bean and No Neck.

"We go in and we come straight back," No Neck admonished.

If Gillian were here she'd probably ask if she was allowed to wash her hands first. Keegan smiled without bothering to explain. Delayed commuters filled the terminal. A disembodied voice suddenly announced the landing of their plane.

No Neck halted so abruptly Keegan walked right into him.

"Holy sh— That's Nathan Orrik!"

String Bean jerked like a puppet. "Where?"

A beefy man in a three-piece suit whirled at the sound of his name. Hatred filled his eyes. His hand snaked to an inside pocket.

"Look out, he's got a gun!"

There was no time to wonder how anyone had smuggled a gun past Security. Keegan was shoved against the wall as the terminal erupted in chaos. He didn't know or care who Nathan Orrik was, nor did he wait to see how it all played out. He joined the frantic throng rushing to escape. For the past several hours he'd had nothing to do but think. One thing was clear. If both cops hadn't died in the flash flood, Gillian was in danger.

GILLIAN TRIED CALLING the sheriff before she left, but he still wasn't in. She wished Keegan were here with her. Rio had sounded…wrong. Yet only Rio had ever had the temerity to call her Gilly.

Why had he picked the closed post office for their meeting? And clear over in Trueblood? If only she'd remembered to pack the battery charger for her cell phone. Unfortunately, her phone had died before the stupid rental car and she knew firsthand that there were no pay phones between here and Trueblood.

Her thoughts strayed back to Keegan. Her father had told her numerous times how he'd fallen for her mother at first glance. Was it possible to inherit a trait like that, along with hair color and a sense of humor? If so, she was very much afraid she had fallen in love with a cowboy.

Gillian pulled into the deserted parking lot and wondered if Rio had chosen this location to be sure she came alone. Reluctantly, she left the safety of the small rental car. Standing in front of the bank on crutches made her feel vulnerable. Rio had always been a quiet, serious boy, but he'd never been weird.

A paneled delivery van pulled to the curb and stopped. Fear gripped her as a man stepped from the driver's side. She recognized him from the night he and his partner had stalked her and Keegan in the rain. He smiled and she prayed he couldn't hear the frantic pounding of her heart.

"Gillian O'Malley? Rio sent me."

Her mouth was a desert of fear. That voice had been in the background when her cousin called. No wonder Rio had sounded strained.

"Get in the van and I'll take you to him."

"I don't think so."

The smile slipped. "It's all right—I'm a police officer."

She shook her head. "I don't care. If you take another step in my direction I'm going to scream so loud they'll hear me in Darwin Crossing."

The smile dissolved. He pulled out a gun.

"Shooting me won't get you any closer to Keegan."

He nodded toward the truck. "How about if I shoot your cousin?"

Her legs threatened to buckle. He'd do it. Maybe he already had. "And draw the entire town? I don't think so," she lied. She shifted her weight, wondering if she could reach his hand with the crutch before he shot her.

"Were you looking for me?"

"Keegan!"

The man swiveled toward the unexpected voice. Gillian brought up the crutch with all the force she could muster. Keegan launched himself forward as the shot exploded. The men went down in a vicious tangle of limbs.

"Police! Hold it!"

KEEGAN STROKED her hair.

"I thought he'd killed you," Gillian murmured.

"He missed, thanks to you."

"What were you thinking, taking chances like that?"

"I was trying to rescue you. I should have known you'd handle it."

She hugged him tight, and he inhaled the fragrant scent of her.

"Fool. How did you know I was here?"

"I called the boardinghouse. Then I called the sheriff. He got in touch with String Bean and No Neck."

"Who?"

He gestured at the officers leading the prisoner away. "Oh." She giggled. "How did he know about Rio?"

The sheriff stood talking with her cousin, who'd been tied up in the back of the truck.

Keegan shrugged. "A police officer with a badge has access to all sorts of information. I knew if he'd seen you with me that night and escaped the flood, he'd come after you."

"So you had to play hero."

"It's the code of the West."

Love sparkled in her eyes as she gazed up at him. "Are you really a financial advisor in Dallas?"

"When I'm not pretending to be a cowboy."

"Thank God. There isn't much call for a research analyst in Darwin Crossing."

She nestled against his chest. Keegan didn't want to ever let her go. "I know it's too soon, but how do you feel about long engagements?"

She tensed and his gut knotted. He should have waited.

She lifted her head. "Annoyed."

Keegan threw back his head and laughed.

COP NEXT DOOR

Julie Miller

CHAPTER ONE

"HOLD THE ELEVATOR!"

Detective Ethan Cross stomped the snow off his black leather boots and strode across the worn tile floor of the Mercantile Plaza apartment building. Located just a few blocks from the Missouri River in downtown Kansas City, the old brick conversion structure had seen better days as a textile warehouse in the early 1900s. The crumbling historic architecture might be more unique than comfortable, but to Ethan's empty stomach and weary bones, it was home.

And after two and a half months of living a lie, it felt mighty good to be home.

"Hey! I said—" He caught a glimpse of silverblond hair and a black coat before the person he'd called to slipped inside the elevator and the doors began to close. "Damn."

He was too tired to mess with this. Ethan's shoulders lifted with a frustrated sigh beneath the army castoff trench coat he wore. He sprinted the last few feet, his long legs beating the rickety pace of the sliding doors. He jammed his palm against one door and wedged his forearm into the closing gap. The combination of his considerable bulk and fraying patience gave him the strength to push the doors open and step inside.

"Thanks." For nothing. Sarcasm eclipsed the easy pitch of his voice as he moved past the woman standing at the elevator panel. Her black-gloved finger was still pressed against the door-close button. But she quickly snatched it back into a fist and curled her arms across her middle, clutching her bag to her chest and assuming the classic protective posture of a woman alone at night in the big city. Late at night. Trapped with a stranger.

Instantly, Ethan regretted his cold tone. Hell. He was one of the good guys. She had nothing to fear from him.

"Sorry." He let some laughter slide into his voice. "I just figured two in the morning was late enough to be getting home as it is. I didn't want to wait another 10 minutes while this old contraption went up to your floor and came back down to get me."

Nothing. No acceptance of his apology, verbal or otherwise. Her only acknowledgment that he had even spoken was to clutch that bag even more tightly.

Ethan rubbed his jaw, letting his fingerless gray gloves absorb the melting January snow that dripped through the scruff of his beard. He froze with his hand on his chin as his fingertips clued him in to the image he must be projecting. An angular jaw that needed a shave was nothing compared to six-feet three inches of a man built like a linebacker dwarfing the confines of an ancient elevator.

He'd gone out of his way to fine-tune this particular streetwise look. He'd let his curling, coffee-dark hair grow down to his shoulders. Errant strands, moist from the snow outside, clung to his cheeks and forehead with the abandonment of a man who didn't care. He'd chosen clothes to emphasize his bulk and mask the gun he holstered beneath his left shoulder. The jeans were expensive but well worn. The boots tough but functional. The trench coat formed an ominous silhouette and had secret pockets sewn inside where he stashed his badge and his back-up weapon.

The mute woman over in the corner barely came up to his shoulders. She had every right to try to steal a safe, solo ride on an elevator without the likes of him along for company. Other than the fact she'd been out in the city at two a.m., she was smart enough to have her self-preservation instincts in place.

Admiring her already for that quality alone, Ethan redoubled his efforts to put her at ease.

"You're new here." He made the observation as matter-of-factly as possible.

Her shoulders hitched with a deep breath and she rolled her neck as if standing in that hunched position was growing uncomfortable. But she didn't speak. She continued to stare straight ahead at the button panel.

He tried again. "I've been gone for a couple of months. But welcome to the Mercantile. Hopefully, the super, Mr. DeMarco, got that leak in my bathroom sink fixed while I was away. Usually, he's pretty good about repairs. But as he gets closer to retirement, I think his arthritis—"

She finally turned. "What do you want from me?"

What did he want?

Green eyes snapped at him. Ethan straightened at the verbal attack, but managed to keep what he hoped was a gentle smile on his face. "Well, for one thing, you could stop cringing in the corner like I'm going to take your head off. Or worse." If he introduced himself, he wouldn't exactly be a stranger anymore. "My name's Ethan Cross. And you're...?"

Pretty, round cheeks, whipped to a rosy color from the cold outside, tightened, along with an equally pretty mouth as she articulated her response. "Mind your own business."

She turned her back on him, resuming her closed stance in the far corner. So much for his first attempt to return to the real world. He'd spent the past 10 hours typing up reports and debriefing this last assignment to his boss at the precinct office.

He wasn't ready to think about the 24 hours before that.

Sure, he felt good about busting up a local drug syndicate and getting hundreds of thousands of dollars worth of speed off the streets. But one man was dead. And another was in the hospital with a slug from Ethan's own 9 mm wedged inside his gut.

He could still see the man's rheumy eyes, glaring up at Ethan from the floor of the bar where the final sting had taken place. He could still feel the man's spit, hitting his shoulder and condemning him. He could still hear the man's words, accusing Ethan of betraying his trust. How he'd counted on Ethan to protect him like a brother.

Ethan had wiped off the spit, ignored the accusations and read the man his rights while the paramedics were loading him onto an ambulance.

Oh yeah. This woman wanted nothing to do with a big, bad cuss like him.

A kind word or a welcoming smile was more than he could ask of her. Of anyone until he got this damn bust and the part he'd played so well out of his head.

Giving in to the aching fatigue that this last undercover case had left him with, he sighed deeply and surrendered to her need for privacy. When the elevator reached the fifth floor, he moved toward the sliding doors and nearly bumped into the woman. Surprised to discover she was getting off on the same floor, he stepped back—determined to show her he possessed a few gentlemanly qualities, despite his appearance. He gestured for her to precede him into the hallway.

The woman dashed out, her bag clutched to her chest like a life preserver, her key already in hand. Her skittish maneuvers to avoid any contact with him made Ethan feel both curious and guilty.

He was even more surprised when she stopped at the door right next to his. They turned and looked at each other—he, mildly curious; she, almost in shock.

The nameless blonde with the shoulder-length tousle of hair finally initiated a conversation. It sounded more like an accusation. "That's where you live?"

"I guess that makes us neighbors." Ethan grinned at the coincidence. The effect of which sent her into a panic as she rushed to get inside. He heard not one, but three locks slamming into place once the door closed behind her.

Ethan shook his head and let himself into his cold, lonely apartment.

So much for a warm "welcome home."

But Ethan Cross wasn't a detective for nothing. He liked a good mystery. He especially liked solving one.

Thoughts of finding out what made his reclusive new neighbor tick kept him awake until nearly dawn.

CHAPTER TWO

CALLIE LEANED BACK against the locked door and sucked in a cautious breath. Had he found her?

Her feet and back ached from the long hours of her shift at the Shamrock Bar. But the physical pain was nothing compared to the overwhelming panic that burned inside her chest.

The man in the elevator—Ethan Cross, he'd said his name was—had been so big. So male. So dangerous. He looked tough enough to shoot two men in cold blood.

Callie closed her eyes and saw again the image of her boss, Michael Revere, as she'd last seen him, slumped in his chair, blood turning the front of his crisp gray suit a dull red.

Twin gunshots reverberated in her memory as clearly as they had that night outside Michael's office.

The argument she'd overheard had been so vile, so full of accusation. And then the gunshots. She'd hidden behind a desk in the reception area when the door opened and one of his business associates, Russ McDowall, walked out.

He'd straightened his jacket as if cleaning up from an ugly fight, then exited through the main doors. She'd assumed she'd just ID'd the murderer. One glance at Michael's body and she'd run to call 911, then stayed hidden until the police arrived.

But when the cops showed up there was no body—
no blood. And then they found Russ dead....

She wasn't crazy. She wasn't!

The notes and phone calls proved that.

The man next door could be the killer. Even though
she'd cut her hair and changed her name and job, he
could have found her. He'd be waiting for the right
opportunity to silence her.

That was it!

Callie clutched her stomach and breathed easier,
sagging with relief. If the man next door was the murderer, he would have killed her already. He'd had
ample opportunity on that interminable ride to the
fifth floor.

She still didn't think she should trust him—but he
hadn't hurt her. Despite his temper when he'd forced
his way onto the elevator, he'd tried to strike up a
friendly conversation.

To tell the truth, she'd been unexpectedly intrigued
by the fresh scents of winter and man that had filled
the elevator. And the articulate sound of his low-
pitched voice had challenged her attempts to ignore
him. Under other—safer—circumstances, she might
have found the easy timbre of that voice comforting.

"There are no other circumstances," she repri-
manded herself out loud and forced herself away from
the door. She couldn't afford to be interested—even
remotely curious—about her neighbor. She needed to
be on guard at all times.

Out of habit, she reached inside her purse to the
one thing that offered her any semblance of security.
Her fingertips touched the cold, flat plastic of a computer disk. She'd been on her way to Michael's office
to ask him about the numbers that didn't add up when

she'd overheard the horrible accusations being flung back and forth behind the closed door.

The accounting on the disk might be nothing, or it might provide a motive for Michael's murder. But until she could figure out what the discrepancies meant, she intended to keep the information to herself. She'd already been dismissed by the police once. She wouldn't go to them again until she had proof of a crime.

With the disk safely tucked away in her purse, Callie tossed her coat over the back of a chair and stripped off her waitress uniform. Padding into the bathroom in just her underwear, she turned on the faucets in the tub and let the water run hot. While she waited for her bath to fill, she made cocoa in the microwave. She cuddled the mug between her chilled fingers and sipped the sweet, creamy liquid, savoring its warmth from the inside out.

Though the hour was late, she knew sleep would be an elusive thing. If nightmares didn't keep her awake, then sheer worry would. So she was still soaking in the tub, letting the moist heat ease the stiffness from her muscles, when the telephone rang in the living room. Despite the temperature of the water, goose bumps pricked her skin. She clutched her arms around her knees and curled into a ball, suddenly feeling ice-cold.

The only person who had her new number was her manager at the Shamrock. Before Callie decided he might be calling to ask her to work an extra shift, the answering machine clicked on and a voice, altered by some device to give it a robotic tone, began to speak.

"I saw you at the bar tonight, Miss Smith. Got your

number from the schedule in the workroom. Changing your name won't hide you forever.

"But don't worry. It's only a matter of time before I hunt you down."

"MORNING."

Callie jumped inside her coat at the smooth sound of the cheerful male greeting. She overrode the instinct to bolt back inside her apartment and pocketed her key.

Her behavior last night had probably already drawn unwanted attention to herself. This was a normal, human voice. Warm and a tad breathless. Not mechanical. Not threatening. She inhaled a steadying breath, wrapped her scarf around her neck and headed for the elevator without responding.

Ethan Cross pulled off a stocking cap and gloves and unlocked his door. He was coming back from a morning workout, judging by the gray sweats he wore. The narrow hallway filled with the warmth and honest sweat emanating from his big, rangy body. His heat and scent assailed her as she neared him, reaching out to her like a peace offering, or even a hug.

Callie slowed as she walked past, savoring the sensation of human contact, even if it was limited to her imagination. Last night's phone call had left her chilled to the bone. She'd left her family and friends behind when the first warning had arrived, and she'd been hiding out ever since. She was beginning to wonder if she'd ever be able to trust anyone again— to touch them, be held and touched by them. She wondered if she'd ever feel warm again.

For a moment, the loneliness and longing got the better of her common sense. She tipped up her chin.

She didn't speak at first; she only looked. The fatigue and polite distance in her neighbor's amber eyes tugged at her heartstrings. Surely a man that weary with the world lacked the strength or compunction to hurt her. "Good morning, Mr. Cross."

His solemn expression melted away into a gorgeous smile and Callie felt her own mouth stretching into a matching curve.

"Hey, you remembered my name." That such a little thing could make his day seemed to be an inordinate bit of power to have over a man. Over the past two weeks she hadn't dropped her guard enough to worry about making anyone's day. It felt good. "I didn't catch yours, though."

"Callie S-Smith." She'd almost slipped and said Sullivan. But if he picked up on her hesitation, he didn't let on.

"Do you always work the late shift at the bar?" he asked instead.

"What?"

That warm feeling of connectedness vanished in a heartbeat.

"Seems we're the two night owls around here. Thought it might be good to be familiar with each other's schedules. Provide a bit of neighborhood security. Water each other's plants. You know."

"How did you know where I work?" she demanded, hearing the threat of unwanted familiarity in his voice instead of the promised protection. She hadn't told him where she worked. She hadn't told him anything.

"I don't." He shrugged, drawing her attention to just how much bigger, stronger he was than she. "Your coat smelled like smoke, but you've got a beautiful smile, so I figured it wasn't you. Plus, you wore the standard black support shoes.'' His unshaven, angular face creased with a sheepish grin. ''I notice things about people.''

Callie retreated a step. ''Don't notice anything about me. Please.''

''Too late for that. I already took note of how your green eyes get little flecks of blue in them when you lose your temper.'' His smile vanished. ''And how you're scared to death of me.''

''I'm not—''

''Please. I'd rather you ignore me like you did last night than tell me lies.'' His broad shoulders sagged with some unseen weight. ''If you want your privacy, you got it. I've dealt with enough lies lately to last me a lifetime.''

With that cryptic comment he dismissed her and turned to open his door. She should be relieved that he was walking away, but instead, she was genuinely curious. ''What is it you do, Mr. Cross?''

''I'm a cop.''

CHAPTER THREE

CALLIE HAD DASHED to the elevator without looking back or saying goodbye. She hopped a city bus to the nearest library branch and paid some of her precious cash for a half hour on its computer. But she couldn't focus on the lists and numbers on the Revere Imports disk she had tucked into her purse.

A cop? After all her efforts to hide herself from the world, she'd moved in next to a cop? She'd never been one to believe in destiny, but she seemed to have a knack for ending up in the wrong place at the wrong time. She'd seen Michael dead. She'd seen Russ walk away from the scene.

She'd seen the looks of suspicion and outright pity in the eyes of Kansas City's finest.

Are you sure about what you saw, Miss Sullivan?

Yes! Michael was at his desk. He wasn't moving. There was blood....

But when the cops arrived, there was no Michael. No blood.

They'd taken pity on her then, tried to keep her hysteria at bay. She'd been so insistent about the argument she'd overheard that the police had driven her to Russ McDowall's house. They'd found Russ sitting in his car in the garage. Very bloody. Equally dead.

How well did you know the deceased, Miss Sullivan? Did you argue with him?

No! He argued with Michael. Russ said he'd kill him!

Then where's the body?

I don't know!

Callie buried her face in her hands, unable to shake the voices and images inside her head. If she hadn't been with the police at the time of Russ's murder, she'd be their prime suspect. As it was, they'd taken a phone number and thanked her for her time. They focused their investigation on Russ's transitory past, telling her they'd call if they had any more questions.

The only one who'd called since had been that sick, mechanical voice. I saw you at Revere's office. I saw you at McDowall's house. I don't like seeing you so much.

Would Ethan Cross report her whereabouts to his fellow officers? They'd probably share a good laugh over the crazy lady who had moved into his building.

If the police could track her down, that meant Michael's killer could, too. Hell. He'd already found out where she worked. He knew her phone number.

It was time to move on.

Callie removed the disk and hid in one of the stalls of the public rest room to count her money. Forty-six dollars.

She'd emptied her small savings to buy a month's rent on her apartment. She'd have to go to the Shamrock and pick up her paycheck, or rather, convince the manager John O'Herlihy to pay her early. Hopefully, she'd earned enough for a new place.

Twenty minutes later, Callie stepped off the bus, wrapped her scarf up around her neck and walked into a stiff, damp wind a block and a half to the Shamrock Bar. Feeling safe enough in the light of late afternoon, she cut across the near empty parking lot to the back entrance closest to John's office.

"John?" She rapped on the locked metal door and waited. "John?"

The dampness in the air took shape and turned to wet, heavy dollops of snow. Shivering inside her coat, Callie knocked again. "John? It's Callie. I know I'm early, but may I come in?"

No answer. Callie looked over her shoulder and scanned the parking lot, double-checking that she'd passed John's green pickup. A twinge of concern had her looking around in every direction, making sure that she was alone.

Maybe it was the cold creeping under her skin. Maybe it was the paranoia of the past two weeks, but Callie had the distinct impression she wasn't alone. Twin pools of imaginary heat scorched her back.

Someone was watching.

"John?" She didn't bother with knocking this time. She reached for the doorknob and twisted it. The door sprang open. Callie paused, peering into the darkness of the interior hallway. Something was wrong. "John?"

Before she could react, a figure dressed in black hurtled out of the shadows. He plowed into Callie, knocking her down onto the asphalt. Pain shot through the back of her head, spinning her vision out of control.

She was vaguely aware of her attacker pausing, then running away. But she noticed nothing more. As the winter slush soaked through to her skin, Callie's world faded to black.

CHAPTER FOUR

"I DON'T NEED an ambulance."

Callie repeated herself, appreciating the uniformed officer's earnest concern for the knot on the back of her head. His height and broad shoulders reminded her of her neighbor, Ethan Cross. But there the similarities ended. Though they were both cops, Josh Taylor wore his blond hair short and neat, and his blue eyes were filled with kindness. Ethan emanated something wilder, more on the edge.

His sad eyes had wanted something from her. Something she'd been too frightened to figure out. Something she had neither the time nor the liberty to give.

And while she might take comfort in Officer Taylor's concern, she couldn't forget that he was a cop. And cops ran checks. And if his check turned up a Calista Smith in the state ID system, her picture wouldn't be the one beside the name.

This interview needed to end before he asked to see her crudely forged ID card again.

She rose from the leather barstool, hiding her shaky legs by bracing her hand on the bar's brass trim. She offered him a reassuring smile. "I'm fine, Officer Taylor. If there's nothing else—?"

"Callie? What are you doing here?" John, her manager, dashed in through the back entrance. His black hair was plastered to his head with melting snow. He butted past Josh Taylor and squeezed her shoulders. His native brogue was in full force. "The officer outside said we'd been robbed."

He released her and turned to the uniformed officer. "I just stepped out for a few minutes. Ran my receipts up to the bank. Thank God the register was empty. Thieves cleaned me out big time last year." He spun back toward Callie, pulling off his black leather gloves. "He didn't hurt you, did he?"

John was just now making his bank deposit? Why hadn't he done it after closing last night? Like he had every other night she'd worked.

Callie shook aside the speculation. John was a rock when it came to running his bar and protecting his employees. But he was hopelessly absentminded when it came to numbers. She forced herself to smile. "A bump on the head is all. I didn't get a good look at the guy. He was wearing black, from his stocking mask down to his boots."

"Mr. O'Herlihy?" Taylor reminded John of his presence. "If you could do a walk-through with me? Make sure nothing's missing?"

"Of course." As Officer Taylor pocketed his notebook, John took Callie by the shoulders again. The pleading look on his face put her on guard. "I know it's been a rough afternoon, but can you work 'til close tonight? Angela called in earlier with the flu."

This morning she'd wanted nothing more than to leave this place. Someone—a patron, a co-worker— had gotten her phone number at the bar. Maybe instead of running away from the danger, she should use this opportunity to track down the connection between the Shamrock Bar and the mechanical voice on her machine.

The police didn't want to help her. Maybe she could do more than just study that disk to help herself.

"Callie?" John prompted.

She weighed the heavy pounding inside her skull with the light weight of her wallet and the opportunity at hand. Practicality beat out comfort. "Sure. Let me get some aspirin and dinner in me, then I'll start setting up the bar."

"You're a peach." He leaned in and gave her an unexpected peck on the lips. He thumbed over his shoulder at Officer Taylor. "I'd better go talk to this guy."

ETHAN PROPPED HIS FEET UP on the chair next to him and settled in with his cup of coffee in the Fourth Precinct's break room. He'd been catching up on paperwork all day, getting up to speed on the precinct's open cases, paying particular attention to anything related to his last drug bust.

"Hey, I heard Josh Taylor talked to the crazy lady."

"Who's that?"

Ethan couldn't help but eavesdrop on the two boisterous uniforms who had walked into the break room.

"You know, that lady who said she witnessed a murder, but there was no body." The two laughed and traded tall tales about her version of the crime scene and what the cops actually found. Nothing. "Today she reported a robbery. But there was no money missing."

"What was her name?"

Ethan tuned in with a sudden, unexpected interest. "Callie."

CALLIE HUNG UP HER APRON in the back room. She didn't know which hurt worse, her feet or her head. She'd worked eight hours straight—skipping her break in order to keep an eye on the bar's clientele.

All the regulars had been there—the two Freds who always started with whiskey shots and ended with beers and lecherous come-ons; Hank, the poor old man who sat by himself at the end of the bar; a coed bowling team that came in promptly at nine. Had one of them snuck into the workroom to find her number?

There were new faces, as well, men and women she recognized but hadn't put a name to. Maybe one of them had stopped by the night before and she'd just been too intent on keeping to herself to notice a particular interest in her.

And what about the part-time bartender, Seth? Or the other waitresses? Did Angela really have the flu? Or had she betrayed Callie to the man with the mechanical voice? Could she trust any of them?

She slipped her card into the time clock and punched out. There was her name, penned in John's clear, precise handwriting, followed by her phone number. Easy enough for anyone to slip into the back room to find.

Though the damage had already been done, she pulled a pen from her pocket and crossed out the numbers. She'd get her phone changed tomorrow and ask John to keep the new information to himself. The caller hadn't found her apartment yet.

Or so he'd said.

"Callie?" She jumped at John's voice in the hallway. He popped his head around the corner and smiled broadly. "Good. You're still here. Here's a little something extra for your tip jar." He slipped a $20 bill into the front pocket of her jeans, then let his hand linger a moment at her waist. Callie found herself backing away from the familiarity of his touch. Maybe his guilt had given their working relationship a more personal interest. "Thanks for helping out tonight. I can't tell you how sorry I am about the break-in. You probably saved me a fortune."

Callie slipped her punch card into its slot. "I thought you took the deposit to the bank this afternoon."

"From last night, yeah, but I keep cash in the safe for emergencies. Thanks to your timely arrival, the thief never found it."

She pulled her coat and scarf and purse from its peg and dressed herself for the cold outside. "I'm just glad no one was hurt. I was worried you were inside."

"You're such a sweet girl." John's Irish brogue teased her ear a moment before his hands closed around her shoulders. "I know you were in trouble when you came to me. I don't want to add to it. If there's anything I can do to help—"

"Thanks." Callie scooted away from the oddly uncomfortable sensation of his touch. Still, she knew his heart was in the right place. So she could smile as she faced him. "Right now, all I need is the job."

Outside, Callie breathed deeply, filling her head and lungs with the biting, refreshing air. She pulled her scarf around her ears and gazed up at the harsh circle of light that illuminated the back entrance. The snow had softened to crystalline flakes floating down to earth. But it wasn't the crisp winter wonderland that enthralled her.

It was the knowledge that just beyond that circle of light lay 30 feet of pitch-dark parking lot that she had to cross before she reached the nearest streetlight. Once she got to the street there'd be enough light to reach the bus stop. As long as the weirdos weren't out. And the 1:20 bus was on time.

It was just those first 30 feet...

Making a mental note to add a can of Mace to her meager shopping list, she stepped from the light into the shadows.

The parking lot was deserted except for John's truck and a black sports car. Normally, she walked straight from the door to the sidewalk. But even before Michael's death, she'd been trained to avoid walking too closely to unknown vehicles. So in her swift, determined stride, she headed for John's empty truck. She skirted the front fender and swung around toward the streetlight.

And screamed.

CHAPTER FIVE

A TALL DARK FIGURE emerged from the shadows and reached for her.

She lunged with her fingernails and pounded with her fists as powerful hands wrapped around her arms and pulled her toward the bulk of a man's chest. "Callie, it's me."

Curling dark hair and the khaki-green trench coat finally registered. Callie froze, lifting her gaze to patient amber eyes framed by rich brown lashes. "Ethan?"

He was so big up close like this. So masculine. He smelled of clean winter air and faint male musk. Callie breathed in the comforting, tantalizing scent, orienting herself to the idea that he hadn't hurt her. But she couldn't afford to savor the fleeting sensation of inexplicable safety. She thumped his shoulder one last time for scaring her so before twisting free of his unresisting grip. "What the hell are you doing here?"

An amused smile split the shadowed contours of his jaw. "I'm headed home. You need a lift?"

"I can get home just fine by myself, thank you."

"It's after one in the morning. Do you know what kind of loonies are out this time of night?" She briefly wondered if he counted himself among the strange creatures that lurked in the city after midnight.

"This parking lot is a crime just waiting to happen. You're female. You're alone. Why invite trouble?"

"You're the only trouble I'm dealing with right now. If you'll excuse me." She gripped her collar edges together at her throat and circled around him, leaving behind a frisson of electricity that had started with fear, but continued with an awareness of him that could only bring her trouble.

"I know about the attempted robbery this afternoon. I know you got hurt."

Callie halted in her tracks. Though he made no noise, she felt the heat of him moving in behind her.

"You told the officers on the scene your name was Callie Smith. But that's a lie, isn't it?" She remembered his words outside their apartments—and his sad, weary eyes when he said he preferred her silence to her lies. But how could she tell him the truth? How could she risk telling another cop the truth? "You're the crazy lady people are talking about down at the precinct. Callie Sullivan."

"You're quite the detective." Her sarcasm faded on a twinge of panic and she turned. "You won't tell anyone, will you? Especially Mr. DeMarco. I registered the apartment under Smith. I can't afford to move yet."

Tiny lines formed beside his eyes. "Why do you have to move?"

He might have guessed her name, but the secret threats she would not share. "I have to go now. I'll miss the bus."

He caught her by the elbow and stopped her. "I'll drive you home."

Callie jerked away. "No."

"We're going to the same place."

A third voice cut short their argument. "Callie, is there a problem?"

Great. John was still in his caretaker mode. Now she had to steal away from two overprotective males.

But before she could make an excuse, Ethan had spun around. He had a good three inches of height over John, and he used it to full advantage as the two men sized each other up. "I'm Ethan Cross, K.C.P.D. Who are you?"

"John O'Herlihy." He had to shift a step to the right and look around Ethan to make eye contact with her. "I run the Shamrock." He slowly drew his focus back to the cop. "Is this about this afternoon?"

"Do you always let your female employees walk alone at night?"

"What?"

Enough. Callie moved between them, waving John back to his truck. "Everything's fine. Ethan is my neighbor."

"Yeah?"

The two men continued to watch each other in silent male posturing. One accusatory, the other defensive. She didn't need this kind of attention.

Neither man moved until she opened the door of the black car. She finally conceded to Ethan's will.

"He's giving me a ride home."

ETHAN GUIDED his Thunderbird through the deceptively quiet streets. Just like the woman sitting in the seat next to him, he knew mysterious and possibly dangerous secrets were hidden behind the silent facade.

"You are the unfriendliest woman I've ever met."

Callie crossed her arms and clutched her leather purse to her chest. "Take the hint."

He didn't know whether to laugh or rail at the dismissal in her closed posture. He opted for a rational argument. "All right, then. So I'm driving you home. I'm a cop doing my job. To serve and protect."

"I don't need your protection."

He noted the nervous sweep of her tongue across her lips, and the way her blue-green eyes darted his direction, watching him even though she kept her face glued to the front windshield. "You need something, lady. You're so keyed up with guarding your back and every word you say, you can't think straight." He took a fortifying breath and turned into the Mercantile's parking garage before he continued. "I work under cover. I recognize the signs. The strain of pretending to be somebody you're not."

She reached up with trembling fingers and tucked a lock of what he'd privately dubbed that "just had sex" hair of hers behind her ear. Though he braced himself for the denial that was sure to follow, he let himself enjoy the image of her silver and gold tresses falling about her face with the abandon of a woman who'd been thoroughly kissed by a man and didn't want to erase the imprint of his hands on her.

Such wanton abandonment would seem to be an alien concept for his tightly controlled neighbor lady, but he nevertheless allowed himself a moment to fantasize that he was the man who had kissed her so well and loosened that cautious reserve of hers.

After he'd pulled into his parking space and turned off the engine, she finally scooted a quarter turn in her seat. Here it came.

"Is that why you look the way you do? To work

under cover? I mean, those clothes, and your hair—
and always looking like you need a shave.''

Okay. Not what he expected. Where was she going
with this? ''Something wrong with the way I look?''

''No, it's—it's scary. You look…like you could
kill a man.''

The observation struck home, nagged his conscience. For a few moments he fell into the pit of
defensive guilt he warred with whenever he came off
an assignment. It was his job to get close to people
and then betray them.

He felt the guilt rising to the surface, tensing his
expression, coloring his words. He quickly climbed
out of the car before he gave vent to his churning
emotions. Before he forgot his efforts to assuage that
guilt by doing something as simple and honorable as
giving a lady a safe ride home. Giving her the benefit
of the doubt when office gossip had labeled her un-
balanced and paranoid.

Then he realized what had just happened. Callie
Smith—correction, Callie Sullivan—had just shared
an honest opinion. Voluntarily. For the first time,
she'd trusted him enough to speak her mind.

He might look the part, but maybe he wasn't such
an ogre, after all.

Ethan circled the rear of the car, instinctively
checking his surroundings for any sign of a threat.
Callie already had her door open, but he reached for
her hand and helped her out of the low-slung car. He
paused, unable to hide the hint of a smile on his face.
''Thank you.''

Her sweet green eyes frowned in confusion. ''That
wasn't much of a compliment.''

''But it was an honest answer.'' Fantasy and reality

mixed together inside his head. He leaned over and kissed her cheek. His nose sifted into the golden tendrils of her hair, filling his head with the pungent aromas of smoke and alcohol she worked with, as well as the fresh citrus scent that was her own. ''Thanks.''

She brushed her gloved fingertips against her cheek as he pulled away. ''I'm never going to understand you, am I?''

In her hushed voice, it wasn't much of an accusation.

Ethan locked the car and took her by the elbow, escorting her safely into the lobby of the Mercantile. ''I suspect you and I have more in common than either of us realizes. I do have one question for you, though.''

''What's that?''

''Why are you lying to the police?''

CHAPTER SIX

WHY?

The man had the audacity to kiss her and then ask why she lied?

Oh, I don't know. Maybe to save my life!

She didn't for one moment think Ethan was talking about the attempted robbery. He'd heard about her "supposed" murder case.

Callie wished she had taken the stairs. Surely, they'd be faster than this damnably slow elevator. At least she'd be able to put some space between her and Ethan.

Her skin still tingled where his lips had touched her. She could still remember the gentle tugging along her scalp where his beard had tangled with her hair. She could hear the whiskey smoothness of his voice thanking her. And her heart still burned with the swift expansion of tender feelings that had engulfed her when she saw the light of interest and life click on in his warm brown eyes.

She'd moved to the opposite corner, but the air in the tiny elevator seemed to consume itself with the heat from their bodies. She'd been so stupid to drop her guard. To give in to curiosity. To even think about turning her head as he kissed her cheek so she could taste his lips on hers.

Stupid. Stupid. Stupid.

She whirled around, giving vent to her temper. "The only thing I lied about was my name. I heard two gunshots. I saw Michael's dead body."

"I read the case report. The CSI team found no evidence of foul play in Revere's office."

"Then they didn't do their job right!"

Callie spun back around, pushing at the doors as they slid open. She stalked down the hallway ahead of Ethan, digging through her purse for her keys. Her head throbbed, her ego stung, her thoughts swirled in confusion. She hadn't expected Ethan to believe her, but she'd never expected him to use chivalry or a wounded heart against her.

As she fumbled blindly through her oversize purse, she dumped out a lipstick that rolled across the floor. When her fingers finally found the keys, she grabbed and pulled.

Clunk. Callie froze.

Ethan bent down and picked up the unmarked computer disk before she reached it. She knew her sudden nonchalance didn't fool him for a minute. Her reaction had already given her away. "It holds the work schedules from the bar. I forgot I had it."

"Callie?"

"Go away and leave me alone."

She snatched the disk from his hand and stormed into her apartment.

She tripped over the sofa cushion that had fallen to the floor.

The shredded sofa cushion with its foam stuffing scattered across her living-room rug.

And the broken floor lamp that lay on its side.

And the dresser drawers turned upside down and tossed into a pile.

Callie hugged her purse around her middle, backing away from the man-made destruction of her temporary home.

She must have cried out. She hadn't heard the noise through her shock, but she must have screamed.

Because suddenly Ethan was there, gun drawn. The long black barrel swept across the room. He curved his arm around her shoulders and positioned himself between her and the violation of her apartment.

When he would have moved away, she turned her face into his chest and snatched up handfuls of his soft canvas coat. "Don't leave me."

"Okay, babe." Her arms moved around his waist and he tucked her closer to his body. His warmth and strength breathed security into her.

But then he pushed her away. He apologized with a gentle touch upon her cheek. "I need to check the other rooms."

He moved stealthily through the kitchen, bathroom and, finally, her bedroom. Each room had been completely and utterly destroyed.

Her intruder had been searching for something.

But Callie knew he hadn't found it.

"There's a message on your machine." Ethan's arm was around her again. His firm voice coaxed her out of her stupor. "I need to listen to it."

"No—" But he had already tapped the play button with the tip of his gun.

That all-too-familiar, chillingly nonhuman voice filled the air.

"I saw you at the Shamrock with your boyfriend tonight."

Her boyfriend? Did he mean Ethan? Or had he

spied on John O'Herlihy's attempts to get friendly with her? Oh, God. Could it be John himself?

"If you want to keep a man, you have to give him what he wants. If you want to keep me happy, you have to give me what I want."

CALLIE HOVERED in the doorway, watching the tall, blond man in the black K.C.P.D. jacket standing in the middle of her apartment. Ethan had called a friend, CSI Investigator Mac Taylor, to survey the crime scene personally. And though her landlord, Mr. DeMarco, had offered to put her up in another apartment, or come spend the night with him and his wife, Callie had declined.

She needed to be here. She needed to find answers. She needed this senseless stalking to end.

Mac stood in the center of her living room, the gray eyes behind his gold-rimmed glasses seeming to be the only thing moving as he studied each nook and cranny from ceiling to floor.

Though impatient with the lack of activity, Callie held her tongue. She hugged her arms around herself, shivering despite the fact she had Ethan's big trench coat hanging around her shoulders, covering her down to her ankles. It wasn't winter that left her cold.

Crime doesn't happen here, Mr. DeMarco had insisted, appalled that one of his tenants had been violated this way. It isn't the best neighborhood, sure, but crime doesn't happen in my building.

But it did.

Callie shivered again. All at once, Ethan, who'd never been far from her side since discovering the break-in, was right there, spreading his hand at the small of her back. "Are you okay?"

She stifled a desperate laugh. "Sure. I'm the crazy lady, remember? Everything you see here didn't really happen."

Mac finally looked her way, his eyes narrowed with curiosity at her sarcasm. "Any idea what he or she was looking for?"

"A computer disk." Ethan answered the question before Callie had a chance. "She had it with her in her purse."

She didn't appreciate him giving away her secrets so freely to strangers. "How—"

"Am I right?" There was no smile on his face. "This is the time for the truth."

Callie's flash of temper dissipated on her next breath, leaving her weary right down to her bones. "It's an accounting record from Revere Imports. The numbers and inventory don't add up. I was taking it to Michael when I heard him arguing with Russ McDowall, one of our customs brokers. And then there were the gunshots and…"

Ethan's arm slipped around her waist as her voice trailed off. He pulled her to his side, sharing his uncompromising strength. She held herself stiff for only a moment, then surrendered. Accepting the support he offered, she softened against him.

"I was working late, trying to make the numbers balance," she continued. "Somebody was stealing from the company. If Michael found out…"

Mac didn't need her to spell out a motive for murder. "I'll want to see that disk."

Callie nodded. Mac knelt beside one of the shredded sofa cushions and resumed his inspection. "This was cut with a short, dull blade. Probably a pocketknife."

"In the wrong hands, a pocketknife can do as much damage as a stiletto." Ethan's observation wasn't reassuring.

Now Mac was sniffing a scrap of the faded upholstery.

"What is it?" Ethan asked.

"Spice and alcohol." Callie straightened when Mac's intelligent, all-seeing gaze settled on her. "Do you wear perfume?"

"Not anymore. I didn't bring much with me when I moved in here. I do use scented shampoo and body wash."

Mac shook his head. "Not strong enough. Since you live alone, I'm guessing what I smell is the perp."

Callie frowned with confusion. "This isn't how—" She clamped her mouth shut, stopping herself from sharing her confusion. Mac was the expert here, not her.

"What?" Ethan prompted.

"This isn't how the investigators checked Michael's office."

"What do you mean?" Mac stood, focusing his curiosity on her once more.

She'd wondered at the bustle of activity she'd seen that night, but the officers on the scene had shooed aside her questions and sent her back to her office. "They moved things around, put black dust over almost everything, took lots of pictures."

"The dust is to lift fingerprints," Mac explained. "What do you mean they 'moved things'?"

"They opened drawers, moved his desk and chair, lifted the plastic pad protecting the rug. I guess they were looking for—'' Callie trembled, leaning back against Ethan's arm ''—bloodstains.''

"But they didn't find any, did they?" asked Mac.

"No." Callie looked from Ethan to Mac and back to Ethan. Their indulgent expressions patiently waited for her to explain the impossible. "I saw blood on Michael's clothes and his chair. But when I went back to talk to the investigators, there was nothing there. Nothing.

"How does a dead body just get up and walk away?"

CHAPTER SEVEN

"Do you know the Michael Revere case, Mac?" Ethan asked.

Callie watched Mac Taylor's gaze drift a million miles away, as if checking an internal catalog of information. He startled her when he blinked. But he had clearly tapped into the info he'd wanted. "The scene was clean. One of my assistants, Jeff Ringlein, headed up that investigation. He told me the place was spotless. No evidence of a crime."

"That's old news." Ethan's smooth voice provided a defense before she could react to the unintentional gibe. "I believe Callie when she says she heard gunshots and found her boss's body. Trashing her apartment like this should prove she witnessed something."

An unexpected burden seemed to lift from her shoulders and she breathed deeply for the first time in weeks. She hadn't realized how badly she needed someone to believe in her. Heartened by Ethan's support, she reached for his fingers at her waist and wrapped them up in a tight grip of her own.

Mac nodded. "Callie, this is important." She lifted her chin, wary, but ready to answer a serious question about Michael's death. "Did the investigators move the furniture before or after they dusted for prints?"

Callie thought back to that awful night. "After. Why?"

"Clean I can handle. Spotless makes me suspicious."

"What does that mean?" she asked, catching the knowing look Mac exchanged with Ethan.

"It means when I'm done here, I'll call the judge and see about opening Revere's office for another inspection."

She frowned, still not making the connection. "But the other investigators didn't find a body, blood, or prints. What would you be looking for?"

Mac smiled smugly. "Cleaners."

"Huh?"

Ethan's deductive skills were working in time with Mac's. "Once you discovered Michael Revere's body, did you stay with it?"

"No." A chill rippled down her spine, flashing back to when she'd opened that door and found all that blood. She squeezed her eyes shut, but the image became more vivid.

Suddenly, a pair of warm, firm lips pressed against her temple. A rasp of beard caressed her cheek and her eyes fluttered open. The horrific image vanished in the reality of Ethan's warm brown gaze washing over her.

"It's okay, babe. Take your time."

She didn't want to look away. But something about brawny Ethan's surprisingly gentle care gave her the strength to continue. "There was too much blood. All over Michael's suit and chair. I couldn't stay. I went down the hall to my office and used the phone there to call the police. That's where I stayed until they arrived."

"How long was that?" Mac asked.

"Twenty minutes."

Ethan nodded. "That's plenty of time to clean house. Especially if the killer planned ahead."

At last Callie understood. The possibility of finding a clue to prove she hadn't imagined the whole thing suffused her with energy. "You should be able to find traces of cleaning compounds where the killer scrubbed the chair and the floor pad underneath. Right?"

She cringed at the chaos surrounding them. "So why didn't he clean up after himself here?"

"We'll find that out, too." Mac pulled a camera from his metallic bag and moved to specific locations in her apartment he must have pinpointed earlier. Now he worked with swift efficiency, jotting notes and snapping pictures. "Physical evidence doesn't lie."

"C'mon, babe. You must be exhausted." Ethan's arm tightened imperceptibly around her, pulling her into the hallway. "Let's let Mac do his job."

"I'm not ti—"

She punctuated her excitement over Mac's determination to find the truth with a big yawn.

"I saw that."

Ethan touched his fingers to her chin and turned her face up to his. His amber eyes gleamed with a searching light that took in the droop of her eyelids and her self-conscious smile. "I want to know if he finds out anything."

"It'll be a few hours yet. All we could do is watch right now."

"But—" He pressed a finger to her lips, silencing her weak protest. Though his gaze never left her face, he spoke to Mac. "Do you need me for anything else, Mac?"

"Not right now. I'll stop in if I do."

"Knock first." Mesmerized by the intensity of Ethan's gaze, Callie couldn't look away. "I'm putting Callie to bed."

Taking Callie to bed had been a rhetorical phrase. But as the warmth and scent and feel of her at his side breathed life into his weary senses, the idea took on a literal appeal.

Callie Sullivan was a smart, pretty woman. Her vulnerable situation pricked at all his protective male instincts. And when she looked at him, really looked at him—out of temper or curiosity or concern—he felt connected to life in a way he hadn't for a long time.

They had enough in common that he understood her guarded defense. But there was something more than a kindred spirit at work here. Her fragile trust touched his lonely heart. She needed him as a cop, sure. When he'd heard her scream, years of training had poured adrenaline through his veins. He'd become one of those fabled blue knights, living up to his vow to protect the innocent.

She'd thrown herself into his arms then, clung to him for security when she'd been too frightened to do more than react. But later, after she'd conquered her fear and insisted on watching Mac Taylor's investigation, she'd reached for his hand. She'd sought out the simplest of contact with him.

Callie also needed him as a man.

It was a tempting thought.

But he'd felt the goose egg on the back of her head. He'd seen the size of her yawn.

Finding his way back to the real world in Callie's arms would have to wait for another day.

Ethan sat Callie at the kitchen table and pushed up the sleeves of his brown sweater. Considering recent events, he left his holster strapped across his shoulders with his gun in easy reach. Then he washed his hands and rummaged through the cupboards and fridge. He'd hardly earn a spot on his own cooking show with his bad-boy-in-the-kitchen look, but he could get the job done.

"What are you doing?" Her sleepy voice danced along his nerve endings like a lover's whisper, prolonging his going-to-bed fantasy.

"I'm fixing some cocoa. You've been wearing a coat all night. I figured you could use something to warm you."

"You have cocoa?" He laughed at the childlike interest that perked up her expression.

"Yeah. I make it the old-fashioned way my mama does." He measured out powdered cocoa, sugar, and milk and heated the mixture on the stove.

Later, as they sipped their drinks, Callie relaxed and they chatted about mundane things, like the snow and aching feet and whether or not the Royals could ever put together another championship team. Ethan's apartment seemed cozy for a change—with Callie sharing the space with him.

He had to admire her stamina. She'd been the victim of not one, but two break-ins in the past 24 hours. And though she hadn't really talked about it, he suspected that message on her answering machine hadn't been the first threat she'd received. She didn't complain. She endured. Against serious odds she kept her head, her conviction, and even brightened his world with an occasional smile.

They ended up sitting side-by-side on the couch. When the cocoa was gone and the warmth had finally left her mug, Callie handed Ethan the cup and he set it on the coffee table beside his. The conversation had ended, but there was no awkward silence as Ethan slipped his arm around her shoulders and pulled her to his side, where she seemed to fit so perfectly.

He chuckled softly at the goose bumps dotting her forearms beneath the elbow-length sleeves of her pearl gray sweater. "Don't you ever get warm?"

"August." She treated him to one of those rare smiles. "That's the one month of the year I don't wear socks to bed."

There was the bed thing again.

Ethan's body was suddenly generating enough heat for both of them. He needed to move before he overstepped the boundaries of their neighborly relationship. "Callie—"

"Don't." He made a valiant effort to move away, but she turned, bracing one hand on the burning hardness of his thigh, and cupping his cheek with the other. "I feel it, too." At this angle the rounded swell of her breast pressed against his chest. But it was the raw need shining in her sweet green eyes that suckerpunched him right in the gut. "I don't know if this is the right time or place, but—

"I want you to kiss me. For real this time. On the lips."

CHAPTER EIGHT

ETHAN HAD NO INTENTION of denying the lady's request.

Catching the tip of her chin with his finger, he angled her mouth toward his.

He meant their first kiss to be gentle and reverent, a patient learning of each other's shape and style. But something sizzled at that very first touch. Her lips parted beneath his, binding her to him with a mad electricity that arced between them.

Ethan speared his fingers into her silver-gold hair, taking special care to avoid her injury. The citrus-scented tendrils fell like silk between his fingers, a sensuous counterpoint to the electric heat meeting his tongue as he swept inside her mouth.

He tasted the sweet chocolate on her breath and reveled in the sweeter taste of Callie herself.

God, he hadn't kissed a woman—hadn't loved a woman—for real, not as part of some sting, for so long. This was real. Callie was real.

His hard, hungry response to her willing kiss was equally real.

And in his feverish brain he was cogent enough to recognize that he wasn't the only one with this fiery need to connect. Callie's fingers had twisted into his hair, tugging his face to a spot where she could graze her lips along his jaw, nip at the point of his chin.

He slid his hands down her back and tormented her with the same scudding exploration of her soft, sensitized skin.

"Ethan…" His name was a breathy plea that scorched him clear down to his groin. Her hands circled his head, clutched at his shoulders as she tried to align herself in a less awkward position. Again, Ethan obliged the lady, slipping his hands beneath her bottom and lifting her onto his lap.

In just reward, Callie curled her arms around his neck, rubbing her pebbled breasts against the frictional plane of his chest. Her mouth opened beneath his in a combustible mix of demand and surrender. Ethan groaned at the sensation of being consumed by Callie Sullivan's fire.

He wanted her. Now. He needed the release of healthy, normal life he'd find buried deep inside her body.

But he couldn't. It was too soon. First kiss. He forced the words into his rational mind, taking control of his body's instinctive desire. "Callie."

He slid his hands to the more neutral position of her waist, but still found her curves hot to the touch. He tipped his face to the ceiling, purposefully moving his mouth beyond the temptation of hers.

She nuzzled the pounding pulse in his neck and Ethan fought the urge to reconnect the powerful current still sparking between them.

"You're tired, babe." He kneaded her shoulders, pushing a bit of distance between them. "You've been through too much today to deal with this."

"No, I—" A yawn, bigger than the one that had clued him in to her fatigue earlier, mocked her protest. As exhaustion overwhelmed her own desires, Ethan cuddled her close, adjusting her weight in his lap so his own body cooled. She pulled her arms to the front of his sweater, but in an unspoken gesture of trust, made no attempt to move away.

"I'm warm," she whispered against his neck. He felt her smile on his skin like a tender caress. "I'm finally warm."

The side benefit of their unexpected flare of passion amused him. But she allowed little time to enjoy the humor of the situation. Moments later, Callie had dozed off against his shoulder. Her soft snore was too sweet. A swell of tender responsibility eased the unfulfilled heat of his body.

Ethan carried her to his bed. He removed her shoes and belt and unsnapped her jeans before tucking the comforter around her.

As he sat beside her and watched her sleep, it registered that she wasn't wearing her uniform. Maybe she hadn't been expecting to work. Or didn't have time to go home and change after foiling the robbery at the Shamrock.

Ethan's professional instincts reawakened. Had the delay been intentional? Had someone planned a phony robbery to keep her away from her apartment so he or she had ample opportunity to ransack it?

Or was Callie the break-in's intended victim?

The coincidences didn't sit well in his stomach. He brushed a kiss across Callie's cheek, then went to the couch and tried to make his long body fit there.

He needed some sleep to keep his senses sharp. Tomorrow he was going to pay a visit to the Shamrock Bar.

ETHAN AWOKE with a crick in his back from trying to fit his long form on the short couch. But the stiffness faded as other observations touched his senses. He heard the sizzle of food frying in a pan. And the tantalizing smells of maple and cinnamon teased his nose and whet his appetite.

With a shot of adrenaline he was suddenly wide-awake. He swung his bare feet to the floor and checked his holster beneath the pillow he'd used. Then he shoved his fingers through his hair, combing it into a semblance of order, as he snuck out to the kitchen.

Thank God. Callie was safe, in one piece, and apparently cooking up a feast.

"'Morning, neighbor.''

Her body jerked as if he'd startled her. But the smile she greeted him with indicated it was a pleasant surprise. "Good morning."

Ethan questioned the rush of pleasure and serenity that swept through him at the homey picture she created. Was this what real life was like? Waking up to a beautiful woman? Sharing simple things like breakfast and bed-head hair?

He sniffed the golden slices of bread she lifted from the pan. "French toast?"

Callie turned off the stove and carried two plates to the table. "I may not make it the way your mama does, but it's edible."

"It looks delicious." She looked even better. Though she wore the same jeans and sweater as yesterday, her hair had been freshly washed, giving the ash-blond strands a distinctly silver glow as they dried and poufed around her face in that sexy disarray he found so irresistible.

"Mac slipped a note under your door. I put it on the table."

Ethan finally tore his gaze from her delightful morning vigor and read the note. "He thinks your break-in was an impromptu search. The perp wanted to find you as much as that disk. He doesn't advise you being alone until he can get into Revere's office and pinpoint a suspect. He must be on to something."

His words doused the energy in the room, plunging it into silence. When he looked up, Callie was hugging her arms around her waist again, in her habitual posture of self-defense. She shouldn't have to be afraid like that. She shouldn't have to protect herself against every curveball life threw her way.

"Ah, babe, I'm sorry." Ethan tossed the note onto the table and reached for her. He uncrossed her arms and pulled her wrists behind his back, stepping into her embrace. "If you're scared and need to hold on to something," he whispered, "hold on to me."

"Why is this happening?"

"I don't know. But I want you to understand that you're not alone anymore. I'm here with you. And I'll stay as long as you need me."

"As my friendly neighbor?"

Blue flecks danced in her green eyes and he lost himself in the vulnerable need he saw there.

"Neighbor. Protector." Something more? He kept the newly formed wish to himself and opted for the chance to make her smile. "Think of a cop next door as a cheap security system."

The expression in her eyes changed, but she didn't smile. "You're more than that, Ethan." She cradled his jaw between the palms of her hands, letting her fingertips stroke the hills and hollows of his craggy face. "So much more."

She rose up on tiptoe and pressed her lips to his. "Good morning, neighbor."

"Morning." He kissed her then, wrapping his arms around her, tenderly consuming the welcoming sweetness of her, wishing he could start every day of his life in the reviving heaven of her arms.

Moments later, Callie broke the kiss. She slid her arms around his waist and snuggled against him. "Thank you."

Ethan willingly held her close, rubbing his chin at the crown of her head. "For what?"

"I was so tired last night, so crazy with everything that's going on—" He felt her cheek flush with heat against his neck. "I was afraid I'd only dreamed about kissing you. I wasn't sure even—" she tried to scoot away, but he wouldn't let her leave the circle of his arms "—if we made love."

"Don't worry, babe." He heard his own voice drop to a husky pitch. "You'll know when I make love to you."

Callie trembled at his promise. She leaned back against his arms and looked him straight in the eye. "Then show me."

CHAPTER NINE

CALLIE ABSORBED Ethan's possessive kiss. She wrapped her arms around his daunting shoulders and buried her fingers in the sable waterfall of his hair.

He challenged her to open up her mouth, her body, her very soul—and accept the healing power of a man and woman sharing their most elemental needs.

He held her with such tender care, kissed her with such feverish desire. She wanted to lose herself in this incendiary passion, rediscover her feminine strengths after so many days of doubting her own sanity. She wanted to show Ethan that she trusted him. And she sensed that this brave, dangerous man needed to be trusted. Just as she had needed someone to believe in her, Ethan needed someone to believe in him.

Callie lifted herself into his kiss, stretching her body along his, savoring the delicious differences between his hard angles and her soft curves—and how she blossomed and heated in all the places that he touched.

His callused hands slid beneath her sweater, skimming circles along her skin like the ticklish rasp of a cat's tongue. Goose bumps prickled her flesh.

The rich sound of his laughter tickled her ears and seeped into the barren confines of her heart. "You're cold again," he teased. "I'd better see what I can do to warm you up."

She didn't correct him about her sensitized reaction to his needy touches. He cupped her bottom and lifted her up to his budding heat, matching that most tender part of her to that most masculine part of his.

His smooth voice had grown hoarse with desire. "Are you sure about this?"

In answer, she wrapped her legs around him. "It may be the only thing I'm sure of."

With her ankles linked behind his waist, he carried her into the bedroom. Callie took no heed of the chill in the air as they stripped each other of their clothes, stealing precious moments to greedily explore each new treasure as it was exposed.

Impatient heartbeats later he was on top of her, covering her with his hardness and heat. He pulled the comforter around them both, cocooning them in a haven of longing and need.

"I want you now," he whispered against her breast before closing his hot, moist mouth over the straining peak. Callie nearly buckled beneath him right then. But she remembered the haunted look in his eyes, the soul of a man who needed to find his way back to the world.

In the ultimate gesture of her trust, she opened herself and invited him deep inside her. She wound her legs around his hips and hugged him close to her heart. "Now, Ethan. I'm yours now."

With one powerful thrust, she shattered all around him in a fiery conflagration that drained them both. And when Ethan collapsed beside her and swallowed her up into his arms, she sensed the winter had forever melted from her lonely heart.

"THERE ARE ADVANTAGES to being night owls." Ethan's voice was laced with humor as he whispered against her hair.

Callie sprawled beside him, his shoulder serving as her pillow. With their legs entwined and her arm thrown across his chest, she felt deliciously warm and thoroughly loved.

"What advantages are those?" she asked, kissing the sensitive underside of his chin.

She felt the answering tremor dance along his skin. He hugged her tighter. "We can stay in bed all day making love."

"Ethan." She swatted playfully at him. He kissed her passionately in retribution.

They'd already showered and made love twice, and she'd been content to laze the day away in the ephemeral security of Ethan's arms.

Callie suddenly stiffened. The entire day? She sat up, clutching the comforter to her chest, sweeping the hair from her eyes and scanning the room for a clock. "What time is it?"

"Ten after four."

"I have to be at work by five!" She slipped from the bed and started to dress.

Ethan sat up in bed. "I don't want you back at the Shamrock. Not until we know who tried to rob the place, not until we find out who's after you. I know how a killer's mind works. He'll be watching you."

She hooked her bra, then whirled around, indignant at his imperious command. "Just because you're some kind of supercop, you can't tell me what to do."

His mouth thinned in a grim warning. "Wanna bet?"

CALLIE POURED three rum and colas, sparing a glance for the man who shadowed her before picking up the tray.

Ethan had nursed the same beer all night back at the corner table, watching her movements as she served drinks. He sat with his long legs sticking out from under the table, forcing passersby to walk a wide berth around him.

He needn't have bothered. With that bulky trench coat and tough, unshorn face, he exuded an aura of lethal power that demanded caution and distance, if not respect.

But what frightened Callie most were his eyes. The laughing amber gaze that had darkened like fine cognac when passion overtook him had been replaced by cold, soulless eyes. Eyes that showed no connection to the world around him.

Was this the real Ethan Cross? A dangerous, closed-up undercover cop? A man who controlled his world—and the people in it—wherever and however he could in order to survive?

Maybe she could trust such a man with her life. But it didn't seem wise to trust her heart to someone who could turn his emotions on and off. A man who could turn a day of fragile trusts into a night of distant guardianship.

She walked past Ethan's table, feeling his deceivingly nonchalant stare on her. Guilt warred with anger and regret inside her. As much as she resented his high-handed tactics, she had used those very same strengths and skills to find comfort and security.

Her time with Ethan had been a beautiful illusion. But she wasn't safe. Not yet. She wasn't free to love.

And he didn't seem able to love.

She might have surrendered her body to him, but

she hadn't surrendered her spirit. With her temper brewing, she set the glasses on the table with more force than necessary, sloshing one drink over a customer's hand and earning a teasing flirtation. "You're gonna have to do more than get me wet if you want a tip, sugar."

"Drop dead."

Callie walked away from the leering taunts that followed, disgusted with the controlling tactics of men in general. When could she have her old life back? The one where she was in charge of her own destiny?

Case in point. As she reached Ethan's table, he stood, unfolding himself to ominous proportions and blocking her path.

"They may be drunken jerks, but they're harmless," she defended the insulting patrons, thinking Ethan had gone on alert to protect her.

But he had no comment about them. "You close in less than an hour. Don't go anywhere without me. I'm going to have a little talk with your boss."

"Take all the time you want. I'll find my own way home."

"You're not going back to your apartment alone. Either you ride home with me or I follow the bus."

Callie opened her mouth to challenge his perfunctory order. But he strode away, turning down the hallway to John's office. She clamped her mouth shut, angry with herself for overreacting. He was just doing his job. Maybe that was all he could find it in his heart to do.

ETHAN FOUND John O'Herlihy in the stockroom, cutting open boxes of hard liquor. With a pocketknife. He'd never liked coincidences. He didn't think he liked a man who took so little responsibility for his female employees' safety, either.

"That blade looks pretty dull," Ethan observed, watching O'Herlihy saw through tape and cardboard.

"It gets the job done." He set six bottles of Irish whiskey on his cart, then reached for a box marked "Imported Rum." He responded to a question Ethan had asked earlier. "I usually take the deposit in after we close at night. But Angela had gone home sick, and we worked extra late closing the bar. That's why I waited until the next day."

"Do you always leave your back door unlocked? There were no signs of forced entry."

O'Herlihy straightened his shoulders in a huff. "If you're suggesting my carelessness is what got Callie hurt, think again. I've got fond feelings for that girl. I locked the door when I left."

Ethan wondered if O'Herlihy possessed enough Irish charm to lie to his face, or if the man was telling the truth. "Then who else has a key to the building?"

CHAPTER TEN

CALLIE GRABBED on to the door handle while Ethan steered the Thunderbird through the quiet streets of Kansas City at two in the morning. His sharp turns and rudimentary stops were the only indications of his temper. His voice was smooth and even as always as he talked into his cell phone.

"Sorry, Mac. I know it's late. Or early. Can you meet me at Michael Revere's office? Bring your report."

He punched the phone off and jammed it into a coat pocket. "Can you still get onto the computers at Revere Imports?"

Callie thought he'd forgotten she was in the car with him. His sudden interest, even if it was professional, surprised her enough to answer. "If the passwords are the same, then yes. I didn't think it was safe to go there, though."

"I'll watch your back. You pull the information off the computer."

"What are we looking for?"

"The names of whoever runs your liquor shipments through customs."

"Why?"

He swerved around another corner. "Your new boss's spare key belongs to his liquor distributor. In case they have to make a delivery to the Shamrock while he's gone."

"Is that unusual?"

He finally spared her a glance. "It is if your distributor is owned by Revere Imports."

"OH MY GOD."

Callie sat at the receptionist's computer while Mac Taylor walked Ethan through his findings in Michael's office.

Russ McDowall.

The man who'd argued with Michael just before the gunshots.

"What is it?" Ethan, tall and dark, and Mac, tall and fair, hurried over to where she sat, framing her on either side like handsome bookends.

She downloaded her disk and matched up the account numbers before she made her final pronouncement. "Russ McDowall was in charge of the liquor shipments. To a subsidiary company called U.K. Spirits. That's one of the accounts that I found with a second set of books. Either they're losing money or—"

"Someone was siphoning off funds," finished Ethan.

Mac frowned. He was unsatisfied until all of the puzzle pieces fit into place. "So Revere found out McDowall was stealing from the company. When he confronted him, McDowall shut him up. Permanently."

Ethan gripped the back of Callie's chair and shifted it back and forth. "But you said the killer switched Revere's chair with a duplicate?"

Mac explained Ethan's question. "I should have

found something on Michael's chair. If not blood or cleaning solutions, at least fibers from his clothes, or a follicle of hair to prove that was the chair he used.'' He thumbed over his shoulder. ''That chair in there is clean as a whistle.''

''So Russ switched chairs,'' Callie reasoned.

Ethan shook his head. ''You told me you hid behind this desk until McDowall left the office. Did you mean this receptionist's office, or the main reception by the outside doors?''

''The outside doors. I didn't want to take a chance that he'd see me.''

''So you heard two men arguing. You heard gunshots. You hid and waited for McDowall to leave. Then you went inside and found Revere?'' She nodded. ''You went to your office to use the phone and 20 minutes later the cops arrived.''

Mac adjusted his glasses. ''That's not enough time for McDowall to come back, remove the body, and clean up the place. McDowall's not our man.''

''But the gunshots—'' She could hear them as clearly in her head now as she had that night.

Ethan's expression lit up with possibilities. Were they about to uncover the truth? ''McDowall wasn't working alone. Someone else must have been here that night.''

Callie picked up his train of thought. ''Then his accomplice killed McDowall. So who else was here?''

Mac put his hand on her shoulder and gave her an apologetic squeeze.

''You were.''

She shot out of the chair and turned on Mac to

defend herself. But Ethan beat her to it. "I don't believe she's involved in this for one minute."

"She could have staged her attack and the break-in. Sent those messages to her machine."

"No! I—"

"You can't fake fear like I saw in her eyes, Mac." Ethan's hand at the small of her back soothed her as much as the conviction in his voice. Maybe he did care. On some level. "She's the victim here, not the perp."

After a moment's hesitation, Mac took Ethan at his word. "All right, then. You have any other suspects?"

"One." He pulled away from Callie. She turned to face him, already reading the doom in his expression. "But you're not going to like it."

"RIGHT, MAC. As soon as I drop Callie off I'll meet you at the precinct." Ethan punched the phone off and buried it in deep in the pocket of his coat.

"You think Michael staged his own murder?" Callie paced the tiny confines of the Mercantile's elevator.

"Who else has a motive for killing McDowall?"

"His accomplice. The one who wants that stupid computer disk."

"Think about it, Callie. What if Michael was the one stealing from Revere Imports? McDowall was on to him, maybe even blackmailing him. How do you get out of that kind of trouble? You fake your own death. A dead man has a perfect alibi to commit murder. He can get rid of McDowall and skip the country. Who's gonna look for a corpse?" She retreated to one corner, hating the detached sound of his voice. "What he hadn't counted on was you finding a second set of books. Or showing up to witness the 'murder' that night.''

She shook her head at the incredulous theory. ''You're grasping at straws, trying to play he-man for me again. I want the truth, not an excuse to keep throwing myself into your arms.''

The elevator's atmosphere subtly changed. ''Was that such a horrible place to be?''

She couldn't lie about that. ''No. But yesterday was a moment out of time. This is reality. I haven't done a very good job of pretending to be somebody I'm not.'' She hugged herself tight, willing him to understand that this wasn't easy for her, either. ''I have to find out the truth so I can go back to my world. And I'm not sure a man who can become someone else so easily has a part in that.''

His amber eyes sparked to life. ''I care about you.''

''But can you love me? Can you give me your heart and trust me to keep it safe?''

He didn't answer. The bell for the fifth floor dinged and she turned to leave.

Ethan grabbed her from behind, turned her into his arms and covered her mouth with a hungry, desperate kiss. He lifted her off her feet, pouring out his hurts and frustrations and raw desire in one all-consuming embrace.

Then he let her go. Tears stung her eyes, mourning the loss of what might have been between them.

''Goodbye, Ethan.''

She dashed through the elevator doors, taking note that he stood fast and watched her until they closed.

CALLIE LET HERSELF IN to her apartment before the ache in her heart had her running down the stairs to catch Ethan.

He'd seemed so alone.

But Michael had been her mentor. He wouldn't put her through this. She had to prove Ethan wrong.

The DeMarcos had cleaned the apartment while she was at work. There was already a message blinking on her machine. She debated about calling Ethan. As a cop, he'd want to know about it. But she had just burned that bridge. Bracing herself for the mechanical voice, she pushed the play button.

And breathed a sigh of relief as John's Irish brogue spoke. "A man left a message for you here. Since you're not on the schedule, I thought I'd pass it on. He says he can help with your computer problem— don't know what that's about. He says he'll be here around five if you want to meet him. I'll be here, too, if he turns out to be some kook."

There was one friend who hadn't let her down.

BY THE TIME Callie stepped off the bus, the snow was falling in earnest, giving her a white crown when she entered the Shamrock Bar.

"John?" She brushed the snow off her hair and coat.

"Right here."

Her smile of greeting vanished as she stared into the barrel of a snub-nosed revolver.

"Sorry about the lump on your head. I didn't mean to hurt you. You were only supposed to be detained by the police."

"You attacked me?"

"After the robbery last year I would have lost the

business if he hadn't bailed me out. I had to do what
he asked.''

"Who?'' The scent of spicy cologne stung her
nose. She understood why John had betrayed her before she turned around.

"Michael.''

"Hello, Callie.'' His gun looked equally deadly. "I
wish you hadn't been such a dedicated employee. I
always thought Russ was the only one who knew I'd
doctored the books.''

"Was he blackmailing you? Is that why you killed
him?''

Michael slipped his arm through Callie's and
pressed the gun against her ribs, leading her out to
the parking lot. "I paid him off for the last time. With
you I think I'll skip the pay-off part and simply get
rid of the trouble. A dead man can get away with
murder as many times as he needs to.''

As they led her outside to a black sedan, Callie had
two thoughts. The first? Ethan had been right about
Michael. The second?

She loved Ethan Cross. But she would never get
the chance to tell him.

CHAPTER ELEVEN

ETHAN EASED UP on the accelerator and swore, cursing the deteriorating weather. If anything happened to Callie...

The red light on top of his Thunderbird spun candy cane patterns on the wall of snow that limited his vision to only a few feet. Backup was on the way. But calling Mac Taylor about the message on Callie's machine wouldn't do him a bit of good if she'd already fallen into Revere's trap.

Damn her quest for the truth!

He'd never liked coincidences. Learning that the Shamrock Bar was tied to Revere Imports should have put him on alert. But the Irishman had been so open. He hadn't lied about the key. Ethan should have recognized that the best way to lie was to blend it with a little truth. O'Herlihy had probably been recruited by Revere.

But he'd been too confused by his feelings for Callie to put it together.

Can you give me your heart and trust me to keep it safe?

Why hadn't he been able to take that leap of faith? Was it so hard to shake the trappings of undercover life that he couldn't accept the beautiful possibilities of a life with her? He needed a second chance to make that leap.

But he had to save Callie first.

He spotted the black sedan a block north of the bar and gunned the engine. He'd know that shock of just-had-sex hair anywhere. Through the back window he could see the black-haired man sitting with her. That must be Revere, because O'Herlihy was driving.

Ethan fishtailed around the corner and floored it. O'Herlihy spotted the lights and took off. But before the Irishman could get away, his wheels hit ice. The sedan careened out of control and slammed into a light pole.

Ethan skidded the Thunderbird to a stop behind them and jumped out.

O'Herlihy was out cold. But Revere had Callie by the hair, dragging her out of the back seat. "You've ruined everything!" he accused. Callie kicked and screamed, refusing to surrender. "I got rid of McDowall's blackmailing behind. But I couldn't leave the country. You had proof of what I'd done!

"Give me the disk or I'll kill her!"

Revere put a gun to Callie's temple and Ethan charged. Revere spun around, pulling Callie up like a shield in front of him.

But Michael Revere had never met Ethan before. And Ethan Cross defending what he loved was not anything a smart man wanted to mess with.

In a matter of seconds Revere was on the ground. His gun was in a snowdrift. And Ethan's hands were around his throat.

"Ethan! I'm okay."

He felt Callie's hands snatching at his shoulders. With two uniformed officers pulling up behind him, he let Revere go and crushed her into his arms. She was real and alive and covered with snow.

She rose on tiptoe and hugged him as tightly as she had ever held on to anything. ''I love you,'' she whispered fiercely.

''I love you, too, babe. I love you, too.''

WITH THEIR TUSSLE in the snow, Ethan and Callie were soaked to the skin. After clearing paramedics and police, Ethan took her back to his apartment with an offer to warm her up.

Now she was curled up beside him on the sofa, wearing a pair of his long johns and sipping cocoa. They'd talked for hours about the case, how Callie had foiled Michael's plan for a rich retirement in Rio. They'd talked longer about Ethan's career as an undercover cop—the terrible things he'd done and seen, and how hard it was for him to leave that world behind when each assignment ended.

As night turned into day, Callie watched Ethan's distant expression transform. This was the kind of healing intimacy he needed. He just needed to be reminded that he was human. That he was a man. And that she loved him.

''I'll miss having you next door,'' Callie admitted.

''Forget next door.'' Ethan set down his mug and slid her onto his lap. ''That's too far away.''

His arms went around her and she cuddled close. ''Are you asking me to move in with you?''

''I'm asking you to marry me.'' She smoothed the hair from his brow and he gently tilted her face up to his. ''I'm asking you to trust me with your heart.''

Callie's answer was as simple and potent as their kiss.

''Yes.''